For my wife, Susan, who's here every morning.

ONE

I'd hate my relationship novel to open with a telling glimpse of me in my natural habitat — at home, by myself in my pink chenille robe and staring at the glow of a computer as I review men's dating profiles like so many DVD covers on Netflix.

But here I am, and here are these men, gazing at me from the screen, thinking they've picked the best possible photograph for me to judge them by: some sitting with one butt cheek on a car fender or a stump out in nature, some with their arms folded like a news anchor in a fifteen-second promo, and some staring out with a cold, blank expression that makes them look like they're on the fine edge of either landing a mate or becoming a serial killer. Someone should really tell them, but it's not going to be me.

I decided to go with Commitment.com, which at least has some realistic optimism compared to Soulmate.com (too daunting) or Match.com (a ridiculously low bar — just match me to someone, I don't care who). When you sign up with Commitment.com, you have to check a box that says, "I am searching for a person to share my life with. I'm not interested in playing games or dabbling in a series of short-term relationships. I'm ready to Commit®." It sounds kind of desperate, but on the other hand they weed out the players this way and save you a lot of time, I'm assuming. I hadn't been out with anybody from there yet when my relationship novel began, just a little while ago now.

The faces flipping by, page after page of them, made me think that by the time you get to Commitment.com you're probably too far gone to attract a normal person. But then again I'm not a normal person anyway and I never get very far with normal men.

By normal men I mean the clean-shaven kind who wear permanent press slacks and Izod shirts, or tweed sport coats over creased, gray pants and who keep their hair short and styled in a way that doesn't offend their bosses, regardless of what line of work they're in. They tend to play golf and enjoy sporting events, mainly basketball and football, neither of which I can abide. They generally have a nice car, a BMW if they're so inclined, or a Land Rover, now and then an American muscle car that beams out nostalgic signals from their youth — Firebird, Mustang, Camaro, Charger — always lovingly restored (or bought in that condition because they're so busy). They like to trade stocks through online brokerages, they like all kinds of music, they have strong political opinions that almost always fly in the face of mine, and the one thing that seems to be common among all of them is their confidence that they know what a woman wants.

A woman wants to be treated right, they think. Okay. A woman wants respect. A woman wants to know that she has her man's complete attention. So far so good. But what they don't realize is that there are all kinds of women, and I'm not any *one* of them.

First of all, I'm a doctor. Many men who are not also doctors are intimidated by this, though they needn't be. I don't bite. I leave my work in the examination room, as it were, unless I'm on call. I have worked for the last ten years (I'm thirty-eight) at a large HMO here in Northern California — a popular one that advertises a lot on television (but shall remain nameless), claiming to be able to help its patrons live magnificently happy lives, judging by the look of the actors they hire. Old people riding bikes, young people eating lots of salad. Everyone's always laughing in these spots, and we joke about that at work because most of the people we see have no reason to laugh. They're sick. Usually they're worse off than they need to be because they waited too long to come in, wanting to avoid the co-pays and deductibles. Also not wanting to hear bad news. I told one older gentleman recently that he had a small esophageal fistula and he said, "I knew it!"

But I'm not hard to get along with because I'm a doctor. In fact, I'm one of the least cocky physicians you'll ever come across because my professional confidence was put through the wringer a few years ago when I sent a little girl home with children's Tylenol only to hear that she died thirty-six hours later from abdominal sepsis. I don't like to talk about it. My colleagues told me they would have done the same, considering her mild symptoms when she came in, but it humbled me and that's why I don't think being a doctor gives me any kind of superiority over anybody else on earth, and I mean anybody.

These men ought to just relax. I'm not going to castrate them.

I was getting tired of Commitment.com when I heard my cell ringing in the other room. I knew it would be my best friend, Jules. All relationship novels have a best friend in them, and Jules is one of the *very* best. She checks in on me every evening to see if I've landed on Mr. Right. Of course the answer is always no, so I didn't pick up. In a couple of minutes an email came in saying, "I know you're there. Call me. J xoxo."

"So," she said. "Have you landed on Mr. Right yet?"

"No."

"Don't worry. He'll turn up. I had a dream about him."

"Really. What's he like?"

"Sort of a McConaughey meets Carl Sagan."

"Interesting. Why didn't you get his number for me?"

"That would be cheating. You know what I mean."

"It's depressing. These guys are all pretty much the same. They're like a many-headed hydra."

"Yuck."

"It's like they all go to one academy to learn how to be men. They're singing from the same hymnal."

"It's not their fault."

"No, it's their mothers'."

"I think it's *our* fault. We've scared them into submission. They can't be themselves, so they put on this kind of generic jumpsuit so we don't run away screaming at their idiosyncrasies."

"None of these guys has an idiosyncrasy. I can tell."

"You can't tell that till you get to know somebody."

"That's not necessarily true. If just one of these men said something that wasn't right out of the dating boilerplate script — I bet Microsoft has it built into Word — believe me, I'd jump on him. They're all so similar."

3

"Now, Sarah."

"They even look alike. Well, there are three or four types, I mean. The J. C. Penney Model. The Dude. The Rugged Blue Collar Hunk. And the Shaved Head With Obsessively Trimmed Goatee. That's it."

Jules was laughing. She knew.

"You slay me."

"Don't ever forget. I helped you find Wayne."

"I know. And I'm fairly grateful."

"If he hadn't come in with the bloodshot eye..."

I had helped Jules through *her* relationship novel a few years ago. Every woman is the protagonist of her own relationship novel, and hers happened to come out before mine. (I was the best friend in that one.) This is why chick lit is so popular. We're hoping to go out and buy our own relationship novel so we can see how everything turns out. Of course, nowadays, all literature is pretty much chick lit because women buy the books and get to decide what they want. Even a man writing a serious novel is actually writing chick lit, because he has to somehow appeal to the women. Look at those dark, brooding eyes of Philip Roth, for instance. Chick lit author. Look at all the lawyer novel authors. Women fantasize over them. Chick lit.

I told Jules about my concept of the relationship novel and how I had a weird feeling mine had begun that very night.

"I worry about you," she said.

"Why?"

"I think you might be too quirky for your own relationship novel. You need to tone it down. I saw your profile on Commitment.com."

"Because I showed it to you."

"You shouldn't brag about your lunchbox."

"I love my lunchbox. 'Land of the Giants' — it's classic."

"But you use it as a purse, and that's a little *outré*, isn't it? Especially for a doctor? Who's inching toward forty?"

"I don't see why. Ouch, by the way."

"And you could use to buy yourself a new car. The '63 Volvo is way too retro."

"It was my dad's. You know that."

I had my own nostalgic signals in play too.

"Yeah, but it's a bucket of bolts now. Always in the shop."

"Thank God I have a good mechanic."

"Why don't you ask *him* out?"

"Married."

"I'm just saying. Maybe we should do a 'My Fair Lady' on you."

"That sounds like gay slang for something really raunchy."

We hung up laughing, like always. I got ready for bed, which is to say I brushed my teeth and shed my pink chenille robe. I kept two pillows on the bed, as if my relationship might show up one night unexpectedly.

*

So I've always been the beat-of-a-different-drummer type. I grew up here in San Francisco, in idyllic Noe Valley, we always called it, and had the run of the city because of my parents' fundamental naïveté. They didn't think anything bad could possibly happen to a nine-year-old taking the bus downtown. They're lucky nothing bad ever did happen, unless you count the time a man exposed his gnarly old penis in front of me while we both waited for the J-Church. I didn't have the heart to tell Mom and Dad about it. It was literally no big deal.

I was kind of like the girls in "The World of Henry Orient," going all over the big city by myself and having adventures. Actually, it was me and Jules doing that. We met when we were seven or eight. In grade school. Jules was the type to march right up to someone — she was the new girl — and say, "I'm Jules Parker, and you are?"

"I'm Sarah Phelan."

She was excited that we had the same middle name. Anne. It was fate that we'd met.

"I'm hereby inviting you over to my house to help weed dandelions in the backyard. My mother will have cookies for us when we're done."

"Okay."

And so began a beautiful friendship. About the only one I've ever really had.

Which, I don't mean to make myself sound pathetic. That's the worst thing you can do at the start of a relationship novel, because people will think, Pity the poor jerk *she* sets her sights on. That's not it at all. It's just that Jules and I were always so simpatico that there was no room for anybody else to elbow their way in, and I was satisfied spending all my free time with her rather than a bunch of others. I mean, sure, there were other girlfriends and even a few gay boys I got along with, but Jules knew me inside and out and there was no way someone could get up to speed with me enough to approach her rarified position. Same with her where I was concerned. She made sure Wayne understood this before they got married, and he was fine with it.

The bad thing about growing up in San Francisco, though, is that if you go to the smart kids' high school, like Jules and I did, you meet only geeky boys or gay boys and your options in romance are limited. When a geeky boy asks you out, your first inclination is to say no because you can't imagine him trying to kiss you. These boys did wear pocket protectors. They had enormous calculators in those days too, so you could say, "Is that a calculator in your pocket or are you just glad to see me," and it was actually funny. Most of them were Asian but had names like Doug or Gary because their parents wanted them to be fully assimilated. The Asian girls were named Debi or Cathy or Lisa. I got along very well with Karen Tseng, in fact, who helped me with trigonometry in exchange for my coaching her for her talent show dance to "What's Love Got to Do With It," a big mistake all around.

The point being, love, matters of the heart — simple lust, now that I think about it — were always going to be a problem for me. Place is destiny.

That's why I went to Washington University Medical School in St. Louis to get my M.D. I thought I'd meet a different kind of boy there, leaving poor Jules behind to fend for herself at SF State. I did meet a different kind of boy too. They were mainly frat types who hadn't yet taken on the veil of seriousness even though they'd been admitted to a top-notch med school. They drank beer by the keg on weekends, showed up for anatomy class so green around the gills that looking into the chest cavity of an eighty-year-old female cadaver just about turned them inside out. I dated a few of these guys for a little while each, always breaking it off when it was clear they didn't think I was legit as a future doctor (sometimes I now think they were right about that) and all they really wanted me for was convenient sex. There were a lot of secret spots in the hospital where two young people could make use of an errant gurney for six or seven minutes on break time. I found it exciting, I must admit, but there always came a point where the guy would lose interest, so I'd end it. I could detect the signs. He wouldn't be waiting for me at the rendezvous. I'd find him later flirting with some nursing student down by the morgue, so that'd be it. I'd cut him off.

*

I'm summarizing, of course. This is where you get to know me well enough to decide whether you want to root for me, and I hope you do. I've already shown that I'm quirky and funny and a little bit vulnerable. Who else do you know who carries around a "Land of the Giants" lunchbox as a purse? And a doctor, no less. I've compared looking at men online to choosing Netflix movies, which is pretty apt, I think, but unusual. It should tell you something about me.

But let me cut to the chase. I *have* known love in my life. I was even married for a while. To Benjamin Cargas. He worked at Left Bank Books in St. Louis, just down Euclid Avenue from the medical center, and we moved in together during my third year of med school — a shabby apartment on McPherson a block from the book store. A shabby but nostalgically beautiful apartment, because it was the scene of our blossoming relationship. It had bars on the windows, and we used to make love beneath the bars with no concern at all that there weren't any drapes and people in upper-floor apartments across the street could look down and watch us if they wanted to. Abandon.

I remember there was an older gay man in the building (I seem to have a trail of them behind me wherever I go) who always

7

called me Carol for some reason. He had dentures and often chatted with me when they weren't in his head. He said, and I quote (lisping a bit because of no teeth), "You and Ben are — I'm not kidding you — jutht the ideal couple together, Carol. You're jutht adorable, you two thweetheart'th."

Ben was an English major fresh out of school who wanted to become a novelist. How ironic, that he wanted to be a novelist and here I am now in my own relationship novel, top billing. Chick lit. I used to wonder if he ever managed to get a book published, but every time I Googled him I came up empty.

Is it strange that a divorced couple would have no idea what became of one another?

Here's what happened. Short version. We met at Llywelyn's Pub on McPherson, catty corner from Left Bank. He was reading from his own work — some kind of open mic for writers, I guess it was — and I was trying to wind down after a horrible neurology exam that day. Nursing a beer, I started listening to him read and I was really taken by his language. Spare, matter of fact, even a little dark, but the character he was describing came through like a spotlight. She was a woman who had burned every stick of furniture in her house because she thought her husband had left her. When in fact he was just working late.

Ben spotted me. Afterwards he always said I looked great there with my lab coat (I'd forgotten to take it off) and my light brown hair down past my shoulders, my black-rimmed geek glasses so uncool at the time as to be cool, long before they actually became cool. Frankly, he said, you looked like a girl in a porn video I once rented, which I took as a compliment at the time.

"So, did you like it?" he asked, this slim, dark-eyed, prematurely balding lad just oozing soul. Soul in the middle-class white meaning of the word.

"It was beautiful. Ironic. If only she'd waited a couple of hours."

"Can I sit?"

"Sure."

"See, it's not that she should have waited a couple of hours. That's not it at all."

"Really? That's sort of what I got."

8

"No, it's that she *had* been waiting. She'd been waiting for *years*. It's like someone — like a depressive who commits suicide? He's been fighting the urge for years but couldn't fight for one more minute."

"Ah."

"I'm thinking of making a novel out of it."

That night Ben was wearing a black T-shirt and blue jeans. It had been a couple of days since his last shave, so the dark stubble on his extremely white cheeks was enticing to me. He looked a lot like Philip Roth, as a matter of fact. Oh, and his lips. He did have wonderful full lips that pursed naturally when he wasn't talking, in a way that made him look like he was on the verge of saying something really profound. His eyes too. They were hazel, deep in their sockets and half concealed in the overhang of his brow.

"Well you've pretty much spoiled the ending, haven't you?"

He smiled. He thought this was wildly hilarious. "I'm Ben Cargas," he said.

"I'm Sarah Phelan."

"You want to take a walk?"

How often do people in relationship novels get started by taking a walk? A lot. And Ben isn't even the relationship I'm getting to.

We walked all around the Central West End, which is a lot like Georgetown or someplace like that — tree-lined, beautiful old houses, leaves dancing along the sidewalks because it was fall. Early November, but not too cold yet. The hour was late. It had rained. The air smelled like tobacco-leaf cookies. I could hear water trickling underground in the sewers.

By the end of the walk, which I had designed to stop at Euclid and the Parkway so I'd have a short trip back to the hospital, Ben had kissed me twice. Once under a streetlamp outside the convent, and once there at the pedestrian crosswalk. He said he wanted to see me again.

"You could get sick and wind up in respiratory therapy. I'm on rotation there."

"Or you could give me your number and let me take you out."

"I don't suppose you're gay, are you?"

"No. Why would you think I was gay?"

He looked genuinely offended. I apologized.

"I've just been led down the primrose path before, that's all."

"You'll find that I'm as straight as they come," he said, which, I later informed him, was one of the worst lines I'd ever heard.

*

Ben came from St. Louis, as a matter of fact — a townie. Suburban but urbane and dreaming of one day living in Greenwich Village and having lunch with his agent to go over foreign rights or a movie deal. Why not dream big?

So when I drew my residency in San Francisco — perfect for me — he was depressed. He had been incubating hopes that I might get something in Manhattan or, at worst, Boston, so he could start sowing the fluffy pods of his literary career. But we were already married, and money talks. What little they were going to pay me at UCSF, that is.

He shifted gears, thinking about the Beat poets now instead of Episcopalian traditionalists like Updike. "This could actually be good for me," he said.

"You could think about graduate school at Stanford. Maybe a Stegner fellowship."

"Yeah, why not?"

We had gone against the wishes of our families and eloped a year into our relationship. A three-minute civil ceremony at the downtown courthouse in St. Louis, where about twenty other couples had gathered to line up one by one in front of a smiling lady judge. A lot of the couples already had a kid or two there to witness the nuptials. I was glad we weren't *having* to get married. It was pure choice, and pure quirky. We went to White Castle afterwards for our wedding feast.

If that had been the end of my relationship novel, I suppose I would now live in the world that characters live in when their books are over. Kind of a foggy void of happiness where nothing happens anymore, which doesn't sound too bad to me. I'd never have experienced the heartache of divorce, or that poor little girl dying. Many of the things that have come to define me, or that at least show up in my face and eyes if you look closely, would never have taken place. I'd be frozen in amber like one of those ancient mosquitoes, in a state of bliss, I have to think, but feeling nothing anymore.

It's like thinking of a figure skater at the top of her miraculous spin, never to touch down.

*

We lived near the UCSF Medical Center, a basement flat on Judah. I'd walk up the hill to work. Ben burned through a few jobs those first couple of years (after my residency) — bartending, landscaping, driving a tour bus — thinking that he could devote himself to his novel if he didn't have to worry about an actual career. This was fine with me. I'd married a writer. His imagination was to be nourished, like a home-grown mushroom. But I did work very long hours and he was alone a lot of the time, in a dark corner of our flat. He wrote at a drafting table and had scene cards, 3 x 5 index cards, taped all over it, and all over the adjacent walls. Jules used to say, "Keep an eye on that boy. He'll vanish into his own world one of these days and all you'll find is his baseball cap and wedding ring."

That's not exactly what happened, but it's not a bad metaphor for it.

One night, maybe six months before the end, he looked over at me as we sat on the couch watching *Survivor* and said, "This doesn't cut it."

"What? What doesn't cut it."

"This. Living like this. I'm not getting anywhere, and frankly I'm not surprised."

I kissed him and told him he was a very talented writer who just needed his big break. It's like anything. If you keep at it you'll get recognized eventually. He was younger than me by a year too. Only twenty-eight and thinking his life had irrevocably stalled.

"You don't get it," he said. "I'm not getting anywhere because I have nothing to say. I have nothing to offer the world. I should be in Afghanistan right now, experiencing something real."

"Oh, I'm sorry. This isn't real?"

"No. No it's not. This is like living in a fucking fish tank."

I didn't say what I was thinking, that he wouldn't last fifteen minutes in Afghanistan, or equatorial Africa for that matter, or anyplace else where someone wasn't taking care of him, because like many men he was something of a baby when in the company of a woman who'd let him be one. Me. I loved him, I really did. He was sweet to me, adoring even, called me his friendly neighborhood goddess and a living work of art, which, honest — I ate that stuff up. But he had this identity crisis going on in his head, and it was much worse than I imagined.

"Then test yourself," I said. "Before you do something stupid and drastic like getting killed in Afghanistan? — go and work in a homeless shelter over in Oakland for six months. See if you have the stomach for ugly stuff."

I was using my terse, school-mistress voice. A tinge of the dominatrix in me. He blinked a few times, completely ignoring the *Survivor* girls' exotically long legs, spectacular breast implants, and hyper-white teeth, then let his smile expand like time-lapse photography.

"I get it. You think I don't have the balls. You think I'm all talk."

"I think I've seen things in the ER that would make you shit your pants. Yes." I'd done my time on late-night ER shifts. It is nothing to sneeze at.

"Oh, that's primo."

"Let's not have pissing contest. I'm a doctor. I've seen more than you, let's put it like that."

"You're daring me!"

"Okay. Sure. I dare you. Go work in Oakland or Hunter's Point. Meet some actual black people. Get your feet wet, and then write about it. Maybe you'll have something to say then."

And that's exactly what he did. He went the very next day to a homeless shelter in Oakland, a bad bad part of Oakland where there'd been dozens of murders already that year, and he volunteered his time and personal welfare. He also volunteered my peace of mind (I think I was bluffing when I challenged him that way) and seemed to be saying, If I die over there it's on your head. There was a little bit of hostility in the act, is all I'm saying.

In nine months or so he'd written a killer piece about his

experiences, submitted it to Harper's Magazine, got it accepted, and was invited to go to New York to study in a famous writer's fiction workshop. The guru had said to him, "I can make you famous," which coming from a famous man like him sounded like a done deal.

Ben left me.

*

"What do you think of the chef, for instance?"

Jules and I were sitting at the dining bar of a small-plate Italian restaurant. The chef was a stocky man with a shaved head, his arms bursting with a Dali-esque array of tattoos. He looked to me like a bulldog that had been trained to stand on its hind legs and cook.

"He's a cross between Shaved Head Goatee and Rugged Blue Collar Hunk Man. They're not my types."

"You like the Permanent Adolescent type. I forgot."

"No. Let me correct you on that."

She was referring to Ben, who she never really warmed up to. Ben wasn't *her* type, which was probably a good thing. She didn't feel competitive where he was concerned.

Jules, by the way, is a short-haired brunette who has a certain boyish quality about her — the naughty imp, the gamin — that used to drive men crazy before Wayne came along with his bloodshot eye. She looks a lot like Sarah Silverman with a bob and can wear anything from a mannish wife-beater tee to a scandalously short baby-doll dress and look amazingly edible. There were times when we joked that we so much liked the other one's style that it was too bad we weren't lesbians. We could end all this endless searching for the elusive soulmate.

"You do," she said. "You like them to be less mature than you. It's a control thing."

"I do not. I've told you. I like them to have a little bit of the teenage boy still in them. Which they let out once in a while. It's a nuance that's over your head, I guess."

"If a guy is still in touch with his sixteen-year-old boy, that's who he really is. The *adult* part is the costume."

"God, you're harsh."

Jules has apple cheeks and sweet brown eyes. When she flashes those eyes it makes you feel like a baby looking at a shiny object. She brought her hand to her nose and scratched, rattling her silver bracelet. I caught a glimpse of her wedding band.

"Remember our rule of thumb? If the guy shows up on a first date —"

"Wearing a T-shirt. Right."

"Not just that. You can make a T-shirt look okay if you wear a cool leather jacket over it, my opinion. Or the right kind of sport coat."

"From a thrift store."

"There's a look to it."

"I remember. It's the T-shirt and the haircut. The Beatle-y haircuts, or Cobains. Or the postmodern faux-hawk shave jobs."

"They're automatically disqualified."

"But the square guys are *so* square."

"Don't let a nice haircut fool you. You keep making the same mistake."

"It's just that my heart sinks when I see a man who looks like his mom combed his hair for him before he left the house."

"It's sad. I know. All those Republicans."

We've had these conversations our whole lives, and our criteria have evolved over the years. Wayne, for example, used to look like his mom combed his hair for him before he left the house, but Jules thinks his personality makes up for that. Plus he went bald. Ben was losing his hair and did not give in to the urge to *comb over the dome*, as we put it, so he looked, at least, authentic. That's the main thing. Authenticity, and it's rare.

"Whatever happened to the guy with the funny T-shirt recently?" Jules went on. She dug into her carbonara while she waited for me to answer.

"The 'Don't Tase Me Bro' guy?"

"Right."

"He never called again."

"Wonder why."

He was definitely one of Jules's Permanent Adolescents, that one. An independent filmmaker, he called himself, and there are thousands of them in San Francisco. Those who can't do, teach; those who can't teach make independent films.

"I asked him — playfully — if he had any outfits that men his age are usually seen in. He was forty, he said. Probably more like forty-five."

"So you insulted his inner man-child."

"I also asked when his film was coming out, and he said he hadn't found a distributor for it yet."

"Red flag."

"I know. It means all he has is a bunch of footage on his computer and has no idea what to do with it."

"You should stay away from all artists, kiddo."

"Tell me about it."

"Or any man with an obsessive interest in anything. Trains, hang gliding, robots."

"I had a robot lunchbox for a while. I'd kind of like to meet a man who's into robots."

"No. They're just computer geeks deep down. Sci-fi nuts. You want no part of that."

"What I really want is an architect. I told you that."

"I don't know why. They wear funny glasses."

"Not all of them."

I didn't go into my teen fantasy of a handsome architect designing a spectacular house for me, maybe situated on a seaside bluff in Amalfi or someplace like that, and he seduces me with hot coded messages in his blueprints. It seemed more and more childish the older I got.

Jules said she had to run. Wayne was coming in to SFO after a visit to his parents in Little Rock, which I always teased her about — marrying a man who came from Arkansas. You never know how you're going to have to compromise your standards.

Later I was walking around the Marina Green and thought maybe I should call "Don't Tase Me Bro" man, just to see. Lights were reflecting on the bay and streaming across the Golden Gate like a line of fireflies, and they made me think I was lucky on some levels, such as being able to live here and have a good career and be close to my mom and all. She lives in Mill Valley, a widow for over five years now. I'm lucky to have her, lucky to have a nice apartment in the Marina District. But there was something about the night and the lights, the foghorn in the distance, the late joggers, the silhouettes of boat masts, and the haunting shape of Alcatraz way out there on the water that made me feel, above everything else, apart.

TWO

A couple of points. One, everything has structure. The human body has structure. Systems, organized patterns of patterns within patterns. Fractal geometry has shown us that even things that seem chaotic on the outside are actually composed of tiny tiny patterns. Structures. So I'm aware that a relationship novel must have a structure too.

By now you have to be wondering what my problem is. All right, so I'm quirky. That doesn't disqualify me from bliss, or it shouldn't. You think, There must be something else about her that she's not telling, something that puts men off besides being a quirky, intimidating doctor lady who castrates her suitors like a reverse Bluebeard. I assure you, though, there's nothing physically wrong with me that would put men off. In fact, I've been told I'm attractive, even beautiful on occasion, but no woman looks in the mirror and tells herself she's really and truly beautiful. Everyone knows that, right? In fact, the more beautiful you might be (in the most objective terms possible), the more insecure you are when you look in that mirror and ask the woman looking out at you, Why do you keep fucking it up?

"I'm not fucking it up," she says. "*You're* fucking it up."

"No, no, no. All I'm doing is putting myself out there like you tell me to do, and *something's not working*."

"Try dropping the stupid lunchbox."

"I can't. It's so *me*."

"Well it's detracting from your outer beauty, okay? Look at me. No. I mean eye contact. Tell me what you see."

"I see the same face that's been looking back at me for thirty-eight years."

17

"No you don't."

"Then what do I see?"

"A rapidly *aging* face that's been looking back at you for thirty-eight years."

"Shit."

So there it is. Ben had me in my glorious, unblemished youth and deposited me (like an abandoned baby) on the doorstep of middle age.

Two. I'm fine physically — I know that in spite of my insecurities — and fine intellectually, so I can hold my own in a conversation with just about anybody, including most artists (though I do try to avoid them), but I might not be so fine emotionally. Okay? I admit it. I have some hang-ups. I miss my dad a lot. He died too suddenly, and if I'd known more about aneurysms of the brain when he had his stroke I have to think I could have helped him. That's part of it. Then there's my sister, Ella, who definitely got the better of the jazz names, lucky in all things but especially in love, which has so affronted me that I've had to estrange myself from her. (That's not really the reason. I'll get to that.) She lives in La Jolla, by the beautiful sea, and has two darling girls who make me cringe every time I get the annual photographic Christmas card. There they all are — Ella, Tucker (the rich husband), Olivia, and Gretchen — all dressed up in their supple velvets and wide silky ribbons and bows (not Tucker), looking out from the surface of the photo with pure smug superiority, each and every one of them, so that it's all I can do not to crumple the thing up and toss it into the john because I don't have a fireplace.

I don't usually get into this stuff with a man until we've been out on several dates, when the time comes to start revealing the tender details of everything that came before. You know how that goes. There's a moment just before you hurl it all out there when you think, Why can't this wait till after we're married? It's not that big a deal, is it? He won't be shocked five years from now. He'll take it in stride. If I tell him now, he might bolt, but I like him and I don't want him to bolt yet, even if he did wear a T-shirt on our first date.

But you tell anyway. You were raised to be honest. You give

him something small first, then he gives you something small. There's a formal pattern to adhere to, a dance. You tell him you ran away from home when you were fifteen, and your parents had to call the police to track you down somewhere between here and Stockton in your eighteen-year-old boyfriend's car. He tells you he was actually arrested once, for pot no doubt, possession, but he was a juvenile and it's not on his record, to which you say, Who didn't smoke a little pot now and then? And you laugh. Your turn.

"I lost my dad a few years ago. Still having a little trouble with that."

"It's hard. I know. You'll be fine."

"Well —"

"Maybe a grief counselor?"

"I don't think so. There's more of a family thing going on. I don't know if I want to get into it."

"Ah."

There's more in that "ah" than it sounds like, of course. He's pulling back. You can tell by the way his chin tips up and one eyebrow lifts involuntarily.

"It's a long story," you continue. "Different reactions after Daddy died, so, you know how it is. Everybody deals with things in their own way, which — I haven't talked to my sister in five years."

"Wow."

That "wow" is even worse than the "ah" that preceded it. Your goose is cooked. The only thing to do is forge ahead with the details, through which you reveal to this near-stranger that you and your sister have never gotten along, really, but you had this sort of détente thing going for a long time just to make your parents happy, even though everyone knew it was all an act and you both more or less despised each other. She had no reason to despise you, but since she was older she had dibs on everything and called even the most trivial shots when it was just you and her alone in your bedroom, so much so — she was such the tyrant — that she made you brush her hair every night, a hundred strokes, so it would be "luxuriant" for the boy she wanted to impress at school. She made *you* run to the corner store for her Snickers, which she was addicted to and spent all her allowance on, and she made you go down and tell Mom that she'd made a mess on her sheets (still not getting the hang of Aunt Flo's monthly visits, as Mom charmingly called them), and all of this comes out in such a breathless rush that your date on the other side of the table has eyes now like a Roman bust. Blank and stony. It's either a case of TMI, or else the details are so humdrum that your rationale for sibling rejection doesn't seem legitimate to him.

You know you're cooked when he doesn't bother telling a reciprocal tale.

I'd been thinking, when my relationship novel began, of just writing my sister out of the story completely. It would make a happy ending much more likely. And believable.

*

Since I work at a medical center in San Rafael, ten minutes north of the Golden Gate in Marin County, I'll often stop in and see Mom in Mill Valley on my way up. This particular morning she was already out in the garden, planting, on hands and knees, a multipack of nasturtiums.

"Those'll take over, you know."

"That's what I want. I want the whole bed full of them. Nothing else wants to grow here."

My mom is a tiny creature with a boy's haircut. A lot of women seem to go to men's barbers once they hit a certain age, which is interesting because they've apparently been busy combing their sons' hair all along. She has a certain Peter Pan look about her, though at sixty-six now the quality of her complexion makes for a pretty haggard-looking Peter Pan, even if she's still full of vim and vigor. I think she's beautiful, though, blessed with June Allison cheekbones and mildly up-slanting eyes, along the lines of a Shirley MacLaine.

(I tend to compare people to actors and actresses for some reason. Maybe it's easier than listing their physical features, as if English words can account for the really minor differences that characterize people. Before a blind date, for instance, I always ask the guy, What famous person do you look like? One poor man said Charlie Sheen and I stood him up.)

With her big gardening gloves, Mom also looked a little like Mickey Mouse.

"Can I bring you anything on my way home tonight?"

"No, I'm fine. I have ten Lean Cuisine lasagnas in the freezer. They're the only frozen dinner I can stand."

"Good Lord. I could bring some sushi for you. We could eat together."

"I eat early, dear. You know that."

"Free food. I'm off at seven if I'm lucky."

"I get it. You don't want to go home."

She's always had this knack for seeing through me. I hadn't told her about Commitment.com yet, but apparently the soul-devouring effects of it showed on my face.

"It's not that."

"You have time for coffee?"

"No. It wouldn't help anyway."

"Sarah?"

"Hmmm?"

"Are you okay?"

She stood up and cocked her head in that way that makes me feel like my nose is bleeding but I don't know it yet.

"Fine. Work has been — frustrating."

"All those sick people."

"They just keep coming."

We laughed. She knew I loved being a doctor. I love being able to do things that make people feel better by the time I'm done with them. Not even the science of medicine so much as the miracle of it, which comes from knowing the patterns of the body, and chemistry, and the unvarying behavior of tiny organisms. Memorizing it all is the real miracle.

"I'll call when I get off. See if you change your mind."

"Love you, sweetheart."

She went on her toes to kiss my cheek. I turned my face a little too far and she wound up kissing my ear.

*

Mom, whose real name is Elaine, became a widow five years

ago and has made no effort at all to meet somebody new. Somebody to spend the rest of her life with. I've asked her about this many many times, and she always says, almost mystically, "I was made to be with your father, dear." She says it in full acceptance of all that it means — that she'll be alone till she dies, that she must content herself with memories, some of them getting quite stale by now at more than forty years old, and that she will never know the pleasures and reassurances of spousal love again. I'd almost prefer that she was religious at this point. She could look forward to that big reunion in the sky with Daddy (real name Pat — Patrick), where they could pick up where they left off when she was way too young to lose him. But she's not religious and does not believe in any kind of afterlife, which, neither do I for that matter. I've dissected the human body again and again, examined its tiniest microscopic components, including the neurons of the brain (where, you'd think, the soul must reside), also its biochemical processes that make everything go, and I can't find anything in there that would suggest the person this particular body was in life could be anywhere else but gone. It makes longing for love seem trivial, all in all, or maybe, looked at exactly the other way around, the most important thing we do while we're here, because what I do believe is that the best way to get along is to get along with another human being, one on one. It verifies all experience. It gives meaning to the daily grind. I know because of Ben, and that's why it hurts so much that he did what he did to me.

So, I was wiping tears out of my eyes as I pulled into my parking spot that morning. Nothing too unusual.

Right away, as I got to the office, Becky at the main desk told me I had two emergency appointments lined up.

I pegged them in the waiting room. One was a middle-aged man bent over in his chair, clutching at his belly with both hands and rocking back and forth. I'm thinking appendix. He probably should have gone to the ER. The other was a mother with her maybe sixteen-year-old son, who was sitting there with his hands glued between his knees and his eyes on the floor. No idea what might be wrong with him, but he didn't seem to be in pain.

"Get their BP and temperatures. I'll do the other vitals."

"Then there's the scheduled appointments after that, Doctor Phelan."

"One at a time, Beck."

Truth is, it was depressing as hell to scan the waiting room and see about twelve people already leafing through the six-month-old magazines. The other doc in our suite, Nilesh Sengupta, was at a renal conference that week, so they were all mine.

I've learned not to make eye contact as I breeze through the waiting room when it's like that.

The man with the belly cramps — fifty-ish, overweight — was a walking myocardial infarction waiting to happen. He was not pointing to the appendix when he showed me what hurt.

"What did you eat last night?"

"Venison."

"Frozen since last fall, I'm guessing?"

"Absolutely. I shot the goddamn thing myself."

"You cooked it yourself too?"

"Wife did. Crock pot."

"No mushrooms you picked yourself in there, I hope."

"Nah."

The last thing I wanted now was a nasty case of mycetism.

"I'm thinking it's the deer meat," I said. "Maybe a little too old?"

"We did have a power failure a couple months back. Remember that big storm? Knocked down trees in Muir Woods."

"Oh my."

He was destined to experience a couple days of some pretty awful diarrhea, I told him. Olympic caliber. Surprised it hadn't started by now. He should keep himself hydrated and take things easy. "It's food poisoning," I said. "Which means dump the rest of that meat."

"That's a cryin' shame," he said.

"Nonetheless."

The teenager was in the exam room alone when I went in. Sheepish looking, he didn't seem to want to look me in the eye when I asked what seemed to be the problem today.

"It's a little embarrassing."

"I don't think I have time to play twenty questions, Brandon.

How 'bout you tell me what part of the human plumbing is messed up? Air, blood, potty?"

He blanched at that last. "Potty? How so."

"Burns when I pee."

"Hmmmm."

"I probly ought to mention —"

"You've had sex with someone new in the past two weeks?"

You never saw a redder mug on an adolescent boy. Under his dirty blond hair his face looked like Lucifer with zits.

"Okay. Okay. I'm not taking names. I *am* taking a urine sample, though, to start, and I'll send you down to the lab for a blood test." I didn't tell him I was sparing him a swab of his tender urethra. He'd have freaked. "We'll figure out what's going on, and then you'll get the hard sell."

Poor choice of words, perhaps. He didn't pick up on it. All he could do was nod.

"Meantime, no more sex. Not till I identify the bug. Even then, you're sixteen, kiddo."

"I know."

"I'm sure she's all that and then some, but you need to be ultra smart at your age. Some of these nasty little things are incurable, you know."

He didn't want the lecture. He wanted antibiotics, and I obliged.

For the next couple of hours I ran through the other patients out there, spending no more than my HMO-allotted twelve minutes with each. I worked through lunch. They kept coming. Two flus, two muscle pulls, two late-onset asthmas, in they came two by two.

Structurally speaking, as relationship novels go, this is just about the spot where they usually introduce the Love Interest.

He showed up in the exam room right on time.

THREE

You know how doctors' offices work. As a patient, you get called long before the doc is ready to see you. A nurse takes your temp and BP, checks your history form, weighs you, and leads you to an ice-cold room where you are to wait. You're told to change into a dressing gown if you're there for a full exam, or to sit tight otherwise. "The doctor will see you shortly." The magazines in there are even more out of date than the ones in the waiting room, and you're probably not interested in them anyway. You're sick and anxious and shivering, trying not to look at the anatomic poster on the wall that shows all of the glistening pink, blue, yellow, and brown organs inside you that are possibly malfunctioning. The view out the window is awful too: the rooftop of another building, packed with air conditioning units and ductwork, dotted with pigeon and seagull poop.

I'd been going from room to room, selecting them by the plastic clock faces on the door, which the nurse sets when she deposits a patient inside. Tells me how long the poor soul has been in there. When I came to Exam Room C, I realized this patient had been in there for twenty-five minutes.

I reviewed his chart. New patient. Physical exam. Reporting sleeplessness, lethargy, poor appetite, weight loss. Thirty-seven years old and clocking in at one-sixty-seven, which is perfectly healthy for a man of six feet tall. (The nurse had actually written 5'11"+.)

He sported the remarkable and unlikely name of Dylan Cakebread.

I tapped on the door and heard a raspy voice, a voice that hadn't spoken in twenty-five minutes, say, "Yes."

Inside, Jude Law sat on the exam table with his stockinged feet dangling.

To the casting director of the relationship movie that comes of this relationship novel, if you can't get Jude Law himself for the part of Dylan Cakebread, you have to find someone who looks exactly like him. Dead ringer. He had Law's tousled blondish hair, eyes so blue they're see-through silver, the jaw of a Viking, and a mildly apologetic but impossibly charming smile, and I'm ashamed of myself for flushing as I think about him there on the day we met, it's so embarrassing. I'm a doctor, for God's sake.

"I'm Dr. Phelan," I said. "Really sorry for making you wait so long."

"That's all right. I think I actually dozed off for a while. Little bit of kip."

"I'm sorry?"

"A nap, I mean."

Yes, he even had an English accent, and though his voice was not quite Jude Law's voice, it was close enough in timbre and tone that I imagined Jude Law might sound this way when he's sick. I was almost ready to believe that this *was* Jude Law, except that the name on the chart was Dylan Cakebread.

"Never heard that before," I said. Pretending to look at his chart. He put his fist to his mouth and coughed.

"I've been in America long enough to know better. I shouldn't use slang from the mother country."

"No, I like it. Kip, you say."

"Right. Some kip."

I could feel myself smiling at him as my head bobbed, till it struck me that too much time was passing. An awkward moment.

"I see you're here for a physical, but you haven't been feeling too well."

Sitting there in his limp, ill-fitting gown, it was evident he hadn't been feeling well. He had raccoon circles around his eyes, easily imaginable on Jude Law, and his complexion was waxy and grayish. It didn't make him any less attractive, of course. Only made me want to mother the bejesus out of him.

"Downhill slide for a while now," he said. "Always under the weather. Losing some weight."

"Probably nothing to worry about. We'll check you out and get to the bottom of it."

He flashed a relieved smile and took a deep breath.

I asked him why he'd come all the way up to San Rafael when he lived in the city, and he said the HMO couldn't assign him to a primary there if he wanted a quick appointment. Reasonable enough. Then I asked the usual questions about diet, exercise, drinking (a bit, not to distraction), smoking (no, thank God), and allergies, then I started the exam. I listened to his polite heart beating away at a slightly elevated rate. No murmurs. I looked at his tongue and throat and peered up his well-maintained nose and into his ears. I shined my penlight into his eyes and looked for dilation response (normal) and signs of lens opacities (none). I stepped to his side and behind him and pressed my stethoscope to his bare back (Britishly wan), ordering him in a kinder version of my dominatrix voice to take a deep breath and hold it. I auscultated him. His lungs sounded mildly congested but without rales. Maybe he'd had a cold and didn't realize it. Busy man. I hadn't asked his occupation yet.

I had him lie on his stomach so I could check his skin for possible melanomas. Nary a mole on him, though. Smooth as Michelangelo's marble.

"Now turn over and lie on your back, please."

"Yes, ma'am."

It was all I could do not to say, "That's a good boy." I'm glad I didn't. Professional discipline, though by now I could feel that my own heart rate was up a little. Hands a little moist.

I palpated his neck glands. His abdomen. No enlarged or irregular organs. He was turning out to be, in spite of his outward symptoms, quite an ideal specimen of a male human being, and very clean too. He smelled like a nice unpretentious soap, maybe Dial.

I started thinking about the Perfect Penis, which was something just between Jules and me. I'll tell you about that later. It just flashed in my head, and I had to blink a few times to chase it away.

"Do you mind standing up now?"

"Certainly."

27

"I have to ask up front here." My voice cracked. I couldn't make eye contact with him. "Always a little uncomfortable, if you know what I mean. The testicular exam."

"Ah."

"Some men don't like the idea of a female doctor — down there."

"I hadn't thought of it, actually."

"Well, if you —"

"No, it's all right."

"I do use rubber gloves."

"That's fine."

"And it's very quick. Just looking for unusual lumps."

"Cancer then."

"Right. Just want to make sure."

"Have at it."

My face was hot. He smiled in a permissive way, and I smiled and cleared my throat before turning and seeking refuge at the glove drawer across the room. I pulled out two blue gloves from the dispenser. Put them on, trying not to snap them in a way he might find threatening. They were lightly powdered and fragrant, lilac I think. I hoped the odor wouldn't put him off.

I positioned the stool in front of him and sat. I told him to face me and approach the stool, legs parted a bit, which he did, bravely.

"Is it turn my head and cough time?"

"Almost. Hold on."

I reached up under his gown and proceeded with my usual technique, my face turned parallel to his stomach and pressing against it ever so lightly. His unseen penis was a patient, gentle weight over my knuckles. My fingertips, even through the gloves, found a pocket of serene warmth. It was a little like milking a cow who was glancing back at me with each tug.

"The glove is bloody cold," he said.

"Sorry." I was looking at the roof of the other building. Didn't want to see his face, to see if he was smiling. I hurried.

"All right," I said. "Everything's hunky dory."

"That's it?"

"Yep. Painless."

28

I had probably done a less than thorough job, I'm afraid.

"Any clues as to my — condition?"

"Not yet. I'm leaning toward something nutritional. Vitamin deficiency. Maybe an environmental allergy, hard to say."

"Maybe I just need to get used to it."

"Oh no. People need to feel good."

Without warning him of the next item on my exam menu, I went back to the counter and retrieved a tube of lubricant. "Would you lie on the table again? Facing the window."

"Of course."

"This part's a little trickier."

"Oh?"

"Normally I could call for my male colleague to do it. He's at a conference this week."

"Are we talking prostate?"

"I'm afraid so."

"Well," he said with a stoic note, "it won't be the worst thing that's happened to me today."

This remark was a little unsettling, and I hoped he was just making light of an unbelievably humiliating situation — for me. Though my trained fingers had probed the prostates of thousands of men, men of all ages, races, and sexual orientation, every one of whom, I imagined, was content enough, as far as it goes, to have a physician like me approaching them with the cool intimacy of a role-playing prostitute, I was having a sudden attack of shame as I lifted the back hem of his gown. It's etiquette to avert the eyes as you begin the rectal exam, letting your fingers do the walking, as it were, but I snuck a peek, totally involuntarily I swear to God, and caught a brief glimpse of his fine, fair, and hairless white bottom. Boyish and clean and smooth and beautiful, and when the words that first came to mind were *Spank it*, I had to distract myself.

"This won't hurt," I said. "You'll feel some pressure."

I heard him gulp.

"So tell me," I said, as I began the, what we call, digital penetration. "What do you do for a living, Mr. Cakebread. Sometimes a patient's trouble is work-related."

He shifted his weight slightly and groaned in a way that was impossible to interpret.

"What's that?"

"Architect," he said.

"Oh no, you're kidding."

I think I hit a sensitive spot at that moment — reflex on my part — because he flinched and made a sound like "unnnh" or "hnnnnf."

Could Jules have sent him in here as a joke? My God.

"What's wrong with being an architect?"

"Nothing. It's a —" I had to swallow. "It's a noble profession."

"Pays the bills anyway."

I was already out and away, sling-shooting my gloves into the bio-waste bin. A drink of water would have been good, or a drink of gin, actually. A stiff one.

"Normal prostate," I said. "Here's a box of tissues. To wipe."

He snatched two or three tissues from the box as he sat up, looking at me bashfully, and I turned away again so he could clean up with a little privacy.

"That was less of an ordeal than I expected," he said. "The last time I had it done, the doctor had fingers like King Kong."

I turned back, expecting to see him with a wry smile of pride at his cleverness, but instead I found him sort of *in flagrante*, right in the middle of his wipe. His head was down and his eyes on the floor or his knees, I couldn't quite tell, and he was grimacing. You can almost imagine Jude Law that way, I bet.

He looked up just then, of course, and his cheeks went English pink. I swirled around to my clipboard on the countertop, scribbled a note on the chart that said, "sjjeifnl wofhcn poemfinth," when I checked later.

"Aside from your symptoms," I told him, still with my back to him, "you're just fine."

"Well, that's disappointing."

"It could be you're getting over a mild respiratory infection. You're still congested. I'm going to order some blood work and we'll see if there's anything else going on."

"All right."

"Other than that — when you're not busy architecting — I

think you should get more rest and take a multi-vitamin. Make sure you're sleeping eight hours."

Architecting. I was not meaning to be funny. It slipped out.

His face changed. Suddenly, as I let my clipboard drift down against my thigh, I watched his expression go from "anxious patient" to "man with the glimmer of an idea." I went from "authoritative professional" to "thirteen-year-old girl drooling over a fan magazine." Could almost feel the mortifying zits popping out on my cheeks as he looked at me.

"Architecting," he said. "That's pretty charming."

"Well, why don't you dress now and I'll write up the blood work order and you can pick it up at the desk on your way out."

He was saying something as I left the room, but I had to leave and I had to leave in a hurry or I'd have made a total fool of myself. When I got a look at my face in the restroom mirror, I saw that I'd gone a humiliating shade of pomegranate.

I also saw, as I finally went in to see the next patient, that I'd spent much longer than twelve minutes with Dylan Cakebread. I'd been in there for forty-five.

*

"If you marry him, you'll be Sarah Cakebread. I like the sound of that."

"You're definitely jumping the gun. Just because I had my finger in him doesn't mean he's obligated to propose."

"In some cultures it means you're already married."

Jules was getting goofy. She had rushed over to my place after work to plot and plan. I'd texted her the news that the man of my dreams had come in for a physical.

"We're getting ahead of ourselves," she said. The pizza she brought over was almost gone. "Before the kids get names you have to figure out a way to go on a date. At least one."

"I'm not going to sleep with him and conceive a child on the first date."

"No, though you've already deflowered his rectum."

"What a story to tell Mouthwatering and Luscious one day."
The Cakebread kids. You can see how stupid this was making me.

31

Jules made a brainstorming face as she gazed absent-mindedly out the front window, which had a sliver-view of the Romanesque Palace of Fine Arts at the end of the block. It was floodlit, screaming out in a way I'd never really noticed before, *Architecture!*

"You'll have to be discreet," she said.

"Goes without saying. Tricky though."

"Probably unethical to use personal information in a medical file to finagle a date out of someone."

"I mean, my God. I know his vitals. That's more personal than a diary, if you think about it."

"But you're entitled to call him as his doctor, right?"

"If there's a reason to call him. A medical reason."

"Well, you can't make something up."

"No. I could go over his blood results with him, I guess."

"Even if there's nothing wrong?"

"I'm sure his cholesterol's a little high." My cheeks tingled. "And if it's not I could tell him it's too low."

"Careful, Doctor Phelan. Malpractice can kill a new relationship."

We agreed on a few things. I couldn't have him come back into the office if there wasn't a legitimate reason. I could ask to meet him somewhere to give him some kind of information, a nutritional pamphlet or something, but only if he didn't think to have me just mail it to him. I could walk around near his apartment, which was on Fell Street, near Alamo Square. We'd "bump into each other," and I wouldn't be wearing my doctor hat. He's fair game.

"Could take a while to run into him," Jules pointed out.

"Yeah."

"You do have a life, you know."

"That's the buzz."

"But it's worth a try. As a first step." Her eyes got that impish look. "I could be there with you. Couple of gals out walking around together."

"I'd have to ditch you if anything started to happen."

"Oh, trust me. To get you hooked up with Jude Law, I'd parachute out of there so fast you wouldn't know what happened."

"Uh huh."

Short of creating a medical crisis for him out of whole cloth, this seemed like the best plan for now. I told Jules I'd ruminate, but I had in mind to go on a Dylan Cakebread safari the next evening. Alone.

*

By coincidence, Dylan's blood work came back in the morning, everything squeaky clean and as reassuring as the diploma on a doctor's wall. And I'm not so professionally rigid that I didn't peek at his HIV results first thing — negative, of course — which is just one of those practicalities that a sexually active woman has to pay attention to these days. And I did hope to become sexually active soon. It had been a long sojourn through the desert since Ben left, with few oases. Arid is just the right word for it.

Tempting to call Mr. Cakebread and tell him that his blood had offered no clues to his lethargy and insomnia. He'd be getting a copy of the results by mail anyway, so it wasn't like I was withholding information. I just didn't want him to go away yet. A day or two wouldn't hurt. And I might spot him on the street before then.

That evening (having told Jules I was working late), I dressed in one of my least doctory outfits, jeans and an arugula-green cowl-neck sweater that Jules tells me does great things for my silhouette, by which she means my boobs. I'm not huge in that area, but Jules thinks my breasts are natural beauties the way they sit, unsaggingly, and because of their overall enthusiasm. That is, according to her they always seem to be looking upward, wanting to see what's going on around them, a thing that Ben always commented on. On her advice, in certain clothes I can go braless without much worry that I'll look too contrapuntal as I walk along. I wasn't about to risk it this night, though.

With the same caution, I left my lunchbox at home too.

Though it was May, it was chilly out. I drove up and over Divisidero and turned left on Oak, then looped back around toward Fell to look for parking. It's a tough neighborhood for parking at night. In fact, it's a tougher neighborhood all around than the yupped-out Marina, making me wonder why an architect, presumably a successful one (because aren't all architects successful almost by definition?) would want to live in a rough-edged place like this. I got lucky, found a parking spot between two driveways on Grove, right around the corner from the Painted Ladies. My '63 Volvo, named androgynously "Pat" for my dad, fit perfectly in the non-red part of the curb. An omen.

The fog hung just above the streetlamps as I walked back toward Fell, Dylan's address looping through my head like a bookkeeper's mantra, *seven forty-four, seven forty-four, seven forty-four*. At the corner store a Middle Eastern man stood in the doorway smoking and looking at me like he knew what I was up to, maybe even knew who I was stalking because women must always be stalking Jude Law around here, that is, Dylan Cakebread. I felt like I could utter some password to him and be led through a hidden back way to a spot where I would be able to see right into Dylan's bedroom window. I kept my eyes down. The man said, "Beautiful evening."

"Not really."

"You need anything? You need smokes and beer?"

"No thank you. Is this the seven hundred block?"

"Yes, ma'am. I have espresso machine. You need a nice cappuccino? Warm up?"

I shook my head and smiled a tense smile. "No thanks. Gotta go."

No sign of Dylan anywhere near seven forty-four. It was a drab brown two-flat, much less appealing than the buildings on either side, which were standard Victorians painted nicely, owned by gentrifiers, I guess. Dylan's was owned by a slum landlord, apparently. Hadn't had a coat of paint in two decades. A crooked awning over the front door, and the garbageman's alley the perfect hiding place for a rapist. I couldn't see inside either flat. The front windows were each blocked with old, thick-slat Venetian blinds, caked with greasy yellow resin. Oh dear.

I told myself a little story about how a successful architect would want to live not in some fancy-pants yupped-out neighborhood like a doctor, but instead down and among the people, the real people, so he'd always be in touch with the fundamental needs of the human animal. It's all about shelter. Form and function combine to keep us mammals dry and as warm as possible, private as is practical. We need a secluded place to cry at night.

I went around the block.

"You come back, eh? I thought you come back!"

"Sorry."

"You want cappuccino after all. I make it for you, okay? This is no problem. I throw in a lotto ticket."

"I'm fine. I was looking for a friend, that's all."

"*I* be your friend!"

He grinned like he was the brightest star in the firmament.

I walked toward Dylan's again with my head down. A cold mist was hanging in the air. My nose felt like it was made of tin. Hands freezing. Spirit on ice. This was stupid.

"Sorry, is that Doctor Phelan?"

I looked up and there he was, the object of my manhunt. Dylan Cakebread was coming from the other direction with two paper coffee cups in his hands and looking quite a bit the worse for wear since I'd seen him. He wore a sacky belted cardigan the same color as his building, a black T-shirt under it and wrinkled khakis, yet it wasn't his physical appearance that discouraged me so much. It was the fact that he had *two* coffees. There must be someone waiting for him at home.

"I'm sorry. Do I know —"

"Your patient," he said. "Dylan Cakebread."

His face looked cheerful. Happy to see me. I took it that way, anyway. "Oh, of course! Right. I see so many people, I don't always —"

"Stupid of me to think you'd remember."

"No, no. Absolutely."

"Though we *were* rather intimate that day, weren't we."

I'm sure I was blushing nightmarishly in that light.

"You wouldn't believe how many patients I get intimate with in a day."

"I'm sure I wouldn't. It must get blurry."

"I *do* go through the rubber gloves."

He thought this was amusing. Flashed a lovely, sweet smile, cockeyed, and a little bit salacious.

"What brings you over this way? I'd have assumed you live over the bridge."

"Oh no," I said. "I live in the Marina. Supposed to have met a friend for coffee but got stood up apparently."

I threw a thumb over one shoulder.

"Still needing the coffee?"

"Better believe it. Where'd you get those? I didn't like the look of the corner store there."

"Why don't you take one of these? They're black, if you don't mind black."

"Isn't one for — for your girlfriend?"

Remember. No wedding ring.

"'Fraid not. I don't have a coffee maker at the moment. I buy one for tonight and one to nuke the morning."

This was the best news I'd had in a month.

I took the cup from him. Our hands touched briefly. Compared with our close contact in the exam room, it was a minor thing but both of us noticed it and exchanged a certain look before withdrawing.

"Would you like to get in out of the cold?" he asked. "My place is right up here."

"Really. I had no idea."

"You must think I'm slumming it."

"God no. It's up and coming. The Painted Ladies right around the corner."

"Aren't you polite. No. I think it's shit. Temporary digs while I have something built."

"That's *right*. You're an architect."

"Why don't you come on up. I'll put on the electric fire."

"Well," I said. "I can't say no to that."

FOUR

"I ought to unfriend you on Facebook." Jules was angry. Pretending to be, anyway.

"It was just something I had to do. On my own."

"Right, and it was selfish. Now I have to wait to see him till the two of you are ready for double dating."

This was on the phone the next day. I told her up front that nothing happened between (new category) English Architect Man and me but that I did see his habitat and drew some important conclusions. One, he definitely was not a slummer. The building was not his style, but his flat was impeccably furnished — he'd even hidden those awful Venetians with damask drapes — telling me that he was between places. Italian black leather chair. Clean industrial-look sofa bed, which made an interesting statement across from the cocoa damask. Nice artwork, modern. Some black and white photography. Billie Holiday on the Bang & Olafsen stereo. I liked his marketing niche.

"All we did was talk," I said. "Nothing physical happened. Double dating is a long way off, and that's if we manage to get together at all."

"This is not a done deal, in other words."

"*God* no."

In fact, I said, we were fairly clumsy with each other as conversations go. He had a halting kind of approach, throwing out feelers to see if I'd jump aboard, then letting me steer for a while, which I don't like to do anyway. I like to ask questions. It can be like an interview at times, something I'm working on to change, because nobody wants to enter a relationship feeling like they're being interrogated.

"What were you wearing?"

"The arugula."

"Oooh, perfect! Your silhouette must have knocked him flat."

"Never caught him looking, really."

"He's subtle. I like that in a man. *Guarantee* you he looked."

The conversation was actually on the dry side, overall. I felt I had to keep it more or less organized around his blood work, so there were definitely some awkward moments. He'd be talking about the tiramisu at some restaurant, and I'd say, "At least you're not diabetic. Your blood sugar was right on."

"God, Sarah!"

"I know. Lame."

"He doesn't want to talk about his blood. He wants to get to *know* you."

"I couldn't drop my façade. We met by chance. What else am I supposed to talk to him about?"

"Did you get into the history dance?"

"No!"

She meant the exchange of embarrassing information I was talking about before.

"Did you tell him about Ben?"

"I told him his sedimentation rate was ideal."

Jules said to hold on. Wayne was talking in the background.

"Wayne wants to know what kind of stereo gear he had."

"Oh for God's sake. Tell Wayne to masturbate to some *other* boy's stereo."

The last thing Jules wanted to know was how far open was the dating door. How'd I leave it with him?

"I have my foot in it."

"The door, right? Not your mouth."

"The door."

"What'd he say?"

"When?"

"As you were leaving."

I'd been saving this part. I didn't want to spoil it for Jules, who loves a good story.

"He said, 'Do you happen to like classical music, Doctor Phelan?'"

"Oh no. And you better have said, 'Call me Sarah.'"

"Of course. And he said, 'Do you happen to like classical music, Sarah?'"

And I said, I *love* classical music, which isn't true at all because my father was a major jazz hound and had nothing but old jazz records in the house, but I wasn't about to tell Dylan that, so I said, I *love* classical music.

"I have tickets to the symphony on Saturday night. The Elgar cello concerto. Should be excellent. Would you like to come?"

"And you said," said Jules, "'Are you sure? Isn't there someone else?'"

She made me sound like a cross between Marilyn Monroe and Betty Boop when she imitated me.

"Yes, and he said, 'No. I bought the tickets months ago.'"

"Which is loaded with intrigue," Jules said. "Could mean he was with someone then and isn't now. Or he was hoping to impress some woman with his good taste and she didn't buy."

"Who cares?" I said. "I'm going to have to grab a CD of Elgar's cello concerto before Saturday, though. I don't want to look like a total philistine."

The last thing Jules advised was, "Sarah? Please: No 'Land of the Giants' that night. Buy yourself a nice clutch purse."

*

The things you learn when you hope to impress a man. I downloaded the Elgar from iTunes and did some reading. It turns out the composer conceived the great work in 1918 (re-popularized in the later era by Jacqueline du Pré's 1965 recording) in the wake of surgery for an infected tonsil. This perked me up. I like when art and medicine intermingle.

I was determined not to try and BS my way through the evening, though. It made sense that Dylan would be interested in an English composer, and I figured he knew much more about Elgar and his milieu than I could possibly cram in two days. It would be suicide to compete. If he wanted to talk music, I would guide the conversation toward jazz and dazzle him with my knowledge of modal improvisation as executed so memorably by

Miles Davis on the seminal "Kind of Blue." (This is how Daddy would have put it.) With any luck, he'd want to talk about something else after that.

Unfortunately, I got a call mid-day on Saturday, while I was shopping at Stonestown Mall for a goddamn clutch purse, calling me in to the hospital where a patient of mine had been brought in for an emergency appendectomy. She was in terrible shape, a fifty-eight-year-old woman with cardiac issues and diabetes. The surgery went well enough, but post-op she was having trouble in recovery and I suspected bleeding for a while. False alarm, thank heaven. Her respiration was shallow and rapid, and she had a high pulse rate too, but after about four hours of monitoring I felt comfortable leaving her. It was six-fifteen. I had to get across the bridge, home, showered, and dressed in time to meet Dylan in front of Davies Hall at seven.

Im-pos*see*-blay. And no clutch purse either.

There was a message from Jules when I got home — six-forty now — saying she had come by and was highly disturbed to find me not there obsessively waxing my legs and trying on eleven different dresses in front of the mirror. Where was I? Did I have any idea how easy it would be to fuck this thing up?

I called her the minute I stepped out of the shower, my hair in a turban towel. I was dripping across the floor and catching a glimpse of myself naked in the steamy mirror, thinking God, are my hips that wide? It had to be an optical illusion caused by the steam and the fact that I didn't have my glasses on.

"Appendicitis," I said.

"Not *you*."

"No."

"Oh my God, not Dylan!"

"Calm down. I was called into the hospital."

"Sarah, you have got to get your priorities straight."

Ignore the profoundly wrong idea that I should have relegated Mrs. Bannerjee to the realm of *Que sera sera* in favor of meeting a near-stranger for a concert. I knew what Jules was trying to say.

"I'll only be a few minutes late."

"You have to call him. On his cell."

"I don't have his cell number."

"Why not?"

"We didn't exchange numbers. It was all, See you there. That kind of thing."

"So he doesn't have your number either?"

"No."

"How was he supposed to call you up at midnight with the 'I was just thinking about you' call?"

"I didn't think that far ahead. Sorry."

"You are way out of practice, girl."

"Give me a chance. I think I can still hit."

"Funny. You better get going."

I settled on a backless black cocktail dress with a touch of gold glitter in it, not ostentatious. Knee length because my calves are better than my thighs. I also picked out a gauzy black shawl and shoes I could walk very fast in if I had to. I was out of the apartment at seven-oh-five.

Carrying, by the way, a small bag from Joseph Schmidt chocolate as a makeshift purse. It was the classiest thing I had in the house, though the chocolate was long gone.

Naturally the traffic on Lombard and Van Ness was insane, backed up because some ninny of a motorcyclist tried to beat the light at California and wiped out in front of a bus. I didn't learn this till I got near the intersection, where a helpful homeless man was going up and down between the cars and telling the story for spare change. (Ninny, by the way, is a word my mom uses, not the homeless man. He said *asshole*.)

By the time I was anywhere near Davies Hall, it was after seven-thirty. Driving slowly past it, I didn't spot Dylan. Maybe he'd already given up on me and invited some other well-dressed and stood-up woman to share the seat beside him. Or maybe he'd dramatically torn up the tickets and thrown the expensive confetti to the ground, stalking away and ruining his life in one impulsive decision.

I always used to say to Ben, It's a miracle that any two people actually get together. The universe seems to conspire against it. Bad luck, misunderstandings, badly timed menstrual cramps — it's all so fragile.

"We managed," he said.

"Only because I needed a beer that night."

"Only because I picked that night for my reading."

"Only because I didn't study my neurology."

"Only because I couldn't take my eyes off you as I read."

It's always a fluke.

I had to park over on Gough. Ten minute walk back to the hall. Most of the people who'd been outside when I passed before had now gone inside. There were only a few lingering as I ran — grateful I'd picked the shoes I picked — toward the doors. Only problem — no Dylan.

The imposing glass façade of the building was aimed at me like the lens of a giant microscope. Made me feel awfully small.

At the doors, a young woman in a Davies blazer who was taking tickets looked at me with a judgmental sneer. She didn't like late arrivals, I guess.

"Was a man here looking for me?"

"How would *I* know?"

"I was supposed to meet him and I got stuck in traffic."

"Maybe he went in without you."

"Did he leave a ticket?"

"Nobody left any ticket."

"He looks like Jude Law. Did you see Jude Law going in already?"

"I don't know who that is, ma'am."

Criminy, as my dad would say.

I took a few steps back so the ticketed late arrivers could stream past me and inside, where by now Jude — Dylan — was probably already seated and tapping his program on his thigh, peeved at his own doctor who'd stood him up without so much as a courtesy brush-off call. No phone on hand because I had no purse, no lunchbox. The nearest pay phone was probably at the Trans Bay Terminal.

From behind I heard this: "I don't mind a late dinner if you don't."

Before I could turn, his hand had lighted on my bare shoulder. I had my shawl wrapped around my upper arms. Somehow, on yet another cool night, his hand was remarkably warm.

He was in front of me now. Smiling.

"I'm so sorry! Some asshole motorcyclist —"

"Don't worry about it, please. I walked over to Absinthe and made reservations for after the concert."

"But — I didn't know we were on for dinner. I thought — I didn't bring my purse. Long story."

"My treat then. You can reciprocate sometime."

This was both promising and a little troubling. *Sometime* is so vague. Why didn't he say *next time*?

"*Soon*," I blurted. "I don't like debts hanging over my head."

That made me sound a bit anal, I think, but Dylan didn't seem to notice. He was already waving the tickets and guiding me very skillfully with the lightest pressure on my shoulder toward the door. There the young woman took the tickets and gave a look that appeared, now, to approve of me. She understood why I was nervous about having missed a rendezvous with Jude Law.

Dylan was gorgeous, obviously, dressed in a dark, tieless suit, with a gray, silky, open-collared shirt — San Francisco casual, people call it — and black oxfords. I imagined he made a dynamic impression on prospective clients as he flipped through blueprints on a big easel in his office. The fact that he smelled terrific too made me want to be close to him. It was like the smell of vanilla beans steeping in some Earl Grey tea. I hoped I could resist the impulse to lick him.

Once we were through the door, he took me by the hand and led me at a good clip across the lobby and toward the near entrance to the orchestra seats. The usher there smiled at him as he showed her the tickets, making me think she knew him or had seen him here often enough that his face was familiar. (He probably had a subscription.) How many other women had she witnessed on his arm, coming in to spend a couple of impatient hours listening to the pretty music before the evening's main event? There was something about that smile.

I realize — like lots of women in relationship novels — that I'm already coming across as paranoid and jealous, even possessive, though I had no right to consider this get-together a real date. The way it had evolved out of our Fell Street bumping-into, it could be seen as a convenient way for him to use a spare ticket. I needed to keep my expectations low. Still, hope springs external, Daddy used to tell me, so I feel sure that my eyes narrowed at that girl usher. She was twenty-two and perfect, with Alice in Wonderland hair and prep school primness. An Englishman would appreciate that look.

At last, we were in our seats, incredible seats, fifteen rows back, just off center toward the right so that we'd have an ideal view of the cellist, a young Czech player who, Dylan whispered, was setting the world on fire with his interpretation of the Elgar.

"Well, I'm used to the du Pré, of course, so he'll have to wow me."

He glanced at me with an eyebrow up quizzically. "Oh, you know the du Pré? It's the gold standard, absolutely. My father saw her play it at Royal Festival Hall."

"That must have been amazing."

"I'm sure it was. But I wasn't born yet, so."

"He must have told you about it."

"Actually he died when I was too young to appreciate Elgar. Car crash."

I reached over and squeezed his hand. It was a good opportunity to broach the hand holding. "Dylan, I'm sorry."

"He wanted to be a concert violinist when he was a lad but didn't quite have the chops," he said. "Though I understand he was pretty good."

I was dying to get into this, if only so I could tell him about my father and his jazz, how he'd met Dizzy Gillespie once after a show and felt like naming my sister Dizzy afterwards. (She was lucky to come away with Ella, in the end.) The conductor and cellist walked out just then, the crowd showering them with applause like bubbling soup.

The music started, and yes, it was beautiful, and I could detect differences between the young Czech's attack and du Pré's, but all I could think about was Dylan's father. It was going to be my avenue *into* him. I'd pick at the small aperture and work it to an opening I could walk through. We had something in common. (Somewhere in here our hands parted ways.) We'd both lost our fathers. Both of us were living with a ghost of grief inside. Of course, I had a few hundred questions that occurred to me between the stark, emotional opening of the piece and the rousing

44

crescendo at the end, such as: Did your mother remarry? Did you love your step-father? Do you have siblings? (I'd want to steer clear of mine as long as possible, though.) When did you come to the States? Do you go back to England much? Is your mother all right? How come no milk-cheeked English girl ever snagged you before you could get away?

See, my mom was attracted to the Irish, and my dad — Patrick Phelan, Pat, even Paddy in some drinking circles — was just the kind to turn her head. But, she always cautioned me, "You have to watch the Irish, dear, and you can probably apply this to other men too. They like a long bachelorhood, but if he gets into his mid-thirties without being married — or these days living in sin with somebody — think twice before you jump into his boat. It could be leaky."

I always thought this was a thinly veiled reference to venereal disease. That would be Mom's style. In fact, she was talking about something more on the psychology side of things.

My thoughts kept skywriting as the cellist went through his calisthenics up there on the stage, flop-sweat visible in the light. Classical music can be very physical. Then I glanced over at Dylan in the middle of the third movement adagio and caught him wiping a tear out of his eye.

A lot's going on in his head, I thought. But I was touched and triply enamored of him at that moment, feeling his pain, like they say, the loss of his father, wanting to share with him, risk the history talk and stay up all night exhausting the lodes of grief the two of us had under the surface, mining from each other as much as we could of the magical ore that makes a perfect, lasting relationship. You mix it all up and put it in the smelter of love, and you cook up the gold that goes, one day, into your wedding bands.

Or not. I might have just been making stuff up.

Still, it was disappointing when, after the concert — the two of us standing once again outside the hall before (I assumed) we were to walk arm in arm down the street to Absinthe for our sexy late dinner — he took my hand and kissed it and asked in a thickened but strained voice if I minded re-*shed*-u-ling our meal.

"I didn't expect it, but the music has me a bit under the bus, I'm afraid. I feel awful to ask."

What was I supposed to say? "Please, no, don't worry about it. I get that way sometimes too. We can do it another time, Dylan."

He nodded conclusively. Then he bowed ever so slightly — 5'11"+ to my 5'6" — and kissed me on the cheek, holding both of my arms in his hands.

"Thank you for the concert," I said.

"Good night, Sarah."

As I watched him walk away (he glanced back once with a very anguished look in his eyes), I knew it had to be me. It's always me. I always seem to do something, or say something or look odd in some way or remind men of someone, that makes the question of a second date moot.

Was it my makeshift purse?

At home I couldn't bring myself to call Jules. Mean of me, I know, to let her think I might be spending the night somewhere else that night.

FIVE

On Sunday, after I phoned the hospital to check on Mrs. Bannerjee, I drove over to Jules's place in Bernal Heights. Wayne made us French toast and roasted potatoes and we ate outside on their deck overlooking a garden of almost nothing but ferns.

"He's obviously got something on the brain," Wayne said. "It's not you."

Wayne looks a lot like Stanley Tucci — not that that's a bad thing. I think they both carry their balding well, as did Ben. Not every man can make balding look good, and not every man with hair is a knockout, of course, so I try to keep an open mind. Jules took a long time getting used to Wayne's hairlessness, nearly a deal-breaker.

"He lost his father when he was a boy," I said. "That's all I know."

"He shouldn't get so fucked up over a piece of music then."

"Jules," Wayne said. "Come on."

"I'm just saying. I don't think it's his father that got him all weepy last night."

I wasn't going to be finishing breakfast. My stomach felt like a hamster was living in it. "He wasn't emotional when he told me about his father. He was calm."

"Did you tell him about Pat?" Jules asked.

"No, the music started. I didn't get a chance."

"Some people cry with certain music." Wayne was the resident audiophile, though in my opinion he wastes his sensitivities on indie rock. I never saw him cry over a record. "My dad cries every time he listens to *Carousel*."

"And the man's not gay," said Jules. "Incredible."

"You're not insinuating that Dylan's gay, are you?" The truth is, this hadn't even occurred to me.

"Not enough data," she said.

Wayne rolled his eyes. "He asked you out, didn't he? Unless they're sadistic, gay men don't usually ask women out on dates."

"He could be *maso*chistic," Jules said, getting delighted at the turn in the conversation. She winked at me over the rim of her samosa. "A closeted masochistic gay man."

"I can sure pick 'em."

"I'm kidding. You're being ridiculous. It's a fact that the man hasn't been feeling well, and the stress of wondering if you'd go home with him was too much. See, that's why women should just tell a guy up front, 'Look, I intend to sleep with you so just *relax*."

"I wasn't going to sleep with him last night."

"You could have told him *that*. Then he would've stopped wondering."

She was joking. I did the same with her when she had Wayne dangling on a string while they were dating. With Wayne she was trying to balance putting out so soon she looked like a skank with *holding* out so long it made her seem frigid. (Another word of my mom's.)

"What girls don't understand," Wayne said, "is that men aren't one hundred percent all about sex."

"Oh really. *You* were. You almost dumped me, you said."

"Because you were cockteasing."

"I was not!"

"Yes you were," I said. "You told me you were."

"All right, maybe so. It was a strategy."

Wayne wanted to be serious. "Listen, I've told you before. Men want the same thing women want. Just on a different time-table."

"That's charming, but it's bullshit."

"No, no, no. We want to settle down eventually. We do. We just don't think there's a big rush. Meeting the right person is pretty much accidental, after all. You want to be out there so you can have a lot of accidents."

I was thinking about this as Jules jumped all over him.

"You don't meet the love of your life by fucking everything that moves till you're thirty-six, *sweetheart*."

His age when they met.

"I was exaggerating."

"I know what he's trying to say." My eyes fell to the fern garden and landed on a hummingbird down there looking in futility for something to suckle at. "He's saying men are human beings."

"That's ridiculous," Jules said with no humor in her voice. "The best you can give them is that they're mammals."

*

The work week took me out of myself. I hope you haven't gotten the idea that I take my work lightly or that I'm not serious enough to be a good doctor, because I am a good doctor. Just not the best. (Few are.) I admit it with a certain amount of irony, though, because perfection in medicine is largely a myth, for one thing. Medicine, you might be surprised to learn, can do only so much. For the most part it's palliative, it makes sick people more comfortable and shortens the course of illnesses that would run themselves out anyway. The art of diagnosis is flawed, our ability to literally cure disease is limited, and if you want to know the truth, we don't even know what we're treating half the time. We throw what we've got at symptoms and hope that we catch the underlying bug in our net. Certainly there are well-known exceptions — polio, tuberculosis — but I'm not talking about vaccines; I'm talking about what you do when a patient comes in with a baffling constellation of symptoms, nothing's confirmed on testing, and things are getting worse. If she's lucky, you guess right. You treat for your best-guess diagnosis and she does get better. If she's not as lucky, you put her through all kinds of hell trying to treat the likely alternatives. And if she's unlucky, she gets worse and worse until she succumbs. I'm afraid it happens all the time.

This is why I have to compartmentalize, like an obsessive mail sorter. If I fretted over every medical decision I have to make, I'd have no happy outcomes at all. It's a matter of trusting my instincts and training. On the other hand, when things go wrong, very wrong, tragically wrong, it's a matter of beating my head against the nearest wall till I can live with what happened.

What makes *me* a good doctor, people have told me — patients — is that I really seem to care. Great bedside manner. I'll hold your hand or bring you a cup of tea. I'll read to you from *The Goddamn Kite Runner* if you ask me to. I want you to feel tended to and pampered when you're in the hospital on my watch. People become childlike when they're sick, and children need to be reassured.

That's why it was gratifying when, on Thursday, Mrs. Bannerjee was released and came straight to my office.

"You look good," I told her. "I was worried about you for a while there."

White-haired and a little tired looking, she gave me a dismissive wave. She was wrapped in a lovely red and gold sari.

"My husband says you sat by me all day Saturday. I wish I remembered."

"I wanted to be ready to pounce."

"Sunil was very impressed," she said. "He wants you to come to our daughter's wedding."

"Oh, I couldn't impose on you. I'd be a total stranger there in the middle of your family."

"He insists, Doctor Phelan. You saved my life. *I* insist too."

"When is it?"

"Next month. In Santa Barbara."

I told her I'd have to look at my schedule before I could commit, and she said she'd send an invitation here to the office anyway.

"My daughter will love to have you. She wanted to come up to meet you, as a matter of fact, and thank you herself."

"Please. You had an appendectomy. Dime a dozen."

"You don't know how *good* you are!"

No, I wanted to say, the problem is *other* people don't know how good I am.

A little bit bolstered, though, I went out at lunch time and got a card for Dylan. It showed a fish gasping for breath on a river bank, and inside was a hand picking the fish up and putting it back in the water. The sentiment, if that's the right word, was, "Help has arrived."

I almost gaffed by signing "Dr. Phelan." At the last second, my hand wrote, Sarah. No surname. I hoped he knew no other Sarahs at the moment.

*

I know you know that relationship novels all have at least one period — probably more — when the protagonist is waiting breathlessly for word from the object of her affection and doesn't get her deserved instant gratification. While waiting, she does things like talk to her best friend, visit her mother, paint her apartment walls, cook a ridiculously complex meal for herself (braised beef cheeks, in this case), and exercise obsessively. That's where we are now, so I won't go into all the details. You've got them down cold, and they are not cliché but necessary.

The point is, because I knew Dylan's address I knew the card must have been delivered by Saturday at the latest, Friday more likely, and because I had shamelessly included my phone number in it I knew he had everything he needed to initiate contact. My return address was on the envelope, so he could even pop by if he wanted. The only thing I'd left out was my email, which I thought would've been overkill. By the way, I threw in the phone number so I could say, "Give me a buzz so I can take *you* to dinner to thank you for the concert. It was fabulous."

In retrospect, I regretted the fabulous. It's such a vapid word and I didn't want to come off that way. Dylan was smart and well-rounded, clearly. His vocabulary hadn't farted all evening, both times I was with him. He hadn't even dropped one *g* in his *ing's*.

Another few days passed. I worked long hours, thank God. I saw Lyme disease, migraine, a nasty wound from a brown recluse that required the resection of a large chunk of a woman's behind, and other miscellaneous problems. They focused me on the important things — that is, until I got home each night and dined on leftover beef cheeks. I didn't even have the pickmyselfupedness to go on Commitment.com and try to start fresh. In a better frame of mind I might have said to myself, Dylan was a pipe dream and you put too much stock in him as a Serendipity Man. (Serendipity Man is perhaps the most coveted type of all and he can be any of the other types.) Time to start the hunt again. But the thing is, Dylan was the one who had led *me* on, if anything. He didn't have to invite me into his well-appointed tenement. He didn't have to ask me to the Elgar. These are the kinds of things that get a girl's hopes up. Plus the fact that he had no wedding ring (and so, sure, might be gay — it would figure), was pleasant and even gregarious at times over our coffee, and smiled a lot at the things I said. It added up — I had dared to think — to romantic interest.

All that was missing, two weeks after our "date," was romance. And interest.

Jules came by one evening with a gift. "I thought it would cheer you up," she said, unrolling a 2' x 3' full color poster of Il Divo, the world-famous hunk tenors.

"God, that's hideous."

"Are you kidding me? They're gorgeous. I see this on the wall opposite your bed, so you can prop yourself up on pillows and go to town with a vibrator."

"My gaydar is telling me they're all magnificently homosexual."

"Well, they're like Chippendales, then. As long as they keep their mouths shut, you can just look and fantasize."

"Thanks. You *have* cheered me up. When I'm happily married one day I'll laugh my head off at this."

"No word yet, huh?"

"Not a peep."

"Listen," she said with a lower, serious voice. "Do you think this guy is faux real?"

Our term for a phony. We liked the pun of it.

"No. Or I didn't *think* so."

"Just asking. Oh hey, I came across a Shaved Head Goatee man you might like. He works at that wine bar we went to once? Over in South Beach?"

"They're not my favorites. The Shaved Head Goatees."

"I know, but he was really nice. He likes jazz. I thought of Pat."

"You want to set me up to marry my father? How Freudian."

"Sometimes a Shaved Head Goatee man who likes jazz is just a Shaved Head Goatee man."

"I think I'm going to hibernate all summer and come out in the fall. See what there is to see then." It was a depressing thought. Weekend trips to wine country with my new man would be out. Summertime love. It's very nice, and I had projected it onto Dylan. Showing a lot of skin, sailing on the bay, taking evening walks, getting sticky and sweaty when you make love in the afternoon under a beam of warm sunlight. *Criminy.* "Oh, by the way. Get this for some pathetic karma. I've been invited to an Indian wedding."

"Like Pocahontas?"

"No, like Bollywood."

"Seriously? How'd that happen?"

I told her about Mrs. Bannerjee, and she agreed that the woman was overreacting.

"I bet she wants to set you up with her *son*. Like an arranged marriage."

"I don't think so."

"No, that's what they do. They're very old-school about these things. The families get together and decide, and the boy and girl — they have no say in it. In a lot of ways, it would make things easier for us when you think about it."

"Mrs. Bannerjee's been in the States for forty years. I think she's past all that."

"*Mr.* Bannerjee is the one to watch. They're super-patriarchal."

"I think she just wanted to thank me for taking care of her. Anyway, I'm not going to go. It's in Santa Barbara. End of June."

Jules was holding Il Divo — more accurately I Divi? — up against my newly painted wall. "I don't know," she said. "I think you ought to maybe shake things up, go in a completely new direction. Marry an Indian man and let him take care of *you* for a change."

"Right. I'm sure that'd work out just perfect."

*

I picked up my cellphone beside the alarm clock. It was two-thirty in the morning.

"Sorry," the voice said, and it took me half a beat to recognize his accent. "Is this Dr. Phelan? Sarah?"

Unlike movie characters who receive middle-of-the-night phone calls, I didn't flick on the lamp. I don't know why they do that.

"Who's this?"

"Sorry. It's Dylan? Dylan Cakebread?"

He sounded like he was asking me, poor man. Identity crisis brought on by an unwise delay in making a move on the woman of his dreams?

"Dylan! Of course. Is something wrong?" And then, though I knew perfectly well: "What time is it?"

"Well." Hesitation. Throat-clearing. I imagined him also in the dark, or maybe seated in his Italian chair, in his robe and with his hair tousled, lit by the small chrome ultra-modern lamp beside the chair. "The truth is, I don't know, really. I was thinking of you."

My God, Jules had anticipated one of these.

"Really."

"Sarah, the thing is. I mean. Last week when I left suddenly—"

"Two weeks. Two and a half, actually."

"Yes. Sorry. The point I'm trying to make — well, the same thing happened this evening and I'm actually getting a bit worried."

What was he saying? That he'd left another woman standing there on the street and this was getting to be a habit?

"So beautiful music makes you verklempt. Really, Dylan, it was no big deal."

"I mean, I feel terrible."

"Sometimes —"

"I'm trying to tell you. Literally, I feel awful. As in sick. I woke up in soaking wet sheets from the sweating, and I'm dizzy and extremely nauseous."

He was ill. He was calling his doctor in the middle of the night.

My heart became a lump of cold wax, but I was getting out of bed as I told him to wait for me. I'd take him to the ER myself.

He was waiting for me at his doorstep, wrapped in a trench coat and looking, in the light of a streetlamp, like a confused vampire. The collar of his coat was up, and his face was pale enough to read by. His eyes were aimed at the gutter, where a Styrofoam to-go container was cocked and fluttering in the night wind. He was mesmerized. Probably on the verge of fainting.

I parked and left the engine running as I got out to help him.

"You look pretty bad," I said. My hand went instinctively to his forehead. No fever.

"It's been happening more often. I can't figure it out."

"We'll get you feeling better. Don't worry."

I had no real right to say so, but it's what you say. I was running a few possible diagnoses through my mind with very little information to go on, and sadly one of the first to pop up was a drug reaction. Maybe our friend from across the sea had a cocaine problem? Got ahold of some bad ecstasy? Who knows, but in a different category of patient I'd think about something like that first.

"Have you taken anything tonight, Dylan?" I led him to the car, seeing that he was without pants under that trench coat. He had slippers on, nice leather backless ones. "Any kind of medication or anything? Maybe you're having an allergic reaction."

"No, nothing. No alcohol either."

He was not drunk. I could see that. His hand was cool as I took it to guide him into Pat's front passenger seat. When the door was closed, he slouched against it, his head on the window, eyes closed.

It wasn't far, and I drove toward the emergency department on Geary without asking any more questions. Dylan might have been sleeping, it was hard to tell. He'd crashed. I had no idea what he experienced that night, or the night we met at Davies, for that matter. Whatever it was, it recurred more often now and it was scaring him. He was too young for a cardiac problem, I believed. I'd seen his blood work. Good cholesterol levels and perfect blood pressure. I knew he wasn't diabetic. I knew he'd had no similar problems in his medical history, nor had his father died of a heart attack or stroke. Car accident, still a young man.

I pulled into the emergency bay and ran inside. At reception the nurse knew me from my occasional ER obligations, all part of a short-staffed outfit. I told her I had a patient out in the car. When I went back outside, Dylan was trying to climb out of the car on his own and making a disaster of it, a sudden bout of syncope by the look of him. I ran up and got an arm around him.

"We'll take care of you now. You let us do the walking, okay?"

"Yes, mum."

He wasn't trying to make me laugh. I thought he might pass out any second.

An orderly came out with a wheelchair and Dylan let himself into it like a puppet with his strings suddenly snipped.

"Get him on i.v. normal saline," I told the ER doc, a man I knew but hadn't much business with, fifty-ish and sporting fairly sexy gray temples. He always reminded me of Eliot Gould. "I'm thinking he could be dehydrated."

"Yeah? What's the backstory?"

He thought he was being funny. "Backstory? He's sick. He called and said he was in trouble."

"Gee, most patients call 911. Get a wife or someone to bring 'em in. This guy gets door-to-door from his physician. Not too shabby."

Insinuating something. The funny thing was, I didn't mind if he thought I was "with" Dylan. I could use some rumors flying around about my love life.

"He didn't know what to do," I said. "Cut him some slack."

"You want to handle him? I'm up to my nostrils in war wounds."

"Oh no. Bad?"

"Must be a turf thing out there. General is full, so we're getting the overflow tonight."

He was talking about gangs. I didn't see much of that up in San Rafael, though one-off incidents did come in overnight sometimes. Gunshot wounds, stab wounds. The ones that really got to me were the innocent bystanders, like the poor kid in Oakland who was practicing his piano one afternoon when a stray bullet came through the window and paralyzed him from the waist down. Surreal. And infuriating.

"I'll take Mr. Cakebread then. Let me know if you need any help."

"Too late for that."

I caught up with Dylan a few minutes later behind a curtain partition, lying on his back with the drip already in his arm. He had his other arm thrown over his forehead as if to keep the light out. One knee was up. He had the bearing of someone who expects another wave of excruciating cramps any moment. Without his trench coat, his bath robe was revealed, a plain plaid number like you see fathers wearing on Christmas morning in TV and movies. A V-shaped slice of his wan chest was exposed, smooth and creamy, without hair. What a baby boy.

I looked at the chart that had been started for him.

"Well, your BP's fine. Your temperature's fine. A little low even. Good pulse."

He spoke without lowering his arm. "You must think I'm ridiculous. Boy who cried wolf."

"Not at all." I sat on the edge of the bed. "You strike me as the type who waits too long to call for help. It must have been bad."

"I thought I was going to pass out. I was getting ready for bed and everything went white on me. Tunneled."

"Seeing stars, are we? Maybe you haven't been eating well."

"Possible."

"Keeping yourself too busy. You have to remember to throw some food down your neck every now and then."

He peeked out from under his arm. "I like the way you speak. Keep speaking."

"Sorry, no can do. I have to start poking around under the hood to see what's the matter with you."

"I'm completely embarrassed, you realize."

"Can't have that. You're sick. Nobody's sick on purpose."

I started with blood tests. Looking for anything I could find — a mild MI, an infection? — the pool of possibilities was huge. While I started a differential diagnosis on the ER computer, I had a nurse practitioner do the physical work-up. He reported nothing abnormal, aside from the patient's nausea and dizziness. In effect, this appeared to be a more acute version of whatever it was that had prompted Dylan to see me in the first place.

He seemed to feel better as the saline got into his system, but that might have been more of a placebo effect all in all. He hadn't complained of diarrhea or excessive urination, nothing to suggest dehydration other than his appearance. The more I looked at the vitals (and now the blood work came back, around four in the morning — normal across the board), the more I was ready to conclude something as mundane as a lingering hangover. He had the face of a man who'd put it away for several hours and then hit the big brick wall of toxicity.

I checked the blood alcohol results. Zero.

"Well, Dylan," I said. "We're releasing you. There's nothing we can find to explain the way you feel."

"Ah."

"All things considered, I think you're probably exhausted and have to rest. Recharge."

"Easier said than done."

"I know the feeling."

I said I'd drive him back to his place. I had to get home too, shower and change for work at eight.

He was silent on the drive to Fell Street. Slouchy over there in the passenger seat, looking like a kid on a long-distance guilt trip. His eyes seemed unfocused, drifting with the scenery as light started to come up and turn the city to muddy shades of gray.

I double-parked in front of his building and went around to help him out. He was mumbling apologies as I headed him toward the steps like the walking wounded. I felt a good portion of his weight on me, but the warmth of his body too, and I can't say I wasn't getting off on this role for myself: the There For You Girl. I'd always wanted to be a There For You Girl. It makes you feel needed, Joanna on the Spot. Of course, you also open yourself to being used — a pretty big risk when you're as fragile lovewise as I've been these last few years. I've heard of There For You Girls who watch helplessly while the man they're there for hunts down and snags another woman like a wildebeest. It's got to be hard. I ran all this through my mind before letting go of Dylan at his door, trying to decide exactly how "there" for him I wanted to be.

"I can't thank you enough," he said.

"Well, you're welcome. I guess."

"I'm mortified, obviously. I almost wish you'd found something horrendous — curable but horrendous — so I could justify all the trouble you've gone to."

"I'm at the hospital in the middle of the night all the time. It goes with the territory."

"I'm just saying — I appreciate it. Your concern. It means a lot."

"Appreciation appreciated. You can stop groveling now."

He was looking down at me with his hands plunged deep into his trench coat pockets. Then — I thought he was getting his keys — he brought them out and took my upper arms and held me for a second, looking into my eyes with sincerity so thick it might as well have been syrup, and he kissed me. I think it was meant to be a mere thank you kiss at first, but it lingered and I helped it linger longer and I pushed myself into it so he'd know it was all right, keep going, and we kissed there under his crooked awning for what might have been twenty minutes for all I can say. I had an out-of-body experience, I believe. Or better, such an intense *in*-body experience that it amounts to the same thing.

"My goodness," he said. "That was unexpected."

SIX

That day was a complete blur. From the office, stealing a minute's break, I emailed Jules and told her that "something" had happened. I didn't go into it, I just said something had happened with Mr. Cakebread and I'd tell her all about it when I could. I also phoned Mom, who'd have missed me in the morning because I didn't have time to stop by.

"I had to work all night," I said. "Emergency."

"You poor thing. Now you're putting in a full day."

"It's all right. I'm kind of high, to tell you the truth."

I didn't say why. I had Dylan's kiss on my mouth. I'd probably refrain from eating so it wouldn't be diluted by a dull cafeteria lunch. I could still recall the mild odor on him of the ER too — *eau de hôpital*. It's a tang that I must usually take for granted and so not notice it, but coming from him, laced through his hair, embedded in his coat and robe, following him like a fog, it was something I couldn't help relishing. Weird, but sort of sexy. It mingled with his natural smell, which was kind of woody, cedary, like the inside of a hope chest.

"Come by this evening if you have time. I'm roasting a chicken."

"Tired of lasagna?"

"The chickens were two-for-one at Safeway."

"I'll try to make it. Day's already getting away from me."

It was not easy to concentrate, but patients do have a way of making me focus. Their misery is attention-grabbing. My maternal instincts, such as they are, make me want to fix their boo-boos and poor-sores. A young man with a fever is just heartsickening to me, a girl with a rash on her pretty cheeks, a little boy with mumps. I can't have it.

The last of them left with his prescription clenched in hand, and Becky started shutting down. I told her I had some paperwork to finish before I could go.

"Can I say something, Doctor Phelan?"

"Sure."

"You look terrible. You've looked terrible all day. Didn't you sleep last night?"

"Unexpected trip to the ER. You remember Mr. Cakebread? Came in a few weeks ago."

"What was the problem?"

Becky is middle-aged and plump, in an appealing way, and she means well. She comes off as a kindergarden teacher or something like that. Has her hair in a bowl cut and always wears dresses in the colors of after-dinner mints.

"Don't know. All the tests were negative."

"Hypochondriac," she said.

"May-be." I hadn't thought about that. "Only I don't think you can fake looking as bad as he did."

"He's the one who looks like Jude Law, right?"

"Does he?" I raised a quizzical eyebrow. "I didn't notice."

When she was gone, I opened Jules's email. It had no body, only a subject line. "*WHAT HAPPENED*?!"

*

Mom fed me her roast chicken and her Rice-A-Roni and brussels sprouts with butter and Bacos. It was heavy on my sensitive stomach — my anticipating, anxious stomach. I wanted there to be a message from Dylan — cell, land line, semaphore, I didn't care — or for him to be standing outside my building when I got home, a sheaf of flowers in his hand. It was hard to think of anything else during supper.

"Get some sleep," Mom said, taking it well. She always could read me.

"I will. Rough twenty-four hours."

"I wanted to tell you," she said. Her back was to me as she fiddled with the dishes. Her hands were in turquoise rubber

61

gloves. "Your sister called today."

"Oh?" You could have recited "Hiawatha" in the pause I dropped there. "What did she want?"

"Just to say hi. No news. Tucker is fine. The kids. They're going to the south of France in July. A colleague of Tucker's has a house there."

"Lucky them."

"She asked about you."

"Did she."

"Wondered how you've been."

"What did you tell her?"

"I said you're busy. Really really busy."

"True enough."

"Sarah?"

"Mom, *please*."

"Don't you think you could just write her a card? A little note?"

Mom was facing me now, her eyes getting that dartboard look she gets when she might cry.

"We hit an impasse," I reminded her. We'd been all through it. Many many times. "She doesn't want to give an inch."

"You don't understand each other, that's all."

"That I agree with."

"You know your dad would want —"

She stopped herself. I didn't have to say a thing.

*

Dylan wasn't at my place. Of course he wasn't. It was late. Nine by the time I got there. If he'd been around, he got tired of waiting. The flowers must have started to wilt.

No messages either.

"He kissed me," I told Jules on the phone.

"That's all? He kissed you?"

I went through it all for her. The lowdown, as Jules and I like to call it. When I was finished, she said, "I thought you were going to tell me he sweet-talked you into bed."

"You're disappointed."

"Not exactly. I thought there was more to it. *Something happened,* you said."

"He was in no condition to do more than kissing. I don't know what's wrong with the poor guy."

She was impressed with my There For You Girl above-and-beyond.

"He'll remember it when he feels better. You think you can pick up where you left off?"

"I know *I* can."

"What about him?"

"He did seem kind of urgent with the kiss. It came up all of a sudden. It took both of us by surprise."

"That means he's been thinking about it for a long time. They can't help it. It comes busting out of them."

"I just hope he's feeling better today. I'd have thought he might call."

"Oh, here we go."

"What."

"How's the sea bass this evening?"

"Huh? I don't get it."

"You're being a waiter."

"Funny."

"You have to take the bull by the horns on this one. He *sounds* too good to let slip away. It's like landing a big old tuna on the deck and watching it flop over the side."

"You have fish on the brain tonight."

"You know what I'm saying. I want you to call him tomorrow. If you can't reach him, I want you to drop by."

"No, I can't do that. It'll make me look desperate."

"You're worried about your patient. You tried calling but there was no answer. You came over to make sure he was doing all right."

"But there's nothing wrong with him."

"Nothing you know of. Besides, it's an excuse. It's almost better if he gets that it's a ruse, see?"

I didn't know what to say.

"How was the kiss?" she asked after a few beats.

"God, it was unbelievable."

"Screw you, then. If you aren't going to make a move on a guy who looks like Jude Law and kisses unbelievably, there's no hope for you."

And that's where we left it. She was right. There was no good comeback to the truth.

*

I had a night of peculiar dreams. Dylan wasn't in them, but there was, in one of them, the recurring character of Faceless Man, who drops by now and then to remind me that I'm chasing a phantom. Sometimes he gets me in a clutching embrace and seems ready to reveal himself to me, but then he turns to mist or smoke and dissolves before my eyes and I'm left hugging my pillow. I remember the comfort there once was in waking from a bad dream and finding Ben there next to me in the bed, and in how he didn't mind if I woke him up to tell him about it as he held me in his arms. He'd say something funny like, The wolf is clearly your id — it wants to devour the rest of you. Other times I'd wake up and find him sleepless and looking at the ceiling, and when I'd ask if anything was wrong he'd tell me he was working out a problem in his novel.

There's a beautiful closeness that grows when two people sleep together for years. Conscious and subconscious intermingle, you show your own vulnerabilities and embrace your partner's. He snores, you sleep-talk. His feet are cold, you get really bad breath. It's all welcomed.

I missed that stuff.

This time Faceless Man went a long way toward showing himself to be Dylan. He led me on a walk through what I recognized to be the Panhandle, the north boundary of which is Fell Street, if you know the city. He was wearing a trench coat that flowed behind him as he walked fast ahead of me. I was in a nightgown. It's not like me to go out in public in a nightgown. Every now and then Faceless Man would turn to look back toward me, reaching for my hand in the same motion, but his profile was obscured by fog or smeared in a way that kept me from seeing who he was. I thought, understanding the game, He's taking me home, to Dylan's, and yes, sure enough, I found myself standing at the foot of Dylan's steps, Faceless Man at the top but in shadows, and he was naked under the open coat.

Oddly, his penis — I couldn't help staring — was bound in kitchen twine, like a trussed-up rump roast. It wasn't very appetizing from where I stood. Large and red and ponderous. I couldn't begin to imagine how to get the string off of it without hurting him — a local anesthetic, maybe? A topical.

Anyway, as per usual, he vanished. I tried the door and it wouldn't open.

When I woke up I tried not to analyze the dream because it seemed to be telling me that Dylan, if Faceless Man were him, was metaphorically deformed. I wasn't ready to believe that. I just wanted to have a goddamn affair with a spine-tinglingly beautiful man, okay? My very own Adonis.

Actually, I just wanted a way to be happy without all the doubt.

In this mood I went down to the garage to warm up Pat for my drive to work. I phoned Mom from there to tell her I wouldn't stop by. Another full day in store for me. I'd have to attend a staff meeting at lunch time too, then play catch-up all afternoon and hope I could get through the crowd in my waiting room by six.

The garage door opened, and there was Dylan standing to one side, peering into the dark. My headlights were on him. He wore pressed tan pants and a dark blazer over a gray-green open-necked shirt. He put his hand to his brow like the bill of a cap, and in the other hand was a large floppy sunflower.

The minute he recognized Pat he flashed a smile and began waving. I pulled up beside him and he mouthed "Don't get out! Roll down the window!"

"What are you doing here? Are you okay?"

"I feel ten times better, Sarah. I don't know what did it, but I put myself to bed after you left and didn't wake up till this morning. It was like my blood was refreshed, if that makes any sense. I hopped right out of bed at daybreak."

"That's wonderful. It's good to see you so chipper."

"Listen. About yesterday morning. On the steps."

"Oh, please, no. I understand. You were in a daze."

"That kiss. I just wanted to tell you. That kiss was — it was millennial. I'm serious. It was the kiss of my life."

I wasn't sure I was good to drive. My pulse was accelerating as I looked at him. The smile. The color — the *colour* — in his cheeks. He was healed, and he was telling me, in his way, that I'd somehow rocked his world.

"I have to admit, it was pretty good for me too."

"It was transformational, Sarah. *Transcendental*. It made me realize something. That I've been living in a cocoon. I haven't been *breathing* — for months now."

"I know what you mean."

"Here." He handed me the sunflower. "I was walking past a florist on my way to the office, and the owner was out hosing down the pavement. She took a look at me and said, You look like you're in love, sir. Take this."

With that, he bent down toward me and I knew to stretch my neck toward him. He kissed me again. He kissed me while smiling, which has a special feel to it, you know, and it makes you have to smile too. I did. He stepped back from the car.

"Are you free tonight? Can I take you to dinner?"

"I'd like to take *you*. I owe you one." I sounded breathless and a little baffled.

"I'm fine with that," he said, laughing. "Call me when you get off. I'll be home before you, I'm guessing."

He walked toward Lombard, presumably to catch a bus. I might have offered a ride but I was too confused. He turned around once to look back, just like Faceless Man, only this time it was someone I knew. He waved good-bye and then made the international gesture that says, *Call me*.

All of a sudden I had very very high hopes.

*

We met that evening at a restaurant on Chestnut, near me, that's often hard to get into. We were there late, though, close to ten o'clock, and a discreet twenty from Dylan to the hostess got us a table for two in the front window. We ordered a bottle of wine and a few appetizers instead of two entrees, because, as Dylan put it to the waitress, "We're feeling eclectic tonight."

He had changed clothes, now in black slacks, a gray knit shirt that clung nicely to his chest, and a leather jacket, while I had picked a black wool skirt and cream sweater that made me look, the way Jules viewed it, like I wanted to be plucked from the convent and defiled. It suited my mood.

"I came over for school," he was telling me. "Decided not to go back when I was finished. To South London. Got myself legal as soon as I could."

"That's funny. There was a time I'd have done anything to live in England."

"Well, both have their pluses and minuses. I'm a full-fledged Californian now, though."

"Bay Area all along?"

"No. Not till fairly recently. San Diego before that."

"No kidding." My sister's territory. "Not La Jolla, I hope."

"I went there quite a bit. Why?"

"No reason."

"Have you ever been?"

"Long time ago."

"Small world."

I felt like I was coming off as tense and harboring some kind of mysterious neurotic grudge. I forced a smile. "So how did you get into architecture? I've always liked — architecture."

He smiled with a wistful look about him. "The great buildings of London, of course. Beautiful. Old. They're in my mind like pictures, so when it came time to think about what I wanted to do, I just thought, why not?"

"Is there anything of yours in San Francisco I could look at? I'd love to see something you designed."

"Not yet. There will be. One of these days." He looked out the window for a moment, then back at me. "Sadly, I've had to prostitute myself with a lot of cookie-cutter residential work for the time being. To get my name out there."

"You're on your own?"

"How do you mean?"

"Not with a company?"

"Oh, of course. No, I'm trying to have a go at a one-man shop."

"Well, more accolades for you, then. You won't be the

anonymous staff designer in a big firm. Takes confidence."

"I could use a little more of that. Sometimes I'm scared out of my wits."

He seemed to be blushing in the low light. His smile was self-deprecating and warm. I'd have kissed him again right there if we weren't in public.

"And how about you?" he asked. "How'd you get to become such an exceptional doctor?"

"You think I'm an exceptional doctor? Please, I'm a family practice cog in a giant heartless HMO. The other doc in my suite calls it McMedicine."

"The way you handled me the other night? Yes, I think you're exceptional."

"That's flattering. I think I did it out of self-interest."

"Is that so."

He took on a lover's look. You know it. Narrowing eyes, wry smile, the slightest hint of a fanged and stalking predatory animal in there. It made me warm behind the breast bone.

"I mean — okay, I'll be honest. I was attracted to you from the get-go."

"In your office?"

"Oh yeah."

"You had me where you wanted me. Half naked and shivering."

"I *tried* to maintain a professional demeanor."

"Absolutely."

The conversation, touching on the delicate now, was surprisingly easy. Still, there was a moment after that when neither of us spoke and I began to feel self-conscious.

"Sarah's a beautiful name," he said.

"Really? It's a little biblical for my taste, and then there's Sarah Palin. Phelan, Palin. People can be cruel."

"That's a shame."

"But I always remind myself it made my dad happy. He was a jazz lover."

"So it's for Sarah Vaughan?"

"Very good! A lot of people don't get it."

"I'm a big fan."

"My sister's named for Ella Fitzgerald."

"Strange name for a girl. Fitzgerald."

"That's good. You're funny when you feel well."

"I try."

"I'm glad you're feeling well."

"You said your father was a jazz lover," he went on. "Past tense. He's moved on to light opera or something?"

"Oh, no. No. He died. A few years ago now."

"I'm sorry."

"Ah, well. You know what it's like."

"No, not really. I hardly knew my father. He's a sort of historical figure in my mind. Like Disraeli."

I felt myself nodding. The difference was obvious. I wished I hadn't mentioned Dad at all, because now the tears were starting to well up and I didn't want to go there. All I needed was for my mascara to run down my chin and into the sunchoke salad.

"You loved him a lot," Dylan said.

Now I shook my head. Not to say I didn't love my father but to steer us away from this kind of talk. I was in too good a mood. My mating prospects were on the upswing. I didn't want to get maudlin on our first date.

"So your folks named you after Bob Dylan, right?"

With a tolerant purse of the lips, he chuckled through his nose. "No. Actually, Dad was extremely fond of Dylan Thomas."

"Ah."

"'Do not go gentle into that good night.'"

"Sad."

"Ironic, anyway. Because he didn't. Go gentle, that is."

I didn't know what to say. Hard to believe, I know. Instead, I took his hand and we sat for a little while, not speaking at all.

SEVEN

I guess I should probably go into the Perfect Penis now.

Other women might be different, but Jules and I developed this idea when we were girls, independently, of what a man's penis must look like in the truthful light of day. Neither of us had been abused or anything like that, and my only glimpse of one was when the pervert showed me his while waiting for the J-Church. I really didn't see it, or maybe I've blocked the reality of it out of my memory, so that what remains is kind of a fuzzy little rodent peeking out from his fly — a gerbil. It was gerbil-colored.

But anyway, Jules and I eventually shared with each other, in high school I think it was, our idea of what the penis must look like in its exotic, forbidden, unimaginable erect state. We could have tried to score some gay porn, I suppose, but that didn't even occur to us. Instead, we preferred and relied on what our minds' eyes served up, and this became the Perfect Penis.

It resembled an ancient fetish object, more than anything, an ivory (if the man is white) or, say, teak (if the man is black) dildo, for want of a better word, whose only identifiable feature is its slightly swollen end, oh, and its distinctive size and shape. We had no idea of its size, really, but its shape was more or less like the tapering leg of a mid-century coffee table, and it would be just as smooth, and probably varnished too, for all we knew. Jules thought that it would look more like the handle of a baseball bat, but with a less pronounced knob on the end, while I had real trouble getting past the idea of foreskin, which I'd heard of but couldn't fit into our prototype. We drew pictures. We tried to imagine this object tucked between the legs of some of our favorite boys. For a little while we even tried to make one, out of pieces of wood we'd find in Golden Gate Park. We whittled on them with steak knives. The best we came up with was way too rough looking and scary — you'd get splinters if you had sex with that thing — so eventually we gave up and just let our image of the Perfect Penis have its way.

I suppose boys were trying to imagine the Perfect Pussy too. Weren't they surprised when they first encountered that wild thing, in its own bushy habitat.

Jules and I were shocked too. An actual erect penis, it turned out, was far more exotic than our simple, smooth fetish wands. It was much more textured than we might have imagined. It had bluish veins crinkling up and down its length, and a thick spongy tube running up the underside like a snorkel. The head was like a mutated plum or shiitake mushroom, with a tiny bird mouth on the end, and, examined closely, it had that weird triangular seam underneath. Talk about eye-opening. Our Perfect Penis was relegated to the whaling museum. Fantasy scrimshaw.

Believe it or not, I was the first to experience the real thing. Who with and under what circumstances aren't important, but I rushed over to Jules's house right after and told her what I'd seen.

"You're *shitting* me!" she said.

"No, it's positively freakish. I can't get over it."

"Too bad you can't take a picture next time."

"I don't know where I'd have it developed. I'd get arrested if I tried to take it to Fotomat."

These the days before digital cameras.

Jules had been so interested in the reality of the human penis that she forgot to ask how the sex was. I wouldn't have been able to tell her. It was over with in milliseconds.

Anyhow, I bring up the Perfect Penis and its mythos now because, after dinner, after a serene kiss outside my building, after vacillating a thousand times between the restaurant and home and not knowing, even as we kissed, what I'd decide, I invited Dylan up for a nightcap.

These things are always about the same. Even though both of us had sex on the brain, I was never a first-date putter-outer and, Dylan said after the fact, he'd never have presumed to go all the way so early in a courting. He was curious about my place. He really did want a nightcap too.

But we kissed again on the landing, and again outside my apartment door. His breath was fresh — he must have snuck an Altoid when I wasn't looking. My breath was probably cheesy and squiddy, but he didn't seem to mind.

Inside, we kissed again, but upon separating he began to look around the place and I rushed to the kitchen to get an antediluvian bottle of cognac from under the sink, and two juice glasses. I had no snifters. No crystal to speak of. At least I picked juice glasses that were unadorned and not my collector Flintstones jelly jars.

Immediately, of course, I was self-conscious about the complete lack of design in my place. Bland Macy's furniture, a few odd *objet d'art*, such as the tin toys I used to drool over in my twenties, the board game boards framed on the wall, and, if Dylan looked closely, the little plastic soldiers hiding in my potted plants.

I love all those things, but, God, what a drip they must make me seem like. I should have thought to strip the place to bare walls.

When I came back from the kitchen, I saw that he'd discovered my "Land of the Giants" lunchbox, which I'd left on the coffee table. He was examining it way too closely.

"Oh, that," I said.

"Interesting."

"It's a nostalgia thing. Even though I wasn't even born when that show was on."

"No, it's beautiful. In a peculiar way."

"I use it as a purse," I ventured. "My casual purse, I mean. Here."

I held out one of the glasses.

"Ta," he said.

"Ta. I love that."

"Sorry."

"Please. It's charming." Then: "*You're* very charming."

"You're very generous."

"Why don't you sit down?"

"Because I'd rather stand close to you."

He put his glass down. I put mine down. He took a step toward me and took me in his arms with just the right amount of assertive pressure and not a whiff of aggression — a fine line many men can't finesse — and we kissed again.

We kissed a long time, I think, until he buried his face in my neck and held my body in a way that felt like he was trying to incorporate me into *his* body. It was magnificent and still gives me shivers to recall. He whispered my name. My legs wobbled.

"Normally," I said. "Typically I don't —"

"Neither do I."

He was swaying me lightly to music that must have been playing in his head. I don't believe it was the Elgar.

"And when I do have a man come up the first time, I never—"

"I wouldn't think you would."

"But I *have* seen you almost naked."

"Yes, you have."

"And I've massaged your prostate, haven't I."

"As it were."

"Dylan?"

"Sarah?"

"When we go into my bedroom, don't be upset by the rubber dinosaur on the wall or the framed mambo album covers. It's just a phase. I can get new things for the walls."

"I think I'll manage," he said, and I led him by the hand to the place no man had ever been before.

In just a little while I learned, with relief, that Dylan's was not the Perfect Penis. Subconsciously I already knew, having checked him for testicular cancer and hernia, but I do think it would have been disconcerting to confront a smooth marble phallic totem when we got naked together. There's such a thing as *too* perfect — I don't want to fuck Michelangelo's David, for godssakes — and, besides, everything else about him (aside from his idiopathic illness) struck me as perfect. Endowed with the Perfect Penis, he'd have been instantly off-limits as far as I'm concerned.

What he was, in bed, was all the things I could ever ask of a man. Responsive, appreciative, willing, creative, passionate, and (very important to me) funny. I have to laugh during sex. If I can't laugh I can't —

Never mind. Dylan made me laugh.

EIGHT

And so we began the honeymoon.

All relationships enjoy one, and all relationship novels show it. It's the warm, silly, invigorating, sometimes exasperatingly wonderful, painfully pleasurable period when you're not sleeping much, your thoughts are magnetically and constantly drawn back to this new person in your life, and you find things like food and bodily functions unbelievably annoying because all you want to do is lie naked with your lover and screw every ninety minutes or so when you're together, which is, let's face it, fairly inconvenient. All you do, besides that, is talk. You talk about your past, present, and newly imaginable future. You soak up his story and study the minutiae of his personality like a philatelist. You know he's doing the same with you, so, like I said before, you try not to let your bigger secrets out, at least not too soon, but you can't help it. The urge to reveal yourself to him completely is too great.

"I haven't laid eyes on my sister in five years," you blurt. Not smart. You're not ready for the honeymoon to end.

"Family feud?"

"Not exactly. More like permanent loathing."

"Well, since you're perfect —"

"Almost perfect."

"Since you're *almost* perfect, she must be in the wrong."

"I wish I could have you talk to her. God."

We were in his flat, lounging on plumped pillows in bed and eating leftover shawarma from a takeout place around the corner. I was surprised at how easy it was to eat naked in front of a man, with tinkling Ravel piano music playing in the next room and a vivid afternoon light the color of persimmons coming in through the window.

"I have a brother back in England I haven't seen in ages," Dylan said. He sounded matter-of-fact about it, as if estrangement from a sibling were common enough.

"Family feud?"

"Not really. We're just completely and utterly different."

His brother, he said, remembered their father well. He was the elder of the two children and seemed to want to follow in Dad's footsteps, which as it turned out, weren't all that promising.

"In retrospect," he told me in a lower voice, aiming his eyes up toward the corner of the room, "it seems my father was — eccentric."

I leaned into him and kissed his cheek.

"I mean, really, anyone who names his child after a poet who died of alcohol poisoning has to be a bit odd, deep down, wouldn't you say?"

"What's your brother's name?"

"Steve."

"Now *that* I don't get."

"Maybe Mum won the naming rights first time round, I don't know."

To get him off the topic of my sister, I asked him more questions about his dad. And Steve. He answered them willingly, without much emotion, that I could see, in fact, with kind of a flatness that made me think he'd been all through it many times, on many levels, and had reached his comfort zone — a place I hadn't yet come to where Ella was concerned. Steve, he said, was a heavy drinker, a bachelor-womanizer, an operator of construction equipment in London. He'd worked on several famous buildings there, including the Swiss Re headquarters (The Gherkin, some people call it, though it looks more like a Fabergé rocket ship) — "So architecture sort of runs in the family," Dylan joked — but seemed to have no appreciation for the actual structures, their design, their beauty or aesthetics, or even their function. "No, in actual fact, he might as well be putting up malls and petrol stations for all he gets out of the work. At the end of his shifts he goes down to pub and gets pissed and grabby with women, then sleeps alone. I tell him — I used to tell him — the clock will run out on that kind of behavior one day, and he says, 'Too right, mate. That's the 'ole point, innit?'"

Dylan's impersonation made his brother sound like a character in a Mike Leigh movie. A real East Ender.

"Different strokes," I said.

"So what's at the root of your problem with Ella? It can't just be sibling rivalry."

"I don't know if I want to go into it."

"Chicken."

"What?"

"I called you a chicken."

"I'm not a chicken. I just think the whole thing is too boring to deal with while we're naked and eating shawarma."

Dylan began to make chicken sounds. *Bawk, bawk-bawk-bawk.*

"Stop it. I'm not being chicken."

"You're not naked. You're covered in feathers."

It didn't take long for him to put his food aside, carefully — he didn't want to make a mess — and to hop up on the bed and do a strutty chicken mime for me, until he had me laughing in agony. I was laughing as much at the way his penis flopped up and down and back and forth and how unaware he was of it as he strutted.

"Oh my God," I said, almost breathless. "You're *whimsical*, aren't you!"

"I'm *not*! How dare you!"

"Yes you are! You're whimsical, you fey Englishman you!"

He stopped his chicken dance and stared me down. "I'm sorry, did you just call me fey?"

"I did. You're whimsical and fey."

"I might be the littlest bit whimsical — at times — but I don't have a fey bone in my body. Them's fighting words, madame."

I threw a black olive at his delicate package but it struck his navel, and he fell on his back and played dead. We both broke out in cramps of laughter. After a little bit of that we screwed again.

*

Jules was the one who pointed out a few days later that our fey Englishman seemed to be over his mystery illness. I hadn't seen her much lately, so this came via instant message. "You cured him, kiddo. Nice work. You should do a journal article on how a little pussy is better than penicillin."

"It would have to be a case report," I wrote back. "I'm not about to do a randomized, double-blind, placebo-controlled trial."

"There's no placebo that would fool any man I ever went to bed with. They know the real thing when they see it. So... How's your love life?"

"D-vine."

"Share."

"Another time. I'm meeting him in half an hour."

"Bitch!"

I'd already told her that Dylan did not possess the elusive PP but that he was an elegant and durable lover. She seemed depressed to hear it. Wayne, she was fond of saying, was either marathon man or Sir Speedy, and which one showed up on any given occasion was unpredictable. I promised myself not to tell on Dylan in the way she did Wayne. Besides, he hadn't made one false move yet, other than that night at Davies.

She was right about one thing, though. Dylan had improved a lot since Elgar. The dark circles under his eyes had faded, his color was much more sanguine, and he seemed to have plenty of energy. Thinking back to the night at the ER, I had to wonder whether the experience had scared him off something he'd been doing or indulging in (alcohol abuse did appear to run in the family, from what he'd been telling me). Or maybe it was the sex. I don't want to sell myself short. We were setting the sheets on fire.

It was the first week of June when Mrs. Bannerjee's wedding invitation arrived at the office. I had forgotten about it in the swirl of things, and not just because of Dylan. Mrs. Bannerjee's recovery was going so well that I hadn't had to see her again. The wedding, I noticed, was going to be on the last Saturday in June, in Santa Barbara, and since it was only three weeks off there was no way I'd be able to make it. There was also no way I wanted to be out of Dylan's reach for more than a few hours. I knew, of course, that I shouldn't even think of taking him after knowing him for just four weeks or so. Presumptuous, *and* risky.

On the other hand, the invitation said I *was* entitled to bring a guest with me.

That evening, Dylan looked a little tired at dinner — I fixed some pasta puttanesca at home — and I had to ask if he was feeling bad again.

"No relapses," I said. "You've turned a corner."

"Sorry. It's business. I found out today that I have to make a trip down to San Diego. Don't want to."

"When is it?"

"Three weeks out. Thursday the twenty-eighth."

"Interesting."

"Why's that?"

"I've been invited to a wedding in Santa Barbara on the thirtieth. We could make it a romantic weekend. Find a room with a spa tub and a view and knock ourselves out."

"I like the way you think," he said, "only I'm not sure my meetings won't get in the way."

"No, here. Here's what we can do. We can fly to San Diego together on Wednesday or Thursday, you do your business, then we'll rent a car and drive up to Santa Barbara and then home. It'll be gorgeous on the coastal highway."

He didn't commit himself right off the bat. He chewed self-consciously. He sipped at his wine. Then, finally: "Can I get back to you on that?"

"Uh, sure. Have your people talk to my people."

We both laughed, thank God. If he hadn't laughed I'd have really been unglued.

"But make it soon," I went on. "I need to work it out at the office."

"Magic," he said.

*

By the next evening we agreed that we'd fly on the Tuesday, then drive to Santa Barbara on Friday so there'd be no rush making the wedding the next day. Everything was lining up perfectly. Nilesh agreed to see as many of my patients as he could, with one of our NP's seeing the rest. I owed him now.

"I hear you're going to an Indian wedding," he said to me in the cafeteria line one day. "You'll be out of your element."

"Really. What do you think my element is?"

Nilesh is a small slender man who reminds me of Omar Sharif. He is never without his stethoscope, even in a cafeteria line.

"Your element? I think your element is — what's it called? Looney Tunes."

"Gee thanks."

"You know what I mean. You have a silly side. Bugs Bunny."

"I was always fond of Pepé Le Pew."

"I think you'll find a Bengali wedding is no place for Pepé Le Pew."

I asked him what it would be like, and he said to be prepared for incomprehensible rituals, a lot of symbolism and color, and mantras. Mantras galore. I'd probably overdose on the mantras.

"Sounds interesting," I said. "You don't scare me."

"Not trying to scare you. I'm just telling you. It's not like a city hall wedding or a standard Presbyterian number. Or even Jewish."

"Were you married in a traditional Bengali ceremony?"

"Me?" He took his cheese-dripping nachos and began heading toward the exit. "No. I married a blonde from Alabama. We eloped."

I never knew that about him. A surprise a minute.

*

Jules and I met for Sunday brunch the weekend before the trip. Wayne was hungover and couldn't get out of bed — partied too hearty with an old friend from college.

"I watched them all evening like I was Jane Goodall," Jules told me. "It was fascinating. I should have videotaped the whole thing."

"You could have stepped in. Spared them the hangovers."

"That would have been intervening in the cruelty of nature. No. I couldn't do that."

"He'll blame you when he feels better."

"I'll make chimpanzee sounds until he stops."

She cocked her head as if to say, I always win. I wondered if Dylan and I would ever get to that point. At the moment, I wasn't interested in defeating him so much as *consuming* him.

"So," she went on, nibbling on a piece of bacon. "You realize you're about to embark on that utterly necessary but ridiculously dangerous First Weekend Romantic Trip together. Nervous?"

"I wasn't until just now."

"You haven't been anxious? God, when Wayne asked me to Palm Springs for our first? — I felt like I was going to barf every ten minutes. A lot can go wrong."

"I don't recall you telling me anything went wrong."

"Nothing did. It was the *potential* for something to go wrong that killed me."

I hadn't thought of this. "We'll be fine. We've been spending a lot of time together."

"How long has it been now?"

"A little over a month."

"A month? Well, well, well."

I knew what that look on her face meant. It meant Dylan and I had hit The Threshold, i.e., the point in a new relationship (again in our own book of rules and regs) when it's safe to introduce the inamorato in question to your posse. Parents, siblings (as *if*), co-workers, Safeway clerks, but most especially *best friends* now get to meet and pass judgment on the object of your desires — your official boyfriend.

"It feels too soon for that," I said, knowing *she* knew that I knew what she meant.

"Frankly, you're overdue. Wayne and I have been wondering what you're trying to hide."

"I'm not trying to hide anything. It's just with his medical issues and all —"

"Pshaw."

"Don't pshaw me."

The truth is, like I mentioned before, the fact that Jules and Ben weren't entirely compatible and didn't exactly relish each other's company had me skittish now. The day those two met, I remember sitting there on her sofa with a column of ice in my chest while they surveyed and circled each other. Ben refused to laugh at Jules's gags, and Jules made a point of questioning Ben's writerly dreams. "Let's face it," she said, "nobody reads real literature anymore. They read chick lit. Are you planning to write chick lit, Mr. Writer Man? Or are you above giving us workaday gals something fun n' sexy to read?"

I knew she was kidding. She plays rough. Ben didn't know it, though.

"I'd rather stick a fork in my eye than write that crap," is what Ben said, and Jules shot me a look that seemed to drive home the point that this guy would not be a good provider.

Ben was not even that wowed by Wayne's hi-fi.

Afterwards, Jules told me that she understood the attraction but Ben struck her as too dour for me. I was nothing if not a goofball. And Ben, having now passed over The Threshold, told me that Jules was what his dear old dad had taught him to watch out for as he went through life: a ball-buster.

"She's not," I said. "Not really."

"Then she's trying to sabotage you by attacking *me*. Maybe she wants you all to herself."

This was too frightening to even think. And this is why I was skittish about The Threshold with Dylan. What if Jules hates him?

"Don't worry," she said, reading me. "I just want you to be happy. If you're happy, I can put on a nice face for a sickly but gorgeous Englishman. Best behavior. Cross my heart."

This was obviously on my mind all day Monday, as I was trying to put everything together for my absence. Becky was able to stop me from ordering a colonoscopy for a teenage boy who had mono — a simple case of swapped charts. She told me I ought to take a break.

"Can't. No time," I said, but it was Nilesh who really unsteadied me.

"Just try to keep a low profile at that wedding," he said. "And don't eat the food — it's too spicy for you. Don't try to be anything but a loose friend of the family, and above all? Don't make a fool of yourself trying to dance like an Indian."

"Jesus, Nilesh, you're scaring me now!"

"I don't mean to scare you. I'm offering practical advice."

As the day of departure neared, I was beginning to feel like a virgin being prepared for a stroll to the lip of the local volcano.

On Dylan's side, nothing seemed especially ominous. He called me Monday evening and said it would be best for him if we met at the airport because he had an early meeting with a prospective client. He'd take a cab from there.

"All right," I said. "We'll hook up at the gate, then. How's that?"

"Perfect. And Sarah?"

"Hmmm?"

"Don't forget to pack your bikini. My thought is to spend all day Wednesday on the beach."

"You've got to be kidding. I wear a one-piece, baby. Otherwise my hips make me look like the Waldo Tunnel."

"Stop it. Your hips are my temple."

I think he had to have sensed my blushing through the phone line.

The next day, I called the office to check on last-minute problems and learned there weren't any. Becky wished me a nice time and said that Nilesh wanted photos from the wedding. I thought what he probably wanted were pictures of me in the midst of the Bengali wedding party, a Bartlett pear in among a basket of light brown M&M's. I'd show *him*.

I got to SFO an hour before the flight and went through security with no trouble at all. I've learned to wear slip-on flats whenever I go on a trip, so I don't look like a fool bending over and untying my clunky Doc Martens or something like that. I'm all about efficiency nowadays; that and looking reasonably dignified whenever possible.

Dylan wasn't at the gate yet. I was sure I'd looked everywhere, including the adjacent, less crowded gates where he might have taken temporary refuge, but no. No Dylan. Boarding would start in fifteen minutes or so. I went and bought a pretzel and a vitamin water (skipped lunch in the rush of getting ready) and positioned myself so I'd be able to see him coming down the concourse with that big crooked smile of his. My heart gave a little tickle in its birdcage when I thought of that.

When there were only five minutes till boarding, my cell phone rang. I didn't recognize the number and almost didn't pick up, but I did, and it was Dylan.

"Don't kill me," he said. "I'm stuck at this bloody meeting."

"I'll wait for you."

"No, don't do that. Listen. Go on down, check in at the hotel, and I'll take a later flight and catch up with you there."

"I hope nothing's wrong. Are you at least going to get a client out of this?"

"It's looking good at the moment."

"Well." I wanted to keep the disappointment out of my voice. "You go in there and kick some arse."

Made him laugh. He liked when I tried to sound British. I'm terrible at it.

"I'll do my best. I think I have him on the run, and don't worry. I'll see you at the hotel. We'll have dinner."

So it was an anxious ride down to San Diego, the spine of the mountains out to the left but vague and surreptitious behind a curtain of haze. A metaphor for something, I imagined.

It occurred to me in the middle of the flight, that Jules's Red Flag Rule had kicked in.

The Red Flag Rule dictates that if a new lover should do something negative and unexpected within the first three months, an official Red Flag has been raised. It means, in that time frame, that he doesn't feel like he has to hide the problem from you, so you don't rate where you should. Red Flag. I was telling myself that because this time it had to do with work, Dylan couldn't help it. There's nothing he can do and therefore the Red Flag Rule isn't governing the scenario. That's right, I thought. If he said he'd overslept or lost track of the time while watching "Days of Our Lives," then, yes, definitely, the Red Flag Rule would be in effect. For work, when a new client is at stake? — I couldn't see being a stickler on the rule.

Jules, when I phoned her from the ground, disagreed. "You know there's no exception for work. Not according to the rule."

"No, I don't know that."

"Think it through. If there was an exception? — men would just learn to *lie* about why they stood you up or whatever. See what I mean?"

"But sometimes it really *is* about work. This time it's about work."

"You're making me sad."

"I'm just telling you what's going on here. He's not standing me up. He's on the verge of landing this client, and he felt like he couldn't get away."

I was at the baggage carousel by now, waiting for my two bags to pop out. The way the luggage tumbled down seemed packed with meaning.

I suppose it's pretty clear that I was willing to cut Dylan whatever slack he needed at this point so I wouldn't have to risk losing him already. A month and a half? That's *nothing*. He was just so damn handsome, so damn endearing, so *unusual*, in my world, that, hell, I'll go ahead and say it: I didn't see someone like him coming along again. Ever. It was worth ignoring one stupid Red Flag.

"Okay, here's what we'll say." Jules paused a moment. "If he shows up and tells you he landed the client, we'll waive the Red Flag Rule. This time only."

"Okay." Wave the Red Flag. I wished I was in a mood to appreciate that.

"But if he gives you some lame tale of woe —"

"Don't do this to me."

"You know I'm right."

"Good-bye," I said. "I can't handle this. Anyway, here's my luggage."

"Have a nice time, sweetheart."

I think she meant that part. But she'd planted the seed, and I would be gnawing at my nails till Dylan showed up at the room that evening.

*

It got to be seven o'clock. Seven-thirty. Eight-ten. Eight-forty-seven. I glanced at the digital clock beside the bed every six-point-four minutes.

The room was lovely, though. Beachfront, with Jacuzzi (as

ordered). Dylan had booked it and said he'd be running the cost through his business, so I didn't have to feel guilty. On the other hand, being there alone and listening to the volcanic rumblings of my stomach was no way to spend a romantic evening, not to mention the way my mind kept anticipating what Dylan would say about his new client. My optimism kept calling it "the new client" as opposed to "the potential client," while my negative side, which Jules often referred to as Cruella De Vil, referred to "that prick" without identifying whether she meant the client or Dylan.

I also drank more than half of the bottle of welcome wine as I stewed. I was fairly loose by the time there was a meek tap at the door. Nine-twenty-one.

He had flowers. The bird of paradise among them looked like it wanted to peck at his eyes.

"Forgive me," he said, leaning in the doorjamb and looking, in spite of the day he must have had, completely irresistible. A lock of his hair had fallen over his forehead, maybe as he ran from the cab, and his shirt had come slightly untucked but to really sexy effect. You always like the thought of a man running to you.

"What am I forgiving you for? You're here."

"For fucking up our first romantic trip together."

The way he'd put it made me wonder if he had talked to Jules. Impossible. They hadn't met yet.

"Well, it was touch and go for a while there, but now I have a feeling we're gonna be jes fine."

A little slurry. I'd been waiting for hours.

I tugged at his sleeve sheepishly, and when he got close enough I leaned into an aggressive kiss that was meant to startle him. I was the startled one, though. He kissed back with the voltage of a Tesla coil. The flowers hit the floor. I could feel an insistent, rooting plug where he was pressed against my belly.

When we broke, he said, "I was thinking room service."

"Later."

It was only after a twelve-round bout in the magnificent bed and a playful refresher in the Jacuzzi that we got around to ordering food (somehow I'd forgotten all about my rumbling stomach), and it was only after the food had arrived and I had gulped down half a dozen shrimp and more than my fair share of an over-anchovied Cesar that I remembered the looming matter of his client. I had more champagne before I asked.

"So. Let's hear the story of your first major contract."

"Pardon?"

"The meeting today. How'd it turn out?"

Dylan looked like a life model for the next generation of the Ken doll, sitting there in his ultra-thick terrycloth robe. His chest glistened from leftover droplets of Jacuzzi water. He lowered his chin and began to shake his head slowly.

"No deal," he said. "I'm devastated."

Jules's compromise fell on me like a shroud. The Red Flag Rule was now in place. "You said it was going well. What the hell happened?"

"Whoa, are you mad at the client or at me?"

"Sorry. How could I be mad at you? I'm furious at someone for wasting your time and raising your hopes like that. What a *prick*."

"Prickette. She's a woman. I think she figured I'd underbid a more established firm in the city, so she wouldn't budge even though my proposal was much sharper."

"So you tried to shmooze her all day."

"More or less."

"And she wound up going with the more established firm?"

"What else?" He raised his eyes to me, puppy-style. "And made me wait while she thought it over too."

"Oh, Dylan." I felt terrible for him. I could have been more understanding. Sometimes the rigidity of the rules Jules and I have formulated over the years is a problem, though they are all borne from hard experience. I didn't want to put him off with my woman-scorned act, though. "I wish it would have gone your way. You need the business, right?"

"Don't worry about me. I'll be okay."

"You look a bit wiped out."

"It is starting to hit me, now that you mention it. I spent quite a bit on the presentation."

"Next time, sweetie."

"At least I've got you to comfort me."

That was sly on his part. It led us back to the bed for one more round before sleep.

In the middle of the night — don't ask why — it occurred to me that Dylan, when he first told me about the meeting that morning, had referred to the client as *him*. At least I thought I remembered that.

Then again, I was drunk and a little dizzy, and he was lying next to me and breathing in and out with such a serene, trusting rhythm that the idea he might have dished me a little fib to cover himself that day didn't seem to me the crime of the century.

NINE

In the morning, we had just enough time to screw, almost before opening our eyes, then to grab breakfast at the hotel. Dylan had his meeting downtown at nine, after which — he was hoping noontime — he would come back and we'd drive to Coronado for lunch at the Hotel Del.

I admit, I was leery of the plan because of what had happened the day before. I didn't want to spend the whole day by myself, trying to figure out what San Diego had to offer besides its climate and an overpriced zoo (forty-six bucks a head? — *criminy!*). Worse, I didn't want to be bopping around town and run inadvertently into my sister, who, granted, was more likely to be dropping Tucker's cash in swanky La Jolla boutiques than the tourist quarters, taking tea and having a massage and God knows what else. She had no shame about spending money. What a weird feeling, though, to know that Ella was within ten miles of me for the first time in years. Oh, I suppose she must have come up to the Bay Area to see Mom a few times (and Mom hadn't mentioned it so as not to upset me), but I didn't *know* it. Here, now, I knew she was close, and the last thing I wanted was a sudden reunion. Wasn't ready.

Probably would never be ready.

For an hour or so, I walked up and down the beach, thinking of what a turning point in my life this was — or what a *potential* turning point. I was falling in love. It's a process. Some women say they knew they were in love with their mate the moment they laid eyes on him, but for me it's always taken some getting-used-to time. Ben, for example. Though I liked the cut of his gib at his reading the night we met, I didn't actually admit that I was really truly in love with him till three months later when we had a pregnancy scare. It wasn't that I didn't have feelings of love *for* him before that. I think we'd been exchanging "I love you's" for quite a while. It's just that he didn't bat an eyelash when I told him I might be pregnant, I'd missed a period. Almost three weeks late. He took my hand and kissed it, then wrapped his arms around me and whispered in my ear that it seemed as good a time as any to ask me to marry him. It floored me. See, in the past I hadn't been able to hang on to a boyfriend through good times, much less scary ones like this. That he wasn't going to bolt at the thought of a baby meant I was safe. I could let myself *fall* in love. He was something soft and cushy to land on, but strong enough to bear up under the (emotional) weight of me.

(The pregnancy scare, by the way, was a false alarm. Seems the stress I was under in med school had messed up the regularity of my periods. So sensitive.)

This time, though: something different. I think I sensed that Dylan — after our strange origins together — knew that I could bear up under *his* emotional weight, and this was equally freeing for me. I could be in love with him and not worry about getting dumped by a guy who didn't really care. Dylan did care. He'd shown his weak side a few times, brought out naturally by his illness, whatever it was, and he'd allowed me to care for him. This is big, to my mind. Like I said, a turning point.

Yet, too, there was a Red Flag pending.

I'm in love with him, I said, barefooted on the beach and carrying my shoes on the tips of two fingers. Have to find the right time to tell him so.

The thought occurs to me that it might be kind of disconcerting that a doctor, a physician, can use a lot of her brain power dwelling on such seemingly trivial, adolescent problems as this. I'm aware of the disconnect, believe me. Many of my colleagues don't reveal their trivial, adolescent side, though you'll see shades of it in their behavior sometimes, their petulance, their tempers, even a sparkle in the eye when they talk about a fancy car they just bought. "Turbo," they might say. "Baby really moves when you open it up on the freeway."

Doctors are people too, so they have all the usual flaws. Many of them are married. Some screw around and get divorced. Others neglect their spouse and children, work too much, think they're God's gift, and so on, but they're not one hundred percent professional one hundred percent of the time. This I know.

Okay, so they don't carry around a "Land of the Giants" lunchbox as a purse. Maybe their eccentricities are better hidden.

After the beach, I went back to the hotel to see if by some fluke Dylan had returned. No go. The room hadn't been made up yet either, so I didn't want to hang around there. I drove down Point Loma and looked at the lighthouse, the sea, the city, and sky from behind the wheel of my rental car.

Now understanding that I was in love with Dylan, I also understood how vulnerable I had let myself become — with hardly even trying. It was a done deal. I'd already walked, voluntarily, over the precipice, and the free fall was going to last a lifetime. That's the plan, anyway. I wouldn't want it to end till *I* did.

"I made it down all right," I told my mother. I'd speed-dialed her on my cell without really thinking.

"Oh good. I was a little worried when I didn't hear from you."

"I always tell you, Mom. If you don't hear of a plane crash on TV, odds are I'm okay."

"I know. I get anxious, that's all."

"I'm glad. It means you care."

"Of *course* I care." She was doing things while on the phone. I heard pots clanging and water running. She's a big multitasker. "So where's your *English* friend now?"

"Seeing to business. We're meeting up for lunch in a little bit."

"Are you staying at the same hotel?"

"Oh, Mom."

"Never mind."

She had never liked the idea of her daughters giving it away before marriage. I'd explained, many times, that I didn't care for a life of celibacy after Ben. Marriage is always a big unknown when you meet someone, but there's no reason you shouldn't enjoy the fruits of physical attraction.

"Sarah?"

"Mmm?"

"I spoke to Ella last night."

This caught me off guard. "Uh huh."

"I told her you were in town."

"Why'd you do that?"

"She'd like to see you, honey. I told her you'd met a nice man. She's free tomorrow if you have time to —"

"I thought we've been all through this," I said, very tersely. It was a tone I used almost exclusively for my conversations with Mom about Ella. "I don't *want* to see her, and besides, *I'm* not free tomorrow."

"She just wants to talk," Mom went on as if she hadn't heard me. "She's willing to listen to you, sweetheart. She doesn't want to try to hit you over the head or anything."

"I can't. You know where we left it. She didn't do what I asked her to do. She said I was being childish. I know you remember."

"Please?"

I could tell she was crying. I heard her sniffle and try to hide it with a dish towel or a sleeve. She took a deep breath, and I started to waver.

"Mom."

"I can't imagine you and your sister being apart after I'm gone. Your father..."

"No, please. Leave Daddy out of it."

"It would break his heart."

"He's gone. Nothing breaks his heart anymore."

"I talk to him all the time. No, he's a wreck over it."

"Now you're being ridiculous. And manipulative."

"All right," she said firmly, pulling herself together. There was a tinge of anger in her voice now. "You're stubborn. I get it. It doesn't matter that *I've* forgiven her —"

"I'll call her. How's that? If I have a chance before we leave for Santa Barbara, I'll give her a call."

"Oh, Sarah, it would mean so much to me, and if there's a spare hour — just an hour, honey! — try to stop by La Jolla and let her see you."

I stopped myself from offering that. I didn't even want to call. The idea of having to see Ella in the middle of this whole thing? — my anxiety was ratcheting up by the minute — it would kill me to have Dylan witness the emotional collapse of his new girlfriend. "I'll see how the call goes, Mom. Are you happy now? Can I get a raincheck on the One Big Happy Family Show?"

She made kissing sounds into the phone, and hung up laughing.

*

Dylan wasn't looking so good when we finally got together. Washed out and wrinkled up. Later than expected too, so I wasn't in a buttery mood myself. With Ella looming over me, the waiting for Dylan to show up had taken its toll. I met him with pursed lips and vampire eyes.

"Tell me this meeting went better than yesterday's."

"It did, actually. Though I'm already in contract with these people." He didn't seem to want to look at me. "They're building a residential development in Escondido, and I'm designing two of the models."

I brightened up. Mostly through force of will. "That's terrific!" I said, and went to kiss him on the cheek. He turned his head slightly at the last second, though, and I clipped his chin, took a mouthful of sharp whiskers.

"It's more of a drag, really. I hate these repellent American houses. McMansions. The people who buy them are closer to the Clampetts than anything else, and every loo has to have two sinks and bloody granite on every horizontal surface."

The forensic image of bloody granite came to mind. I pushed it away and managed to laugh at him, his faux rage. "I'm surprised you know the Clampetts. You and your British good taste."

"I've lived here since I was twenty-one," he said bluntly, no smile. "Remember? I've picked up some of the culture."

It felt like we might be on the verge of our first fight. I didn't want that so I fell back to defend a position closer to the capital. "Listen. You're pooped. You look like you need some food and maybe a martini. How's that sound?"

"Magic," he said.

Half an hour later we took a table on the outdoor patio of the Hotel Del Coronado, viewing the ocean through an intense ball of fire descending slowly toward it. Having to squint wasn't so bad, but it was also hot out there. Yet we didn't ask to go inside. We put on our stiff upper lips and ordered the cocktails. Dylan's hair blew beautifully into his eyes, though I did notice that he had a feverish look, running on fumes.

"I hope you're ready to drive back to the hotel with one martini on board, because I'm having two."

"Why's that? I'm making you neurotic with my fussiness?"

"I promised Mom that I'd call my sister."

"Really."

"She went behind my back and told Ella I was in town. God, I love gin. Ice cold gin."

"So you're making a gesture for Mum's sake."

"I can't stand it when she cries. She melts me when she cries, and she knows it."

"Maybe something positive will come out of it."

The waiter, a young man named Jaime, came right then and took our lunch order, and that's when I told him to bring a second martini. I ordered ceviche and Dylan went with grilled salmon. We couldn't *not* order seafood, sitting where we were, the beach laid out like an apron. The big red cone-shaped roof of the hotel hung in the air.

"Nothing positive comes from any interaction between me and Ella," I went on after Jaime was out of earshot. (As if he might report back to her.) "We're like —"

"Oil and water?"

"More like human flesh and napalm. *I'm* the human flesh."

"Abrasive, is she."

"You could say. At least napalm is warm."

"What's behind all this?" he asked. Innocent eyes. And he'd asked with enough cool objectivity that I felt I could tell him more or less the truth.

"When Daddy died," I began, then stopped.

Dylan took my hand under the table. He squeezed it with fatherly reassurance. It felt awfully good. "You don't have to revisit that. I understand."

I took a breath and kept talking. "See, Ella was feuding with Daddy at the time. Daddy wasn't very fond of Tucker — Ella's husband. Fiscal conservative."

"Your father or Tucker?"

"Tucker. My dad was practically a red diaper baby. He had an autographed picture of Noam Chomsky in his den and would give his last dime to someone who needed it, where *Tucker's* the kind of man who's content to watch homeless people shitting their pants in the street rather than toss them a nickel to help. Bootstraps and all that bull, even though he grew up affluent and spoiled."

"So they were at odds."

"They were always at odds. But it was worse near the end. Ella had talked Tucker into throwing Daddy some kind of bone — like, I don't know. See if you can't clean yourself up a little, open a record store or something. She thought he was a child when it came to money — had nothing to show for his life. Said he ought to think about Mom for a change. It was insulting, and Daddy took it that way."

And then — and this is the part I couldn't bring myself to tell Dylan — after Daddy returned the check, Ella called him one night and scathed him up and down like she was punishing a beagle that had wet the carpet, saying he'd made her look idiotic, going to bat for him, when all Tucker was trying to do was help. She told him he'd wasted his life, said he was an embarrassment, and he'd better not come crawling to her — to Tucker — when he needed help because it was out of the question now, considering how ungrateful he was.

Later she had the gall to tell me this was her idea of tough love. *Tough love.* Because my sister loves people for the tangible, for the firm, actual things she sees around them and the security and clout they must, in her mind, represent, so that when they don't seem to care all that much for the tangible she has to toughen up on them. Me, I loved the lovely, loving man for all the *intangibles* he had hovering around him. My love could never have gone tough on him because I loved nothing more than who he was.

Mom overheard the whole thing and saw how upset Daddy was, and that night Daddy had a stroke.

I've read some of the research. Emotional stress can precipitate a stroke, and Mom knows that I believe Ella upset Daddy enough that night to cause his. I've never told her as much, but I know she knows. She'd probably say, if we hashed it out, that something else would have upset him later on, a traffic jam on 101, a stupid comment on talk radio, whatever. And I'd probably throw out some bullshit about proximate cause and whoever is the proximate cause of something is responsible for the outcome. But I'm not sure I even believe that where Ella's concerned. I don't know. I don't want to blame her and I don't want to think that we have to be so gentle with each other — everyone, not just family — that we can't speak our minds without thinking it's akin to manslaughter. That's not what I believe. What I think Ella is is thoughtless and self-absorbed. She wasn't looking out for her own father's dignity.

That's why I haven't been able to see her ever since.

"He died a few days after their last argument," I said. I was crying. The food came.

"The lady is all right?" Jamie asked.

"I'm fine. You brought the martini?"

"Yes, ma'am."

"It'll work wonders," I said, and managed a hopeless laugh and a grimly ironic smile that, judging by Dylan's face, broke his heart.

*

That evening, after we'd napped off our gin buzzes, Dylan went out in search of something to eat. Take-away, he said. He knew of a Texas barbecue place on the road into La Jolla. I kept forgetting that he had lived down here till not very long ago.

After he was gone, I splashed water on my face, felt my heart rate climbing, fingers tingling, and the shortness of breath I always get when I'm about to speak before a crowd of doctors. I picked up my cell phone and dialed Ella's number.

For Mom, I told myself. This is just for Mom.

"Hello?" A woman's voice. Deeper and more weary than I remembered Ella's being.

"It's Sarah."

"Oh my God. You called."

"Mom asked me to."

My eyes were closed. Clenched, was more like it. I was holding myself with one arm around the belly as I sat in bed wearing one of the hotel robes.

"I'm glad you did. I don't care why you did it."

"Well."

"We shouldn't have let this happen, Sarah."

In the background I heard one of the girls saying, "Who is it? Who is it?" Ella shushed her and sent her away.

"I don't know what we can possibly say to each other."

"Say what you need to say."

"I told you. Mom asked me to call so I called."

"How are you?"

"Magic. How are *you*?"

"We're fine. The girls are getting big."

"Children do that."

"Their dog had to be put down a while ago. Big ordeal."

"I'm sure."

"They kept asking if you could come down and cure him. They know you're a doctor."

"What did you tell them?"

"I said you're a people doctor, not a doggie doctor."

"Fair enough."

"But they still don't understand why you don't come see them."

"Why don't you just tell them the truth?"

Ella didn't answer immediately. I heard her inhale through her nose. "They wouldn't understand."

"If you were willing to explain the truth to them, I think they'd understand."

"What would you have me tell them?"

"You really want to go there?"

"I have nothing to apologize for, if that's what you mean."

"God, you haven't changed at all, have you."

"Look, I know you think I'm a monster. I'm not. My problem with Daddy was between me and him, and he understood that."

"Uh huh."

"We talked more often than you know. He loved the kids. He tolerated Tucker, but that's fairly common with in-laws, in case you didn't realize."

"Why, because I'm not married?"

"You *were* married."

"Right, and I loved Ben's parents. They loved me too, believe it or not."

"You see what you're doing, right?"

"What."

"No matter what I say, you're staking out the opposite side. I can't win, can I."

"Are we playing some kind of game? I didn't know we were trying to win anything."

"Jesus Christ, Sarah."

I could tell she was crying now. It was very very hard to make Ella cry. She of the stone-cold heart. The Stoic Amazon. When she did cry it was usually out of anger.

"I feel sorry for you," I said. "I think you ought to know that I've always felt sorry for you and that's why I put up with your bullshit for so long."

"There. You said it."

What gorgeous sarcasm. I could almost see the curl of her lip.

"You had to hurt Daddy by becoming someone he wouldn't even know if he didn't happen to conceive her."

"He loved me. Now you're just trying to put me down."

My teeth were grinding. She wanted me to believe that she and Daddy had this special relationship that was different and apart from the one I had with him. She was cruel to him because what they had together allowed it. Or demanded it. That close, they were. Was I as close as that?

Finally I pacified myself enough to speak again without screeching. "If nothing's any different, we really don't have anything to say to each other."

"I'll tell Mom you called."

I was already hanging up as she said it.

*

When Dylan got back, he could tell that I was having some kind of episode. A female thing, maybe. He didn't want to probe right away.

"Ribs," he said. "And four Lone Stars."

"Hair of the dog that bit me, huh?"

"You're feeling bad?"

"Just one of those dull headaches." I hadn't gotten up from the bed. I sat there with my arms crossed, looking at him in the doorway. "I called my sister while you were gone."

"Ah," he said. A wise nod as he came all the way in and set the bags on the TV console. "And how did that go?"

"Not very well."

"Would you like to talk about it?"

"Only if want to watch me turn into Medusa before your eyes."

"All right then."

We ate our entire meal in relative silence, got our fingers all saucy and sticky with the ribs and drank our beers like we were strangers at some morbidly seedy Amarillo bar. He made a production out of tearing open the moist towelettes and laying one out for me as if he were a maître d', saying, "Madame?" He'd cracked me. I laughed.

"Took long enough," he said. "It's like chipping a live woman out of a block of ice."

I told him the story. How relentlessly unresponsive Ella is, how rigid and mean. At the end of it all, I said, "Are you sure you want to dive into this with both feet?"

"Yes please. I love you. I'll take the whole package."

"Really?"

"I'll take your side in all and sundry conflicts," he said. "I'll be your vigilant St. George. If you want me to I'll slay every dragon you point me to."

"Contract murder. Not a bad idea."

His relationship courage had made him horny, I could tell. The look. He got up and came to me, standing behind, and pressed his lips to the top of my head. It felt like a gentle electric current from a twelve-volt battery, pouring down through my body.

"I told you I love you," he said. "That means I'm your partner in all things. I'll always build you up, no matter what. Promise."

I turned my face up to him and received a convincing upside down kiss. He meant what he said.

In the morning, though, before my eyes were even open, I heard his voice. It could have been in a dream, for all I knew.

"You were so upset last night I didn't want to upset you more."

I opened my eyes. No dream. He was leaning up on one elbow in the gray morning light. I could hear the ocean deep in the background.

"What's wrong? What time is it?"

"It's just after seven. I have to go."

"*Dylan*. Jesus."

"I had a call last night while I was getting the food. They want me for a few hours today. Apparently the powers that be don't like what I've done with the breakfast nook."

"God, I don't *believe* this. I have to spend another day by myself?"

"I feel terrible," he said, already pulling away from me. "I honestly thought we'd be able to mix business and pleasure."

"At least I'll have you all to myself at the wedding."

He did a double-take.

"Wedding? What wedding?" He looked like I'd tricked him into eloping, like Nilesh and his corn-fed blonde.

"Santa *Barbara*. Remember? The reason I came down here."

"Right. Sorry. I'm distracted."

When he was dressed and ready to head out the door, I asked when I'd see him. "Before dark, I'm hoping?"

"Can't say for sure. I'll ring your cell."

"I'll be on pins and needles."

He kissed me. The man has a natural sedative in his kisses, I swear.

"Dylan?"

"Yes?"

"I love you too."

*

If I'd been able to spend a warm romantic day with my lover on the beach, I wouldn't have done it. I wouldn't have driven up to La Jolla with a mind to run into Ella on Pearl Street, where she'd be shopping for jade jewelry or a new Louis Vuitton. I'll give her this — she has fine taste, along with the money to support it.

But Ella wasn't anywhere on Pearl Street, that I could see, and lunch at an Afghan restaurant put me off more, considering the war and everything. Visions of terrorists on monkey bars. Bad mood. I wrote Jules a terse text message straight from the table, and she wrote back almost instantly, saying, "R U on ur . or something?"

Outside, I phoned her.

"No, I'm not on my period. It's just, everything's going unbelievably shittily. Dylan has to work again today, I got myself all steamed up with Ella on the phone last night, and —"

"Whoa, hold on. She got in touch?"

"No. Long story. Mom guilted me into calling her, and now I'm in La Jolla pretty much stalking her because she basically *won* last night and it's killing me."

"Wow. What'd she say? Didn't you say any of the things we rehearsed?"

It was true. Jules and I had role-played the conversation many times. She was Ella, I was me. "Just the one about how I feel sorry for her."

"Well, that's a good one. What'd she say to that?"

"'There, you said it.'" I made it sound very sarcastic.

"How snarky."

"Over-the-top snarky. And she tried to make me feel like she was closer to Dad than I was."

"Right. She used to refer to him as Che. Now, that's close."

"I don't know what to do."

"Maybe La Jolla wasn't the best place to go today. What if you do run into her?"

"I was thinking I'd do my classy shtick."

"Yeah. Supercilious. 'Hello, Ella. You've lost weight, I see.'"

"No way she's lost weight. She's constitutionally unable to avoid a cookie if one comes within ten feet of her."

We moved on to Dylan. I told her the "love" part was phenomenal, when we happened to be in the same room at the same time. I confessed to being a little sore. Physically. "I'm not used to this," I said.

"Please. I'm jealous. It's a good kind of sore."

"I just wish he'd have told me up front that these clients might monopolize him."

"Nice guys don't like to disappoint. He was afraid you'd cancel the trip."

"But I wouldn't have. I just would have liked a heads up."

"Don't worry. He'll pay for it in Santa Barbara."

"I guess."

"Show him what he was missing."

"God, I don't think I'm physically capable."

"Get creative. Do I have to draw you a diagram?"

She laughed hard at that, then signed off with the reassurance that San Diego would be forgotten the moment we hit the county line. With a new love, it's all about the here and now.

I walked to the car muttering to myself that it's not fair I always have to take the backseat. But I'm a little sister. Little sisters always have to take the backseat to every other category, and it's not fair: big brother, big sister, even little brother. I'm a thirty-eight-year-old woman with an M.D. and I shouldn't have to take the backseat to Dylan's clients, for one. Or to an older sister whose only accomplishments in life were to have married strategically and brought two sickeningly adorable daughters into the world.

She lived in the hills north of La Jolla Shores. I remembered the way — I'd been there a few times, before.

TEN

I parked on the street so Ella wouldn't be able to see me coming. To anyone looking out their window as I walked toward the strangely unassuming house (from the outside), I probably looked like one of those overeager activists for green causes, marching door to door. I had on a light brown hemp blouse and jeans that had become a tad tight in the last few months, big sunglasses, a jute bag that Jules had bought me for the trip so I could leave my lunchbox at home. My hair was in a severe ponytail. I was loaded for bitch.

The urge to throw up came right after I pushed the doorbell button. I bent at the waist and tried to keep dizziness from taking over, deep breaths to oxygenate my blood ASAP. No sounds from inside the house immediately, but that didn't mean she wasn't home. School must be out for the year by now, so the fact that the girls weren't racing to the door surprised me. Mail was sticking out of the incongruous colonial-style box mounted on the sidewall.

Tucker had given my sister one hell of a life, I had to admit. The house alone had to be worth four million, mainly because of where it was. Like I said, on the outside it looks like a plain, Bauhausian shirt box, constructed of white-washed brick with shake shingles on the roof and a three-car garage to one side. A driveway of slate paving stones. A magnolia tree out front, and otherwise low-water landscaping that looked like a sculpted desert scene from a zoo diorama. You expect an iguana to walk by. Inside, the house was sprawling, five bedrooms, three baths, and featured a ten-by-twenty foot window overlooking the ocean. Each evening, a magnificent sunset was painted on it that couldn't be surpassed anywhere on Earth, as far as I'd seen in life. Yet Ella frequently complained of the radiant heat that came beating through the glass every afternoon.

I was still bent over when Ella appeared. Two-thirty, but there she was in her flannelette nightgown, her hair down over her shoulders like a mad queen who has just seen Christ in her shower door. Her breasts, unencumbered by a bra, were the heads of two overly protective footmen.

She had been crying. Hard. Years since I'd even laid eyes on her, but she looked like I did on the night our father died. Utterly gutted.

"Perfect," she said, then turned around and went back in the house, leaving the door wide open.

I went in. Closed the door behind me. The house was shockingly cold, AC up all the way and every blind and every drape drawn so that the only natural light was coming in through the skylight down the hall.

The place smelled like Ella. A cooking smell I could never put my finger on. Allspice?

But she had disappeared. I started wandering to find her. Not much had changed since I was last there — same high-end leather furniture in the huge living room. Same artwork on the walls, that kind of anonymous modern stuff that people buy for the color and texture more than the artist's name. Dylan would be peeved at the enormous granite countertop in the kitchen, the island there fitted with its own fridge and sink, the built-in Sub-Zero and ornate artisan-copper stove hood. But there was something about the place that made it seem badly aging too, overused maybe, just slightly out of time. The blond shag in the living room, the vertical blinds, I don't know. It felt like a set in a lost Stanley Kubrick movie.

Ella reappeared, having left me only to retrieve her drink where she'd left it. The ice tinkled.

"Belvedere," she said. "You want one?"

I noticed, with her hair down, that she had many more untended streaks of gray than before. Her cheeks were ruddy, either from age or the vodka. Didn't matter which. She was only forty-two, though. No reason to surrender.

"I'm driving. I don't need any trouble with the Highway Patrol."

"Well I'm staying in, so."

"Knock yourself out."

She passed me and made her way to the kitchen. Refilled.

"This is obviously a bad time," I said. "I should have called first."

"You wanted to bushwhack me. I get it."

"No. Well, yes. But I didn't think —"

"Water? Crystal Light?"

"No thanks."

"Fine. I'm going to sit."

She took the steps down into the living room tentatively, wobbly. She'd been drinking for a couple of hours, I guessed, alone in the house. Not a good sign. I didn't think I'd upset her that much the night before.

From behind, I saw that her hips really filled out that nightgown. She had gained weight. In fact, she was definitely in the obese category now, by my quick reckoning of her BMI.

We sat in black leather Eames chairs on opposite sides of a low, rough-cut marble coffee table.

"I couldn't let things stand the way they were last night," I said. Her eyes weren't on me. They were on a ball of patina'd wire that rested on the coffee table, a sculpture. Its complexities were too much for her. "I just thought if we're going to have a misunderstanding we might as well make sure —"

"Tucker's leaving me," she said, and she fell apart right there.

*

Ella didn't seem to mind that it was me, her estranged sister, she was unloading all this to. The need to let it out was too great. I'd never seen her like this, the Countess of Control — her eyes red and glazed and bleeding tears like a statue of Mary, her cheeks aflame, and her voice hitting such notes of anguish that I almost cried a few times as she keened.

"That mother*fucker*," she said. "He's been seeing this — *slut* for three years now behind my back, spending *our* money on her, depriving his own daughters. I swear, I felt like I could strangle him when he told me he wanted a divorce."

Something told me the trip to France was off.

"When was that? You didn't sound all that bad on the phone last night."

"He called from Phoenix this morning, the fucking coward."

"I guess he wanted you to have a good night's sleep." I was thinking of how Dylan gave me his bad news earlier.

"Well, he's not going to be sleeping well from now on. I'm going to destroy him. I haven't worked in fifteen years, and he's going to keep me and the girls in the lifestyle we're used to. It's all they know. They're not giving up equestrian, I'm telling you."

God forbid. But if I knew Ella (and even she'd have to admit that I knew her almost better than anyone else — we'd shared a bedroom for a long long time), I'd wager she was more concerned about the trimmings of her own life than the girls' equestrian. I wanted to tell her that I didn't mean it last night when I said I felt sorry for her, but now I really did feel sorry for her and had not one ounce of envy. There were times I was sick with envy over her. Especially over her marriage, though Tucker was definitely not my type. In fact he repulsed me, the smug, baby-faced conservative bastard in his casual golf-wear, like Garanimals for Men. But the idea of a long marriage — relatively speaking — with two disgustingly precocious and adorable little girls? I often wanted to vomit from jealousy. Ella didn't deserve it.

She didn't deserve this either, though. Everything I'd been feeling about her I had to take off the stove for now.

"Maybe this is just a phase he's going through," I said. "He'll have his fling and then beg you to take him back."

"A three-year fling? I don't think so." She sneered. "He's basically been paying this girl's rent. A downtown condo, and you know what? All the times I couldn't reach him at lunch? He was basically at her place shagging in front of a view of the Coronado bridge."

"Wow."

"And get this. She's a market analyst at a hedge fund. They speak the same language."

"What are you going to do?"

She looked at me directly for the first time in years. It was an evaluating gaze, judging my sincerity. I think she was trying to figure out if she could trust me.

"I'm going to be single," she said. "There's no two ways about it."

As I was getting ready to leave, standing in the open doorway and looking at her with what I hoped came across as some level of compassion, she struck me as needing a hug for maybe the first time in her life. When I reached out to take her hand, though, she snatched it away like I meant to push a rusty nail through it. Even in a crisis, the heart of ice didn't begin to melt.

I tried to keep myself from nodding in sarcasm. Instead, while she wept into her flannelette sleeve, I told her everything would be all right, whatever happened was going to be for the best, that we could work things out too, in time, and maybe it would be easier now, in some ways. I don't know that I believed all these things, especially the last. But I said them because I'm a doctor. I wanted her to feel better.

It was too ironic that I was at the very start of a new love and she was coming out the poop end of hers. Only twenty-four hours earlier, I might have lorded my life over her, rubbing it in like the snot she thought I always was. Now, though I wasn't forgiving her over Daddy (she had never asked to be forgiven), I was treating her like any patient who needs a little help.

Mom would be so happy.

*

Dylan was waiting for me at the hotel. He had put himself to bed.

"God, you look awful," I told him. "What happened to you?"

He was fetal, staring out at the wall and unable to lift his head toward me. "Turn for the worse. It just came on like a lorry, knocked me right down."

I sat on the bed and felt his cheek for fever. If anything he was cooler than normal, but his eye rings were back in a big way and his color had him in the sickly wan and bluish range.

"Do you feel bad enough to go to the ER?"

"No. Nothing like that."

"You can't go out in this condition. I'll bring in some won ton soup, how's that."

"Not much of an appetite."

I sat there stroking his head as he closed his eyes and shuddered. "What are we going to do with you?"

"Put me out of my misery."

"Hilarious. Want me to suffocate you with a pillow?"

"You sure you want to dive into this with both feet?" he asked, echoing me from before. A tiny laugh escaped his lips.

"Too late. I've already doved. Dived."

"So you're my nurse. For better or worse."

"Hey, that rhymes."

"I'm a little scared, Sarah."

It's always troubling to see a young man, a youngish man, regress to a boy because of an illness or an injury. He was a little boy in that bed, and I was his mummy. What was making him feel so bad I had no idea. All I could see was that he'd left that morning feeling well and came back flattened. I told him there was nothing to worry about, we'd covered everything last month and had come up empty, pathology-wise. I said he might be allergic to something he came into contact with in his meetings, and it was likely something he also had contact with at home. It could be a toxin of some kind, a chemical. It could be a particular kind of pollen. Or, I ventured, it could even be stress.

"No," he said. Adamant, and he managed to look up at me to reinforce it. "It's not stress. I've always thrived on pressure. There's nothing these people are asking of me I haven't been through a million times."

"It was just a hypothesis, Dylan."

"I put myself through university, worked six days a week and carried a full class load. I've had plenty of conditioning where stress is concerned. I'm not a pansy."

"I wasn't saying that." He protesteth too much, I thought. "All I'm saying is it sometimes causes physical symptoms and since we know you don't have a bug—"

"I'll be fine tomorrow. Wait and see."

On that note, he rolled over, facing away from me, and

appeared to will himself to sleep. He was probably faking it.

I went out, too edgy to stay there with thoughts of Ella on the brain and Dylan a classic case of hypochondria. Maybe Becky was right. Possible that — whether it was stress or not — he was translating it into a physical state that might as well be an illness. I considered chronic fatigue syndrome. I'm sure he'd deny it, but he did have many of the symptoms and lacked the blood and urine evidence that would exclude it. A lot of the time, something else is behind CFS, such as — here it comes again — substance abuse. I didn't know him well enough yet to say whether it was out of the question, though he'd bristled when I raised it before. Why would he admit something like that to me that early on? I could understand the hesitation. If he wanted me as much as I wanted him (imagine!), he'd keep the truth from me as long as he could.

Maybe he was just lovesick. Oh my heart.

At a Chinese restaurant in Hillcrest, I ordered noodles and ate them slowly as I thought all this through. I sent Jules a text message. "Alone again tonight," was all it said, and in just a few minutes came a reply.

"U R scrood. Call me."

When I finished eating, I ordered won ton soup for Dylan and went outside to wait. Jules must have had her phone in hand the whole time, because she picked up instantly.

"Where are you?"

"In front of a restaurant."

"And I take it he's not with you."

"Sick again."

"Seriously? This guy's practically an invalid."

"I think he's really sick. I just haven't been able to figure it out yet."

"Sarah?"

"What."

"I'm going to have to raise another Red Flag here."

"No!"

"You're not objective enough to make the call at this point. I'm the de facto referee, and I don't like what I'm seeing down on the field, okay? He might have a lot going for him, but this mystery disease of his just about neutralizes everything."

"You're not."

"I have to."

"No, Jules. He's not —"

"Damaged Goods."

"No, no, no. There's too many pluses! He's funny and smart and unbelievable in bed. He's an *architect*."

"I know how you are about architects, sweetie. But architects can be Damaged Goods too. You know doctors can, and if doctors can then architects certainly qualify."

"I saw Ella today."

"Whoa!"

"Tucker's leaving her. He has a chippy on the side. A hedge fund analyst chippy."

I told Jules about the whole surreal visit, how vulnerable the Ice Queen was and how she actually seemed to trust me. Oh, except for rejecting my hug, that is.

"You didn't go into Pat, I assume."

"No. I still have some degree of class. Even where Ella's concerned."

"It'll come up eventually, you know."

"I know."

"How will you handle it?"

"If it gets that far — I mean, I'm glad she lives down here and not closer to me — but I think I'll suggest that Tucker had her basically brainwashed on Daddy and now she can see things clearly enough to apologize. Start anew."

"The old start anew thing."

"If she's smart, she'll start anew."

"What if she's not so smart?"

"Then she'll live in a four-million-dollar house with an ocean view she doesn't appreciate and two sickeningly adorable girls to keep her company. Sans sister, though."

"You're tough."

"Well, we've been all through it, haven't we."

"Can I say something else about Dylan?"

"My soup's ready. I should go."

A Chinese waiter in cheesy silk embroidery popped out and handed me a to-go bag.

"Take a step back," Jules said.

"Dylanwise?"

"Right. Be a little cooler. Objective. Make him come to you. For all you know, he has a thing about being nursed. Or even worse than that—"

"Babied."

"Bingo."

"At least we're driving up to Santa Barbara tomorrow. He seems to be allergic to San Diego."

"You have that in common at least."

By the time I got back to the hotel, Dylan really was asleep. Sawing logs with a distinct English accent. It was kind of charming.

He'd left me a note on the table, though. It said, "Forgive me. I really am quite the annoyance, I'm sure."

*

What a relief to get out on I-5 in the morning and head for that county line. I'd phoned Ella first thing and left a message on her machine (she would have a Belvedere headache all day like a blowfish in her skull), saying that I would contact her when I was home again. We had a lot to talk about. She had told me the day before that the girls were staying with Mom's sister, Aunt Dina, for the time being, up in Anaheim. She was unsure how long she'd have to medicate herself with expensive vodka and didn't want them to see her unsteady.

Meanwhile, Dylan *was* better in the morning. And he got progressively better the farther we got from San Diego, which told me that I was closer to the mark than not in thinking the whole thing work-related. There we were, cruising up the highway with the ocean on our left and the golden hills of Camp Pendleton on our right, and a healthy pinkness blooming on Dylan's cheeks. I drove. He could take over when I was absolutely sure he wouldn't pass out at the wheel.

"Whatever it is," he was saying, "I don't want to talk about it anymore. It'll pass."

"Here. Go 'glug-glug-glug.'"

"Pardon?"

"'Glug-glug-glug.' It's truth serum."

"Does it taste good?"

"Of course. Nobody would take truth serum that doesn't taste good."

"What does it taste like?"

"Whatever tastes good to you."

"Your neck."

I had to smile. It was too hard to be cool and objective with him. "All right. 'Glug-glug-glug.'"

"'Glug-glug-glug.'"

"Okay, you just drank truth serum."

"Right."

"Have you ever had this happen before? Your mystery disease?"

"Sare-*uh*. God."

"You just drank truth serum. Come on."

"*No*. Okay? No, I've never had this mystery disease before."

"Sure?"

"Positive."

"Because I'm trying to rule out some things, and I'm just wondering."

"Well I've told you now, so you can stop wondering." He glanced past me at the water. It didn't appear to make much of an impression on him. "I came to see you when I started feeling bad."

"Right away?"

"I gave it a couple of weeks."

"That's not good. You could have waited yourself right into a coffin. A lot of things'll kill you inside of two weeks."

"I'm going to be cremated. No coffin for me."

"An urn, then. You could have waited yourself right into an urn."

"Let's talk about something else."

I told him about Ella.

"God, that's brutal," he said. "Behind her back for three years?"

"Yeah. Ouch."

"At least he's sure about it. He didn't make an impulsive decision."

"Oh, Tucker's nothing if not analytical. He was probably waiting for the chippy to reveal her flaws. Poor hygiene. Crazy mother."

"He's still an arse, but you don't break up a marriage on a dime."

"No. Not in a perfect world anyway."

"Right. Which does not exist."

"Hey, Mr. Altruist. Nice to meet you."

"You know what I mean. We've both seen our share of real life." His face went a bit dusky, maybe a side effect of the truth serum I made him drink. "Marriages fall apart all the time and usually for reasons nobody knows but the couple themselves. I take that back. *One* of the two. The other's completely in the dark — like your sister. The older I get the more I see there's no such thing as fairy tales."

I was getting a little uncomfortable. He was serious. My suspicion was that, for whatever reason, his family was on his mind — his lost father, his no-account brother. The failure of people he counted on. When I get blue, it's usually that kind of thing that makes me that way — that and the ridiculous humiliations you have to put yourself through to fall in love. (Commitment.com is only a metaphor.) Aside from his mother, who lived in Tampa, Florida, Dylan was more or less alone. (Mrs. Cakebread had married an American man, "Bob," after the boys were grown, though "Bob" died some time later.) He might be thinking (I thought) that if he loses me because of his stupid mystery illness, he's got nobody. He's alone in his business, alone in San Francisco, alone in California, and for all intents and purposes alone in life. That *is* depressing.

"Well, we have each other," I said, ignoring the fairy tale crack, and reached over to take his hand. This prompted a weak smile, but a smile anyway, and he squeezed my hand. He leaned over and kissed me on the ear.

"We have each other, and we're on our way to a Bengali wedding, of all things."

"Yes we are. Life is full of surprising detours, isn't it?"

He didn't answer. He settled into his seat with his arms crossed and watched the scenery flowing by like streamers.

ELEVEN

Our hotel was a fine hacienda of superbly brilliant marshmallow white, with a terra cotta tile roof and purple bougainvilleas growing up the door-side trellises. Dylan had picked it out. The wedding guests were all over at the Four Seasons, and we thought it would be nice to be away from them.

All we did once we checked in and unpacked was screw. (And maybe you wonder by now why I always say screwing and not "making love." Frankly, to me "making love" just sounds too Hallmarky for what the bodies involved are actually doing. Think about it. Really. "Screwing" captures the physical mechanics much better, but if there were a word such as "flungeing" or maybe "wrucking" or "striggling" — that might do the trick too.) Dylan was especially amorous for some reason and had me every which way he could think of, including on the rim of the Jacuzzi tub, steam wafting up around us as if to make it all look like a dream.

What if I *am* dreaming, I thought. Son of a *bitch*!

We dined at an uncrowded patio restaurant — fantastic fish tacos and immaculate margaritas, creamy snow slush with a mule kick. Both of us got a bit looped on them.

"I'm glad you're feeling better," I said. We were both glowing under the heat lamp. The sea breeze was shooting up from the beach and giving me goosebumps like aquarium gravel. "I really have been a little worried about you, you know."

"Me? Heavens. I'm a steamroller."

"You were this afternoon."

We both laughed and looked down into our drinks. People our age, carrying on like horny teenagers. What had gotten into us?

114

"You do something to me, Sarah. What can I say?"

"Whatever you want. Go on."

"Begging for compliments?"

"No. Insisting."

"Well then. Let's see." He looked up into the night sky, which was lit by Santa Barbara's sienna glow. "I've never known anyone quite like you."

"Good, good."

"You bring out my carefree side."

"You have one?"

"Can't you tell? Here it is."

He shrugged and held his hands out like *c'est moi*. Then he made his lips do a fish mouth and started flapping his hands behind his ears like gills.

"I guess we can keep working on that."

"Seriously." Now he reached out and took my hand. "I never knew that I could feel what you make me feel. It's very very — unexpected."

"Unexpected? That's not exactly a good romantic word."

"But it's the right word. I didn't expect —"

"What."

"I didn't expect to find love. I love you."

I felt my upper lip twitching, the way it does when I'm emotional. And I felt my heart ramping up toward the low end of ventricular tachycardia, which — please, I thought, no EMTs, not tonight. "I love *you*, Dylan," I said, and lowered my head in a way that invited a kiss on the temple, very close to the eye, which he provided. Sexy.

Later, after making lo — after *striggling* yet again, in moonlight like flickering spring water, I told him something that I'd never have said if I had a chance to think about it. Lying in his arms, my face in his warm, sweet neck with its sandy whiskers, I flattened my hand on his chest, right over his heart, and I said, "I'll spend the rest of my life with you, if you'll have me."

*

Jules texted me in the morning after getting my message. "'If you'll have me?' WTF?"

While Dylan showered, I called her. It wasn't that early.

"I told you to take a step back, be cool," she said. "You understand what you've done, right? You've surrendered the high ground. Why is the high ground so important?"

I recited our catechism with a military grunt's voice. "Because the high ground is the only safe defensive position, SIR!"

"And?"

"And it is important to be able to feel superior to the male in question, SIR!"

"So that?"

"So that when the shit hits the fan you don't get your goddamn heart trampled to pieces. SIR!"

Jules paused with a deep breath. "You know the rest."

I did. I wouldn't say it though. *The shit always hits the fan.*

"It's different this time," I said. "It's like you and Wayne. He never trampled your heart to pieces."

"Oh didn't he."

"No!"

"*Really.*"

The ironic tone meant I was forgetting something big.

"I'm sorry. I don't —"

"Vegas?"

"Shit. Vegas."

"I can't believe you forgot Vegas."

"You never told me what happened there. Maybe I'd have remembered if you would have told me."

"I can't talk about it."

Obviously, I'd always assumed the worst. Prostitute at Bachelor Party. She denied it.

"Well maybe you'll tell me when you feel stronger."

"I'll never get over it. I'm just saying. If you think you're like Wayne and me, it ain't all champagne and rose petals, all right? Wayne likes Ultimate Fighting."

"Okay, okay."

"So get your butt back up to the high ground. Make him think you didn't mean it." I heard her blender in the background blitzing a smoothie. "What did he say when you said that awful thing you said?"

I didn't want to tell her. Truth is, I didn't want to think about it again.

"Tell me."

"He said." She had to have heard me swallow hard. "He said, 'That's awfully sweet.'"

"*Sarah!*"

I had to hang up because Dylan came out of the shower then. Smiling. Almost as if he'd heard the whole conversation.

*

We arrived at the Four Seasons in the midst of a wafting parade of Bengali costumes —saffron, ocher, pomegranate, spun gold. Mrs. Bannerjee, dressed like an Indian goddess in her short-sleeved, lacy white gown, saw me from across the lobby and came running. She beamed as she took both my hands.

"Dr. Phelan! I'm so happy you could make it!"

"Please, call me Sarah. We're nowhere near an exam room."

"Mita will be so glad to see you. I've been telling her all about you ever since the operation."

A few yards away, in a forest of potted palms, wedding guests erupted into laughter and applause as the bride and groom entered. The bride was a picture of exotic beauty, dressed in the traditional flowing sari of mainly reds and silvers, with a gold ribbon running down the part in her ink-black hair, and both lovely brown arms clustered with gold and silver bangles. Her face was made up with ritual turmeric powder her bridesmaids (said Mrs. Bannerjee) had devotedly ground with mortar and pestle and applied that morning. A lot had gone on behind the scenes, she added. "Things the Indians would care about but not the Americans. Funny little steps we take to make sure the couple is truly blessed. What the Americans like most is the party afterwards, I think."

"She's stunning," I said. I'd have loved a lunchbox with that bride's face on it. I also noticed that her hands had been painted with elaborate swirling designs done in red and brown henna. It

117

looked like she was wearing splendid sheer gloves that wound
around her fingers like ivy. "And the groom is beautiful too."

He was. Crisp white slacks with an embroidered floral long-
coat and a red and white garland of flowers around his neck. He
looked more anxious than Mita, who, under her red and silver
head scarf seemed to have the poise of a statue.

"Is that the word?" Dylan asked, looking a little sheepish.
"Beautiful?"

"I'm sorry, Mrs. Bannerjee —"

"Lili, please." She was grinning hugely at Dylan, waiting for
the introduction.

"Lili, this is Dylan Cakebread. My —"

"Ah," Lili said.

"What would you say you are, Dylan? My what?"

"Adoring stalker?" He reached out and took Lili's hand.

"This is Lili Bannerjee," I said. "Mother of the bride. Acute
appendicitis."

"I see. You look radiant, Mrs. Bannerjee. I'm glad you're
feeling better." He glanced toward the crowd. "This is all very
impressive."

"Boyfriend," I said. "I guess he's my boyfriend."

"Oh, how wonderful!" Mrs. Bannerjee cried. "Maybe he'll get
an idea here today."

My unsmart love line from the night before echoed through my
head. *If you'll have me.* Probably running through Dylan's too. He
said, "There's nothing wrong with a respectable period of
courtship, is there? We've known each other — what, Sarah? All
of six weeks?"

"Something like that."

Mrs. Bannerjee was shaking her head as he spoke. "No, no, no.
You must not let a prize like her get away, Mr. Cakebread — what
a lovely name too!"

"Yes, I inherited it from my father. It's a bit embarrassing
sometimes."

"No, it's *special*," she said. I looped my arm through Dylan's
and looked up at him with gooey romantic eyes. He felt a little
stiff against me. It occurred to me he didn't much care for the
performance of social situations. "I've never met a Cakebread in

my life."

"Everything is absolutely beautiful, Lili," I said. "*Including* the groom."

"Technically Mita and Palu shouldn't lay eyes on each other till the *potto bastra* —" I had no idea what that meant. "— but we're being more American today and throwing caution to the wind."

"I'm sure it'll be fine. There's no such thing as bad luck."

I'm afraid my face probably didn't make me look like I believed it. I squeezed Dylan's arm tighter to ward off demons.

"We're having the main ceremony outdoors," Lili said. "Wait till you see." Someone was calling her over from the large group. You never saw so many multicolored saris and amazing silk suits. Men and women of all ages, speaking with jubilation in a language I didn't recognize. "And then there's the reception in the La Pacifica room. The wedding is in the Mariposa Garden. One sharp. Don't get lost wandering around like lovers, you two!"

When she'd left, I asked Dylan how he was holding up.

"Not badly," he said. "I'll survive."

"I know you don't know anybody. I only know Lili, after all, but maybe you'll get some leads on potential clients."

"I left my work in San Diego. This is all pleasure."

"Some of these people have real money, though. Don't look a gift horse and all that."

"You're quite the shark, aren't you."

He seemed happy. No sign of the rings under his eyes. He looked terrific too, I have to say, in his cream linen suit with a light tan silk shirt and coral tie with little blue droplets. It brought out the lightness in his hair and made him look like a British colonial bureaucrat in Ceylon or some such place, 1956. I was giggly inside to be seen with him.

As for me, I wore a springy yellow dress that billowed a bit in the wind and made me feel like a tulip whose petals might blow off inconveniently. Jules had said I looked "succulent" in it, which made me think of cactus. White sandals with a few crossing straps made me wish I tanned. My feet looked like peeled potatoes.

Dylan and I wandered out to the garden about ten minutes before things were to get rolling and took seats near the back of the hundred or so white folding chairs. The view was spectacular. Lush green garden dripping with flowers, then the Pacific laid out like a jewel-encrusted tablecloth under a sky of ungodly blueness. The multitude of Hindu gods had pulled out all the stops for these two. An aunt of Mita's approached us to let us know that this was not entirely a *traditional* Bengali wedding, since many many rules were already being broken and rituals sacrificed for the sake of convenience, which she found appalling.

"There's a reason for these steps we take," she said, wagging her finger at Dylan as if he were the one causing the lapses. Some lingering colonial resentment, I guess. "The idea is to set the bride and groom off on the right foot, isn't it? To make sure their life together is *permanent*. I'm afraid these two —" Her voice trailed off and she wandered away.

"Unhappy camper," Dylan said.

"She'd have screamed at my wedding. There wasn't even a photographer."

"My little iconoclast."

"Awww. You like that about me?"

"Absolutely. Very appealing, though I'd pay a few bob to see pictures of you from then."

"No way. I had the worst hair."

The garden filled up quickly. All eyes were on the canopy set up in front, with that view laid out behind it, a billowing white tent with two French provincial chairs and a low wooden stool, along with a table that held all the items the priest would be using during the ceremony — herbs, puffed rice, spices, brass bowls and pitchers. Us Anglos were in the dark as to how they'd come into play. There was also a small square fire box on the ground in front of the chairs, stacked with enough kindling, it seemed to me, to roast marshmallows once the fire got going.

"Have you ever been to one of these?" I asked Dylan. "Back in England?"

"No, never. I've walked by houses where they were going on — usually it's at the bride's home, I think — but all I recall is the ululating women."

At that very moment a number of Mita's aunts and sisters began to do just that. Ululate. It was a celebratory but kind of unnerving sound in that particular place. They were doing so because here came the groom and entourage from behind us, Palu and his posse, who were a variety of friends and family members. Palu wore a remarkable white pointed hat now, something like a sparkled wedding cake perched atop his head. The sitar band whined its way to a sizzling crescendo with adamant drums on the side. I was actually getting jazzed.

The groom took his seat under the canopy and relatives of the bride began to offer him things like nicely folded garments of some kind, which he accepted without much affect. Maybe he was nervous. He set them on the table beside his chair. In a moment the bride, with a matching cake on her head too, was led by Lili and several other women to the canopy, looking more than radiant with ten pounds of dazzling rubies on her chest and her sari flowing around her body, her enormous eyes like a black velvet painting, and her all-around gorgeousness. I don't know how an Indian man would see her — maybe she was par for the course in that world — but to my American eyes she had all the allure of the exotic yet all the lovely modesty of a girl approaching her wedding altar. The priest was coming in behind her, an older gentleman in equally colorful duds, sprinkling puffed rice as he went. Mita sat on the low stool, cross-legged, like something on the cover of the Bhagavad Gita. Ululations continued. The sitar and some other twangy stringed instrument did a "Dueling Banjos" pas de deux. I squeezed Dylan's hand. "Isn't this amazing?"

"Very."

By the way, the colors there among the wedding party and all the Indian guests were like an entity unto themselves. Amber, amaranth (I'll just go alphabetically), baby blue, bittersweet, capri, cerise, cinnabar, fuchsia, fulvous, gamboge, heliotrope, jazzberry, lust, magenta, mango tango, maya blue (of course), Nadeshiko pink (all right, I admit I looked some of these up), orchid, pumpkin, puce, purple mountain majesty, rufous, saffron, of course, sinopia, teal, tickle me pink, ube, urobilin, vermillion, wild strawberry, xanadu, plain old yellow, and, bringing up the rear, a popping shade of zaffre. All accounted for, and many present at once on some of the ladies. They put the flowers to shame.

Now, to my surprise, as the groom moved his chair toward the center, five or six men surrounded Mita and picked her up, little bench and all, and began walking around Palu. There were chants and more ululations, and someone, I couldn't see who, was blowing into a conch shell or something, an oboe da'mare. Obviously the words of the mantra were lost on me. Just as Latin is whenever I attend a Catholic wedding. We do love our ancient languages for really giving a ritual some heft, don't we? Everything's heightened when you can't understand what's being said.

By my count, the men took Mita around the groom seven times, which I guess was a way of weaving him into her metaphorical spider web.

With Mita still hovering over the ground at four feet or so, she and Palu exchanged flower garlands, hanging them around each other's necks. Then everything got very quiet as those in the know realized what was coming, though I didn't, of course, nor Dylan. We just watched. The bride and groom responded to something the priest said by looking at each other for maybe thirty long seconds — the gaze of eternal love — and somehow neither of them cracked up laughing. I would have. Not that the idea of eternal love is a laughing matter. It's not. It's just that looking into my lover's eyes with that kind of intensity would remind me of that thing that makes me laugh, and *that* would spoil my concentration, I'm afraid. I remember with Ben, in fact, as the judge mispronounced his name Carcass instead of Cargas — well, we both lost it. Mr. and Mrs. Carcass indeed.

After that, the bride was allowed to stand on her own two feet and then sit in one of the chairs beside the groom. Each was presented with a large heart-shaped leaf of strikingly bright green, which they held as the priest sprinkled what might as well have been fairy dust on them. Then the priest beckoned them to stand, and Mita's grandfather, I think he had to be, formally handed her over to Palu. The two held their hands out toward the priest, who began to tie them together with a length of silver string. They were now literally bound together.

I wanted to cry at this point, thinking how maybe if we did our marriages so literally — *tying* ourselves to each other — the divorce rate might not be so goddamn high in this country. Again, vis-à-vis Ben (and it's no wonder he was on my mind so much that day), I wondered what it would have been like for us to go through a ceremony like this one, witnessed by both extended families, photographed, videotaped, recorded for posterity, and *sealed*. How could we ever have separated when we'd been through a multilayered and colorful extravaganza like this? Every time we had a spat, we'd have had to think back to the day Ben's brothers carried me around him seven times on my little flying stool.

Though it wasn't over yet, this ceremony would make even the most elaborate and tacky American wedding look like a barn dance. It was solemn, it was earnest, it was beautiful, and it was to be taken seriously by everyone there. Including the Caucasians like Dylan and me. And it made me push Ben off to the side a little bit, now that it was apparently coming to its religious conclusion (the couple seated before that brazier as the priest threw puffed rice and other spicy powders into the flames), and think about *this* man. We were still new, but I had the strongest feeling there and then, with that ocean and that sky as my witnesses, that he and I would one day tie ourselves together. Maybe not as literally as these two, but as earnestly, as believingly. I looked at his profile but couldn't read his thoughts, since he was a kind and well-mannered man and had the respectful expression of a wedding guest. What I did appreciate in him was his willingness to be there with me that day. He'd chosen to do that.

The bride and groom stood and circled the fire seven times, holding hands. What must that painted hand of Mita's feel like in Palu's? Warm, I thought, maybe a little moist from nerves. Definitely small and comfortable, though, a perfect fit. Her eyes were down, while his searched the crowd for friends whenever he came around the front. There were many ululations, and that conch-shell Gillespie was going to town.

After the groom applied some kind of wedding masala to the part in the bride's hair (the priest having delicately removed their hats for this), Palu's mother gave Mita a length of sari fabric, which Mita then laid on her head as a scarf, and when the priest uttered some energetic and throaty syllables into the air, it was seemingly done. They were married.

The music kicked up with rigor, the crowd got to their feet, the applause soared, and the ululations gave me a zing up and down my spine. Everyone was laughing. From the midst of the crowd — I really hadn't noticed them — dozens of children ran out onto the lawn in front of the canopy and began dancing in spontaneous circles as the adults looked on.

In those festive moments, I squeezed Dylan's hand again but got no squeezing response. I looked at him and saw that his face was blank and pallid as he watched the children running their ring-around-the-rosies in loud, breezy laughter. It was as if he was seeing himself in there with them, from long ago, before his father died, maybe — that lost innocence that everyone wishes to get back somehow, but — impossible. I squeezed again, starting to worry about another relapse.

"Would you excuse me for a minute?" He began to get up.

"Are you okay?"

Inexplicably: "I need to get some air."

We were sitting in an outdoor garden with the sweetest air on earth coming off the sun-speckled water and filtering itself through jasmine, wisteria, and roses as big as baby heads.

Mr. Bannerjee, a stately man in a dark suit and with gorgeous salt and pepper against his brown temples, called for everyone to head for the La Pacifica room. Then he and Lili led the happy procession from the garden into the hotel, Mita, the bride, walking head-down with graceful humility as she and her new husband passed me. I let everyone else go, wanting to give Dylan some time to catch his breath — or whatever it was he needed to do.

Those words were going through my mind again. *Damaged goods*. I tried to push away any sense of embarrassment — I mean, there was literally nothing to be embarrassed about. For all anybody knew, he'd answered the call of nature. I guess in the back of my head, though, I was dealing with images of a lifetime of this. Moments alone while my husband retired to a quiet place to pull himself together.

Oh my.

I waited ten, fifteen minutes. Dylan didn't show. Soon Lili appeared at the garden entrance and called out, "Sarah! Collect your handsome Englishman and join us!"

It took me quite a while to find him, my handsome Englishman. I wandered all over the ground floor of the main building, peering into empty banquet rooms, internet cubbies, maids' pantries, and all the loos, totally neglecting the most obvious possibility. The bar. When an Englishman is distraught, he goes to pub.

Dylan was sitting at the ornate marble and inlaid wood bar, shoulders hunched and chin poised over the tumbler of clear liquid with ice and lime. I wagered it was gin.

"This is to get you through the rest of the afternoon? They've got a bar at the reception, you know."

He looked at me with woe in his eyes. Real woe. I couldn't begin to guess where it was coming from.

"I needed a few minutes by myself. Sorry."

A weak shrug. A couldn't-help-it. I wondered, offhand, if there was the slightest little chance he was a real alcoholic and had managed to hide it from me all these weeks. Under the social stress, he'd finally given in.

I sat beside him and waved off the bartender. From the look in Dylan's eyes, and the used napkin with a drink ring in it, pushed away from his glass, I figured this was his second.

"Want to talk about it?" I rubbed his back in a gentle circle. He didn't relax.

"Not especially. It's not what you think."

"I'm not really thinking anything."

"You're thinking the mystery disease is back yet again. Thinking you can't take me *anywhere*."

All right, I was *sort of* thinking that. I was more focused on the alcoholism thing, though. I didn't admit that.

"I'm just thinking I wish I could help."

He smiled at me wanly. The kind of smile that's a hundred percent effort and still falls short. "Anyway, it's not the illness. I just had a moment of — you know. Wondering what it's all about."

"Weddings can do that to me too."

"Weddings. Baptisms. Happy families. You understand."

"Yes, I do."

"You get to a certain age and you just start thinking —"

Well, here we were, pretty much on the same page after all. I'd been slaving away as a G.P. for almost fifteen years, single for nearly ten of them, and I had not a lot to show for it. He'd been busting his nuts — sorry — his *bum* as an architect, trying to get his shop off the ground, and it gets to you. It just does.

"But you know what?" I said. "We have each other now. It's something to fall back on. When you feel the crummy stuff."

"Yes," he said, but his voice was noncommittal.

"And you know what else? We have the kind of amazing hot sex that turns workaday problems into confetti. I was rereading *Lady Chatterley's Lover* a while back and thinking, Wow, I could go for some of what they're having, and —"

"Sarah?"

"Mmmm?"

"Can we make a brief appearance at the reception and spend the afternoon on the beach? I can't make myself be all that — *on*, I'm afraid."

*

Of course, Lili was disappointed when I made a terribly lame excuse half an hour later, saying I'd gotten word that one of my patients was in the ICU with an aortic aneurysm (these things just pop out of me sometimes), and rushed the bride and groom over to Dylan and me.

Mita, who up close was even more stunning with those red red lips and enormous Cleopatra eyes, thanked me profusely for coming and for saving her mother's life.

"Oh, that was the surgeon's doing," I said. "I just handled her post-op."

"Well, she's been a whirling dervish ever since. Doesn't she look awesome?"

It always saddens me when the beautiful young multi-culti's sound just like white-bread valley girls.

"She's radiant," Dylan said, recovering a bit. Putting on a show for me. He reached out and kissed Lili's hand, then did the same with the bride.

Palu, the groom — shorter than he'd looked at a distance — shook our hands and said he was the luckiest man on earth.

"I'm fairly lucky too," Dylan said. "*This* one here." He cocked his head toward me, and I remembered he must be a little bit looped after the two quick gins.

"Palu's the lucky one today at least," I said.

"No, you *are* lucky, Mr. Cakebread," said Lili. "Now do what I said before and get her into a wedding dress!"

"And then quickly out of it!" Dylan gave me an Eric Idle nudge.

Everyone tittered. I think embarrassed Indian people are good at tittering. They're too classy to show when they're really appalled.

"Well then," I said stiffly. I think Dylan could tell I was irked. "We'd better be going."

Afterwards, back at our hotel, he apologized in almost believable remorse, on his knees, claiming that it was indeed the gin talking. He wrapped his arms around my waist as I stood in front of him, his face pressed against my lower belly, and I thought, Oh no, he's not going to propose *now* is he? I won't say yes to a ginned-up proposal. You should never say yes when he's drunk and you're ticked.

Instead, as he began to reach under my gauzy yellow dress and peel down my panties, he said, "All I could think about in there was getting you on your tummy and having my way with you."

Maybe this was still the gin talking. I don't know. It didn't matter, I guess, because he had me where he wanted me in fairly short order, and as I lay there on my tummy, naked and not wanting to get too distracted from his slow-dance above and behind (very hard to concentrate), I thought it might be okay to take this man warts and all. The pluses really did seem to outweigh the minuses.

Jules probably wouldn't have agreed at the time.

TWELVE

"It's all going to fall apart in the Middle East. I've been reading some blogs, and *they* say that the whole thing is unsustainable."

"Everything is unsustainable these days," Jules told her husband. "*Blogs* are unsustainable."

The three of us were at a sidewalk table on Union Street, drinking mojitos and pretending to enjoy the strangely warm summer evening in San Francisco. It was what Dylan and I called one of our "dark nights" — nights we didn't get together. He caught up on work and I ran to Jules so I wouldn't have to be alone.

"Everything *is* unsustainable," Wayne said. "We're living in the Apocalypse Years, right? Nobody knows when the shit's gonna hit the fan, but it's pretty obvious that it is."

Jules, in her clingy white sleeveless top, looked bored and sexy. She had a few loose bracelets up and down each evenly tanned arm, and I thought how lucky Wayne was to have snagged her, even if she said their marriage was no Shangri-La. And, in a weird way, she was lucky to have snagged him too — a unique type of man, not the usual macho conservative truck-drivin', gun-lovin', beer-swillin' kind of man so many of them are anymore. He was an eclectic soul, and nice looking enough that Jules didn't have to feel like she'd married down.

"I think he's right," I said.

"Say what?"

"Pretty much everything is unsustainable. There's too many people and not enough stuff. Minerals. We're running out of molybdenum, I read somewhere."

"Molybdenum? What the hell is that?" Jules was affronted at our ganging up on her.

"Lithium too," Wayne said. "It's because of China."

"Right. They're using everything up. And don't get me started on overpopulation." One of my bugaboos.

"Oh, here we go."

"No. Just don't get me started."

See? I could still talk about other things than how my relationship novel was developing. I read newspapers and web sites, random magazines in the waiting room — actual books too — and I listened to talk radio while driving to and from work. I could opine on just about any topic, even when, in the back of my mind, Dylan was squatting like a half-naked jungle boy.

Jules said — rightly too, I think — that it didn't matter if everything was unsustainable because there wasn't a goddamn thing people like us could do about it. "It's true," she said. "You can buy all the fucking fluorescent light bulbs you want and it'll only make a tiny little dent in the energy crisis. You can stop buying bottled water, you can adopt one of those poor kids from South America, you can give to the Humane Society and *Médecins Sans Frontières* —" Her French was impeccable. "— and we're *still* fucked."

"I love it when she cusses," Wayne said. Glee in his eyes. He took his wife's hand and kissed it.

"Fuck off," she said. "You tell me what I can do to end my vile addiction to foreign oil, huh?"

We all fell apart laughing. The mojitos were good.

Walking to their car, Jules and I got ahead of Wayne as he stared into the window of a high-end audio store. She said, "Now let's talk about what's *really* on your mind." Her arm looped through my arm and I let my head tip and touch hers.

I'd been too busy to update her on Santa Barbara. Work was crazy, and frankly I hadn't wanted to wallow in it so soon. She did know that we left the reception early but still spent the night at our hotel. She thought that was romantically naughty, since Lili could have found us out, if she'd cared very much.

"The thing is," I began. "He's — he's a little off, I think."

"Yeah." That sing-song, told-you-so-tone of hers.

"But so far he's been off in a not-too-awful kind of way. He's eccentric."

"So was John Wayne Gacy."

"Jules!"

"So what happened?"

I told her everything, the upshot of which was, Dylan was generally fine in my company, alone in a hotel room or either of our apartments, *making love* — the usual prosaic relationship acts — but out in the world he tended to melt.

"Like a too-big ice cream cone," she said.

"Exactly."

"It looks phenomenal, but when you start to eat it you realize it's going to get all over you before you can finish."

"I don't care for the metaphor, now that you put it like that."

"I'm really sorry."

"What, no advice? No Damaged Goods speech?"

"No. I think you ought to just enjoy it while it lasts."

Like he was a terminal patient! Or *I* was.

"*I* think we're still in the getting-to-know-you period. It can take a year to get through that, right? So you've seen someone during the holidays, in a swimsuit, handling an umbrella."

"Sure. Does he hold it over you mainly, or him. I get it."

"But you're not going to give me any encouragement?"

"No."

"Why not?"

"Because, babe. You're a smart one. You can see for yourself. *He's* unsustainable."

When I was home later, *alone*, I went over things and realized that the list of Red Flags I was keeping was actually pretty paltry. The pluses *did* outweigh the minuses. Dylan was a knockout, witty, charming, classy, intelligent, English. And a goddamn *architect*. I'd seen him completely naked — I didn't need to see him in his Speedo. As for umbrella etiquette, I was one hundred percent sure he would hold it mainly over me. He was a gentleman above almost all else.

Jules would see. Technically it was time for The Introduction, and the only way she'd admit he *was* sustainable and he *was* wonderful, and a girl *can* be forgiven for overlooking a few Red Flags, was to meet him and eat some crow.

*

Mom and I had lunch at Larkspur Landing a day or two after that. The topic was not Dylan. Furthest thing from it. The topic was Ella, of course.

"I'm still in shock," she told me. "Not as bad as your sister, but it kills me that Tucker turned out to be such an — *asshole*."

I couldn't remember a time when my mother used that word. Or any profanity at all. This was really affecting her.

"The signs were always there, Mom. He drives a Ferrari."

"True."

"He said he modeled himself after Dick Cheney."

"I don't know what Ella saw in him."

"Dollar signs."

"Oh, Sarah. Don't talk about her that way."

"She was always money-grubbing. You know that. She'd send me down to the corner store to buy her a Snickers bar, and she'd always demand the three cents change. I could've saved it up to buy my *own* Snickers bar, but no."

"I know you don't hold a grudge for that."

"No. It's that other thing."

"But she tells me you were nice to her. In San Diego."

"I tried."

"It was an icebreaker. There's no hurry, you know. Now that she needs you —"

"She doesn't need me. She needs someone to commiserate with, that's all."

"She can commiserate with you. *You're* divorced."

"Thanks for reminding me!"

"I'm sorry. I just mean, you've been through what she's about to go through. And survived."

"What, I was supposed to commit hara-kiri?"

"You know what I mean."

"Ben didn't have diddly squat. Ella's going for the pot of gold."

"There's the girls. She has to think of them."

"But she wants to castrate Tucker too."

"I suppose so." Then after throwing a sly look at me: "And I don't really blame her."

I picked at my salad while Mom stared at my forehead. Her fondest wish for her daughters was reconciliation, and she saw this as our opportunity.

"Give her a call once in a while," she said.

"Look, all I can promise right now — and please stop staring at me like that — is I'll be nice to her during all this. Neutral. I won't do anything *hostile*, how's that?"

"It'll do. For now."

"She owes me an apology, Mom. She knows. I left it in her court, but she's too proud to say she was wrong."

She killed me sometimes. Instead of nodding at the fact that Ella had at *least* insulted Daddy before he died, she sat there looking sanctimonious and said, "We all make mistakes, sweetheart."

*

Let me see. What were *my* mistakes? What did *I* do to deserve being single and childless (not that I ever really wanted children) at the age of thirty-eight and three-quarters?

Well, I suppose I didn't detect Ben's nagging discontent over our few years together. Or his secret resentment of me. If it was secret, how was I supposed to spot it? And I guess I've so plunged myself into my work — which I love — that I've subconsciously made it very hard to meet someone, much less the right someone, so the question would be why. Why'd I do that? Do I have that idiotic fear of intimacy people talk about? Do I feel like I'm so goddamn superior — *Doctor* Sarah Phelan — that there's probably no one out there on my celestial level? Don't think so. In fact, I'm probably the only doctor you'll ever meet who feels like she's no more elevated than the average Joe or Josephine. All I did was go to school for a long time. I came out with all the fears, doubts, and flaws everybody has, and I recognize them. I'm afraid I make life-and-death mistakes at work. I doubt my own expertise, my personal stability (sometimes), my social skills, my intuition. And my flaws? Too many to go into, even if I don't consider my lunchbox purse a flaw, or my old car, or my nagging suspicions that Dylan was in some kind of trouble.

That very week, once we'd settled back in after our trip, I began to try drawing him out.

At his apartment one night I cooked him the liver and onions my dad made famous. I brought over an inexpensive chianti to have with it, and a green bean salad from the Italian deli near my place.

Digging in, he said, "This is offal."

"Yes, I know."

We smiled at each other across his small round table. The lighting was romantic, dimmed to almost what's-the-point. The music was an Oscar Peterson and Ben Webster record my dad loved. I was so delighted to find it in Dylan's collection.

"So," he said. "We're back."

"Yes we are."

"Busy this week?"

"Crazy busy."

"All those sick people."

"Right. At least you're not one of them, though."

"Knock wood."

We both tapped, ridiculously, on the glass table top.

He seemed a little reticent. "Can I ask you a question, Dylan?"

"You just did."

"No. I mean, something probing. Personal."

"Oh Christ. Here it comes."

In his tight black V-neck he looked completely devourable. I hated to go where I was planning to go.

"I think we have to start poking around under the surface, so to speak. Under the hood."

"The bonnet, you mean?"

"Right. So I was just going to ask — please don't take this the wrong way."

"Don't I get a blindfold and a cigarette?"

"Funny." I took a deep breath. "Dylan, do you think you drink too much?"

This as we were nearly finished with the chianti.

He began to nod, a subtle knowing expression coming into his eyes and mouth. "So that's what's been bothering you. My gin pick-me-up at the wedding."

"I think you had two."

"I did. And I might have had three if you hadn't come along." Humor leaving his face now. "But no, Sarah. I don't have a drinking problem. I don't drink that much. Not at all. But I was feeling a bit overwhelmed that day, and —"

"Overwhelmed? By what? Nobody expected anything special out of you. Not even me. Just stand there and look beautiful. Make me the envy of every girl in the room."

"*That's* not a tall order. Nooooo."

"Not really. But you got frazzled before we even made it to the reception. Outside in the garden."

"One can have things on one's mind, can't one?"

"Don't talk Britishy to me."

"Sorry. I did have something on my mind."

"What."

"Pardon?"

"What was on your mind that took you away from that unbelievably beautiful place, that spectacular ceremony. Your ravishing date?"

I wanted to get him to laugh. He didn't.

"Not the need for a drink."

"Then what, Dylan? Criminy!"

"Did you say criminy?"

"You heard me."

He shook his head, stood, and began clearing the table. He muttered to himself as he went back and forth from table to sink. *I don't know why I'm getting the third degree all of a sudden. She should have brought this up at the time if it bothered her so much. I didn't realize there was an unspoken limit to the number of drinks I could have without being called a bloody dipso!*

"I'm not accusing you of that." I was pretty sure I knew what he meant.

"No. You're just *asking*."

He was so close to me now, standing there with his arms folded stiffly over his chest, that I couldn't help myself. I wrapped my arm around his near leg, high on his leg, and pressed my head into his hip. I felt the warmth of him coming through his gray slacks. I didn't want to fight. I wanted to screw him.

"I'm sorry," I said in my little girl whiny voice. I hate when I do that. Women think men like it, I guess, but I hate it. "I'm just *worried* about you, baby."

"Are we done with the probing questions?"

"Well," I said.

"What."

"You could just tell me a few things without me having to ask." I let go of him and looked up. The back of his hand grazed across my cheek as he smiled a little bit smugly, like he was winning. "You *are* pretty closed-mouth sometimes, you know."

He backed away, poured the dregs of the wine into *my* glass, and said, "In good time, doctor. It all doesn't have to come out like data in a journal article."

"For all I know you could work for the CIA."

"Oh, that's too scabby!" He threw his head back laughing. "You really are a classic."

"No, that's how tight-lipped you are! I mean, I know what little you've told me about your family, but that's about it. And you never go into any detail."

"I'm *sparing* you the detail, for Christ's sake!"

"Dylan, I love you. The details are all part of you, so I love them too. No matter what."

"Really."

"Yes, really."

This had begun to feel like a fight. I still wasn't ready for our first fight. I reached out toward him and prayed to the ceiling fan that he'd take the offer.

He did. He pulled and I stood up, and we moved seamlessly into a gentle two-step to go along with the music, though there didn't have to be any music at all as far as I was concerned. He held me close to his body, one hand flat, firm, and assertive on my back and one soft but sturdy under my hand. His mouth was touching my ear as he said, "Patience, love. I'm like a good book.

Everything you want to know gets revealed eventually."

This was so cheesy I let my head fall onto his shoulder, my face blazing with a hot flush. But I loved him for saying it. He could have tossed out a few more dry morsels of personal stuff, I guess, and I'd have had to accept them. This way, at least, I knew we'd be together long enough (the way he saw it) to get to the meat of him.

So to speak.

He turned out the lights but left the music playing.

*

So it was on the heels of *that* scene that I arranged the big unveiling. Jules meet Dylan, Dylan Jules.

It happened on neutral ground, a trendy restaurant everyone had been dying to try in the Fillmore District, not all that far from Dylan's place in fact. I'd turned down Jules's offer to cook for us because I didn't want her abusing home-field advantage in some way I couldn't even imagine — not enough toilet paper on the roll? a wobbly chair for Dylan to balance his bum on all evening? — and this she basically understood.

"You need to get something, though," she told me on the phone the night before. "I don't *want* him to fail. I want to be pleasantly surprised. I want you to live happily ever after."

"Let's hear the but."

"The but is, forget the Red Flags and he seems too good to be true, that's all."

"Don't do this to me."

"I'm just watching your back."

And I appreciated it. Just like I appreciated it when Ben came along, and she appreciated it when I monitored things with Wayne. And with every other applicant who came along over the years and lasted more than a couple of months.

Naturally, reservations at eight were impossible so we got shoehorned in for six-thirty, meaning that Dylan would have trouble getting there precisely on time. I explained this to Jules and Wayne as we stood in front of the restaurant waiting for him. He was almost twenty minutes late. No call.

Inauspicious start to The Introduction. Of course I was remembering Ben's. Wishing I'd popped a Valium before heading over.

"Fashionably late," Wayne said, leaning close to kiss me on the cheek. He understood what was at stake. "How European."

"It's his job. He's been trying to land new clients and it's running him ragged." I laughed. Inappropriately. Jules gave me a look.

"Sweetie," she said close to my ear, "don't worry. We're not doling out demerits or anything."

"Nice to know."

Wayne was looking down Fillmore toward Geary. "Good-looking dude running across Bush almost got hit by a taxi," he said. "Is that him?"

I turned. It *was* him. He *was* running. And he had a fistful of generic flowers and what he called his *portmanteau* when he wanted to tickle me. His overcoat — it was chilly on this summer evening in San Francisco, as usual — flapped behind him like unfurling sails. He was already shouting something as he approached.

"Christ, he *is* gorgeous," Jules whispered so Wayne wouldn't hear.

"I tried to tell you."

"So sorry!" Dylan was saying over the traffic noise and the pounding of my pulse in my ears. "Got stuck in downtown traffic, and my phone ran out of juice. I hope we haven't lost our table."

I trotted a few feet and met him. I pasted him with a kiss to his chin, then tugged him by the coat toward Jules and Wayne.

"So." We all looked at one another, fleetingly, then their eyes landed on Dylan to stay a while. It was getting a little weird when I said, "This is Dylan, you guys."

Dylan, with his superb timing, held up his flowers. "These are for the fragrant Jules. I'm so glad to finally meet you."

She almost spit, trying not to laugh. "Oh my."

"Not that Wayne isn't every bit as fragrant," Dylan threw in.

"Old Spice," Wayne said, provoking hearty laughs, and he reached out to shake Dylan's hand. Then Jules, holding her flowers away from her body, went in for the first hug. I saw Dylan land a perfectly polite and acceptable kiss right in the bull's-eye of her cheek — not too close to the mouth or to the ear, either of which would have been too intimate. He was good.

"Well." I couldn't feel my fingers. "I guess we'd better go in and grab that table before they give it to someone else."

On our way through the door, Dylan whispered to me that he was mortified and would make it up to me. All I could say to that was, "Break a leg."

And things went — pretty well. Dylan was content to give Jules and Wayne center stage, asking them loads of questions, responding to their humor with warm, genial laughter that didn't seem the least bit phony, to me. When they asked him about his own life (Jules probing into areas I already knew would prove barren), he answered politely, "It really wasn't that thrilling to grow up in South London. You know how it is. Mum, Dad, a series of dogs whose names you can't quite remember now."

I tried to signal to Jules that this line of questioning was not great for my own comfort and well-being, but she kept at it. At least until Dylan, revealing just a sliver of perfectly understandable annoyance, said, "And what about *you*?"

"Me? I'm not the one who's sweeping our Sarah off her feet. *I'm* her overprotective bubby who wants to know all there is to know about the new boy toy."

"Cheeky."

"Better believe it."

"Well, all I can say is —" God, I hoped he wasn't going to deliver that line about a good book. "— I understand completely. It's just that I'm cursed with this congenital British humility. We don't like to talk about ourselves for fear of putting people off. Or worse. Boring them."

Then, as if realizing he had to offer something juicy enough to distract these two dogs, Dylan told a story of being taken by his father to a violin recital at Wigmore Hall in Central London, and how, though he had no appreciation at all for the music and no grasp of what it meant to his father, he was stunned, and moved for possibly the first time in his life (he was only about five at the time), to see that Dad was crying.

"And the thing is, I could tell," he said, "that it wasn't the kind of crying *I* specialized in, the sort that's meant to get you something you want or a reaction to pain or embarrassment. I didn't understand that it came from pure emotion, pure appreciation, and that it was as involuntary in him as a sneeze. I just knew it was different, and a little bit scary, really."

This went a long way with them. They listened, captivated and touched. I knew he was telling me something too. He was explaining the evening at the Elgar concert.

I held his hand under the table.

By the time I got home, a couple of hours later, Jules had already emailed.

"He's totally dreamy," she said. "Enjoy."

THIRTEEN

Transition point. Relationship novels always have one. Obligatory. It's the point where the feel of the new relationship — after the gaga honeymoon period — suddenly changes, and never for the better. How could it get any better, right?

At first I didn't even notice the transition point was upon us. I had a busy week or two, and so did Dylan. We agreed to two or three dark nights in a row, whimpering on the phone that it was temporary and just one of those things. He had to make a big push on the San Diego project, and I had more patients in the hospital at one time than I could ever remember. That might have been an omen.

Soon I looked up and August was almost over. August is when I usually head for a Tahoe cabin, where I put medical thoughts out of my mind (Nilesh taking care of my patients) and satisfy my brain's need for downtime by reading sleazy magazines and chick lit. Or interchangeable mysteries and thrillers. I think there's really only one enormous thriller out there now, made up of the hundreds of thousands of them that are published every ten minutes or so, and our job as readers is to somehow knit them all together. We're the ultimate sleuths. There's no other explanation I can think of for so many goddamn thrillers.

Before you go running from a doctor who reads chick lit and thrillers, let me just pacify you by saying I can read only so many medical journals, only so many meeting abstracts and pharmaceutical alerts. And I do have a soft spot for genuine literature, such as the D. H. Lawrence I've already mentioned, but also E. M. Forster, Thomas Hardy, Ford Madox Ford, Joseph

Conrad — I guess I have a thing for the Edwardian English. Ben might have done that to me.

Oh, but I can't stand Jane Austen. Which is probably ironic because she's the queen of Empire chick lit and here I am in the middle of my own latter day Jane Austen novel, if you look at it a certain way. How can the capable, pragmatic single girl land the man of her dreams and so ensure her eternal happiness (and, in those earlier days, security) without losing something of herself in the process?

Dylan said he couldn't take the time away from work to go to Tahoe with me, so I canceled. There'd be time for Tahoe later. Just like there'd be time for him to let some of those secret details fall like so many autumn leaves.

Most weeknights, except the "dark" ones, Dylan and I would meet at one apartment or the other, then go out for a casual dinner or now and then some music or a movie. Sometimes just window shopping, strolling along with our arms around each other like you're supposed to do when you're newly in love. Dylan seemed to be in a more solid place now, no recent signs of his illness coming back, and he surprised me by giving me for no reason at all a Brady Bunch lunchbox he found in the Haight. I was over the moon.

"Anorak, we say." He wasn't finished kissing me after the big surprise. "When we're really really chuffed to bits over something. We're anorak for it. Like hopeless nerds."

"I love that. Chuffed to bits is pretty good too."

"I'll teach you so many more."

This was at a bench we'd dibbed as our own on Marina Green, with its glorious view of the Golden Gate Bridge, Alcatraz, the twinkling bay. Late dusk, a peach and violet sunset. Very crepuscular — a word I love because it's as rare as such moments.

"I'm anorak for *you*, then," I said.

"Why thank you, dear. And I for you."

We didn't speak much after that. I didn't tell him I really don't care for the Brady Bunch. (Embossed on a lunchbox they're fine.) He didn't offer up any more childhood tidbits or a latent confession that I might be able to sink my teeth into, but then again I was enjoying the quiet and very easy intimacy between us there on our bench. It was getting cooler and he wrapped his arm around me tighter. It was getting darker, and he kissed me on my earlobe.

"You know," I finally said. "I've been thinking."

"Always dangerous."

"Aren't you the funny man. No, seriously. I was just looking ahead a bit, the way I like to do, and it occurred to me. We might want to think about getting a place together. I mean —"

"A place? Sorry?"

"You know. An apartment. A two-bedroom maybe? Lower Pacific Heights or someplace like that, so it's easy for both of us to get to work."

"Wow," he said.

"Wow? That's it? Not, Fantastic? Not, You must be psychic?"

"Well. After all." British hesitation. No eye contact. "There's a reason I rent that dump of mine. It's *cheap*."

"Exactly. And the two of us chipping in would cut our rents in half, right? You'll actually *save* money."

"I'm not much of a roommate, I'm afraid."

"Oh, come on. You're tidy. You have great taste. I can't imagine anything you could possibly do that would make you hard to live with."

"I —"

"What is it?"

He tried to look at me but couldn't hold it. The foghorn on the Golden Gate blasted out a huge long note.

"I just wasn't thinking like that yet. That's all."

He studied his hands, balled into a knot between his knees. I studied them too. Tense and maybe a little angry. I put on my cutesy optimist face.

"Okay! No big deal! Maybe it's a little soon, I can see that. Maybe when we've seen each other in swimsuits and handling umbrellas —"

"Sorry?"

"Never mind."

After a few minutes of almost no talk at all, he took my hand and squeezed it. Kind of hard. And he said, with a voice that sounded like when a man doesn't want to be seen crying, "We'll know when it's the right time."

Strange. I felt like *I* knew.

*

A couple of weeks later, I finished my rounds early and decided to surprise Dylan with takeout from my favorite Chinese place. Four entrees, three appetizers, a hot and sour soup that was practically a cure for the common cold. He'd take the leftovers for lunch the next day. From where I had to park four blocks away, I shlepped the two bags of food to his building, a big involuntary grin growing under my nose the closer I got. He'd be tickled with my fanciful spontaneity and my taste in Chinese food. I was sure.

But after three buzzes and no answer, I gave the door a good pounding with the side of my fist. I knew he was in there. I heard music.

The door opened, snapping the chain tight inside.

"Yeah, who is it?" An English accent. Not Dylan's.

"Is — is Dylan home?"

"No, he ain't. Who's that then?"

"It's Sarah." I hemmed. Or hawed. I'm not sure which. "His girlfriend."

"His *girlfriend*, is it. Well well well. Come in, why don't you?"

The chain dropped, the door opened wide, and I stood there with my Chinese feast looking at a large hairy man in Dylan's familiar white robe.

"Who are you?"

He'd already turned away from the door, heading back inside. I hesitated. What if this was one of those burglars who comes in and makes himself at home? Where the hell was Dylan?

When he noticed I hadn't followed, he turned and faced me with his hands on his hips. "Coming or not? You're letting in cold air."

"I asked who you are and you didn't say. Where's Dylan?"

"I'll tell you if you come in and share your Chinese food," he said, then landed on the sofa with his arms sprawled out wide.

*

143

Steve Cakebread. Dylan's brother.

I was too unnerved to eat now, but I sat across from him and watched as he wolfed down the twice cooked pork with special enthusiasm.

"Good," he said. "Care for a beer?"

"I'd better. Let me get it."

Steve Cakebread was so unlike Dylan that I had a hard time keeping my eyes off of him. He reminded me of a grungy shipmate in some '40s seafaring movie. Heavy, bearded from collarbone to cheekbones, and reeking of East End manners like those Dickensian types who eat with their fingers and wear the napkin stuffed into their shirt collar. Since he was in Dylan's robe, he kept his napkin bunched in one hand.

I delivered him an Anchor Steam. I was already figuring to have two.

"So then," he said as he ate. "Like I told you, he's away at a conference. Some colleague asked him to present his talk since he had some sort of emergency."

"Dylan didn't say anything to me about this."

"Didn't he? How long have you two been going out?"

"Four months. Plus."

"Not exactly forever, is it."

"We've been spending a lot of time together."

"Is that right? Well, then you probably see it takes a while to get to know me brother. He's not the most readable book on the shelf, is he."

From what Dylan had told me, he and Steve were more or less estranged, so it was very puzzling that Steve was installed in Dylan's apartment as if it were his own. The place was cluttered with casually dropped jackets, undershirts, and abandoned shoes, like Steve was the kind to disrobe while strolling from the door to the fridge.

"Where is this conference of his?"

"L.A., I believe. I think he mentioned L.A. Maybe Long Beach. Or was it Santa Monica?"

"He wasn't clear on where he was going?"

"I'm sure he was. I just wasn't clear on listening."

He made himself laugh. I felt myself shaking my head without meaning to.

"I'd better call him," I said.

"You can if you like, but he told me he was turning his cell off. He's up to his neck with work and has a real bastard of a boss to keep happy."

News to me. "What boss? He's his own boss, isn't he? He has his own company."

"Oh hell now," Steve said, pausing with his hands over the rice carton. "I've spoiled one of his little fibs."

My beer went down fast as he told me the story. He was in fairly frequent touch with Dylan and knew for a fact that he worked as a draftsman for Perry, White & Dawson, a mid-size firm in the City. I'd heard of them. They were trying to make a name for themselves in the green design movement, with tricks like rain collection tanks built into homes, lawns on roofs, building materials made out of old newspapers. Dylan had never mentioned them. He'd never let me meet him at his office, come to think of it. Said it was near the Embarcadero but never told me exactly where.

"*Shit.*"

"Don't get me wrong. He *wants* his own shop. Busting his arse trying to punch up his bona *fee*-daze and build a list of clients. That's why he was all right with this conference on a dime. Networking." Steve pointed to his temple like, Smart, eh?

"I'm —"

"You can see why he stretched the truth a bit, though. Lovely lady like you. He wouldn't want to disappoint you." Now he dug into the sesame beef — Dylan's favorite — and nodded with satisfaction. "And what's your line of work, Miss Phelan?"

"I'm a doctor."

"Too right!"

"I am. I work for an HMO up in Marin."

"So you're in his boat as well. No practice of your own. Wage slave in the American version of our National Health."

I got my back up a bit over that but didn't show it. "When does Dylan get home?"

"Couple of days. If you don't mind, forget to mention I blew his cover, will you?"

Steve winked.

"I thought the two of you weren't speaking a lot."

"Is that what he says?"

"He says you don't see things the same."

"That much I can agree with." Steve laughed hard, a guttural laugh, almost infectious. Dylan never laughed quite so easily. "But he phones me now and again and I phone him every couple of weeks, I'd say. Aside from Mum, we're the only Cakebreads left. Other than the kids, I mean."

"The kids. What kids."

"Oh hell now."

"What are you saying? Whose kids?"

Steve took a deep breath through his nose, laid down his fork and knife, which he'd been using Continental style, pushing meat up the back of the fork that peculiar way they do, and folded his hands on the table.

"I think I'd best keep my bloody mouth shut."

"Whose kids, Steve. Come on."

"Whose else?" He gave me a generously sympathetic look. "*His* kids."

*

He gave me "some space." I gave up on the Chinese food and threw myself onto the couch with a corrugated pillow over my face, trying to digest what Steve had just told me.

Seems Dylan had two kids. A boy. A little girl. A pair of little Cakebreads.

Steve treated himself to another Anchor Steam and then a shower, and when he came back I was sitting upright again, hugging the pillow against my belly and rocking back and forth like a schizophrenic. I *felt* schizophrenic, actually. A foot in two different worlds. One world the world of my wonderful new love affair and all its sweet trimmings, the other the world where my lover is a two-faced, two-timing, wage-slave bigamist wannabe with a quasi-Marxist brother and God knows how many more secrets I'd be learning drop by drop as the months went on. It was emotional waterboarding.

Steve sat next to me on the sofa. His dark hair was slicked back and he smelled of Dylan's avocado soap. "There there," he said.

"Nobody's ever said *there there* to me. Nobody ever *had* to say *there there* to me."

"I've been doing some thinking," he told me.

"Always dangerous." I almost cried, quoting Dylan.

"You got that from him, didn't you. Charming. Anyway." His big hand clapped down on my knee and patted a few times. "All right then. I take it he hasn't told you about Gloria."

"*Please* don't tell me he's married." Such goes the cliché.

"Divorced," Steve said. "But it's been rough. Brutal, actually. The two little ones, him having to be away from them, but he had the job opportunity up here and felt like he had to take it or set himself back years."

"I can't believe this."

"Gloria's suing for full custody now. Accuses him of abandonment, but you see, he *had* to at the time, or the job would have dried up, and Gloria, in actual fact, led him to believe she was willing to come up to Frisco."

I was officially in tears now. Blubbering. "We don't call it that," I said. "Frisco."

"Sorry. How's San *Fran*?"

"Oh shit. I don't care. Call it Frisco if you want."

He took a big gargly drink of his beer and nodded as he considered what to say next. "Truth be told, it's been months of really gritty stuff going on, nasty things in court down in San Diego." So *that's* why he'd been going there so often. I bet myself there *was* no residential project down there. It was his cover story. "He'd settle for shared custody, of course, but Gloria wants no part. She's finished with him and for some reason wants to hand him his arse in a plastic bag."

"What did he do to deserve that? Did he cheat on her?"

"I know for a fact he didn't cheat on her. He's not the type. But he's not been very frank and open with me on the wherefores and whys. Dylan's always been a bit on the locked-up side, sort of, especially when it comes to his personal life, so there's nothing I

147

can do but speculate — which I'm happy to do."

"Let's hear it."

"Really?"

"I think I need to. This is the transition point."

"Sorry?"

"Never mind. Tell me what you think's going on."

He heaved a musical sigh, three ominous notes coming out through his nose and skimming over his big bushy mustache. "See, what I think — *I* think Gloria's a bit of a volatile thing. And I think — Well, very simply. *I* think she got a bit *bored* with old Dill. And she saw the Frisco job thing as a chance to make a change."

I sat there for a few moments trying to let all this sink in. I felt suddenly sorry for Dylan, but that got swept away immediately by the voice in my head that screamed out, He lied to you! Then my softer side said, He didn't want to lose you by telling the truth too soon.

It would be hard to stake out a position somewhere in the middle.

"He didn't want the divorce?" I asked. Definitely afraid of the answer.

"Are you kidding me?" Steve said. "It hit him like a fookin' train."

"He still loved her?"

"Gloria?" he said, chuckling in a helpless way that didn't bode very well. "He was anorak for her."

*

That night, in bed, after I'd emailed the revelation to Jules knowing she would be asleep, I ran it all through my mind fifteen thousand times. The Story of Dylan and Gloria. Steve had filled me in, seeing as how I was a sniveling basket case the rest of the evening. He had to. He hated to see grown women embarrass themselves, he said.

The long and short of it is, Gloria was Dylan's Ben. Only Dylan got quite a bit further along in life with his Ben than I did with mine. Two kids' worth.

They met in college, back east — Pennsylvania, I think (I wasn't registering all the little details) — and fell ridiculously in love. Dylan was in his mid-twenties, going for his masters, and Gloria was (you can't make this stuff up) in the drama department. She caught his eye doing Lady MacBeth in the college production, really nailing the part that goes, "I have given suck, and know how tender 'tis to love the babe that milks me: I would, while it was smiling in my face, have plucked my nipple from his boneless gums and dashed the brains out, had I so sworn as you have done this," blah blah blah. (I admit, I looked this up.) He approached her backstage and told her he'd never seen the role done so *rampantly*, was his word, and there'd never been such a ravishing Lady MacBeth on *any* stage.

I guess an English accent lets you get away with such crap.

Anyway, they began dating, and Dylan got his degree, and within a few months had a job offer in San Diego, where Gloria knew there was a respected rep company she could audition for (she did, but didn't get the gig). They married, and their life together went along like a pleasant car trip. They lived in a nice part of town, near the water — not far from Ella, as it turns out — and several years into their marriage Gloria got pregnant. They hadn't been trying. It just happened. The girl was named Vanessa.

A couple of years later came the little boy, Andy. Andy Cakebread. Can you beat that? Dylan and Gloria and Andy and Vanessa. The Cakebreads. Of San Diego.

Steve told me that he'd never seen Dylan happier than those middle years, the years when the children were still very small and Gloria hadn't begun to think about what her life might have been like if she'd followed her bliss and played Lady MacBeth at the Aldwych in London. National Shakespeare Company. As if. Purely delusional thinking, of course, but when a lovely volatile woman like Gloria (and she *was* beautiful, Steve said, long light red hair, a complexion like pearly silk, green eyes that dazzle a man — oh, *barf!*) gets a bee in her bonnet there will be casualties. Still, he told me, this didn't explain why she became so bloody hostile toward Dylan. I thought it might be classic transference: I feel too guilty about it all so I'm blaming you. But it was pretty clear now that I didn't know either of them so it could have been

149

anything.

Something occurred to me. What had unsettled Dylan at the wedding. It was the children, dancing around so joyfully and carefree after the ceremony, singing and running and looking so cute and innocent, just like his own. He couldn't handle it.

Knowing what I knew now, I couldn't really blame him.

*

You understand that I throw Jules in now to show another obligatory moment, when the Best Friend tells the Betrayed Heroine that it's over and her dreams have been officially crushed. The Object of Her Affection has crossed a line that is sacrosanct when it comes to new relationships, the Trust Line. A betrayal like this can never be undone because you can never really believe a thing that comes out of Said Object's mouth again, no matter how much bended knee he might indulge in, no matter how sad and contrite he seems there in front of you with his Yugo-sized bouquet of roses and his first-class tickets to Paris (I'm talking real chick lit shlock here). He is now a suspect. It would take years for you to stop wondering if he has any more horrible secrets he's had to keep from you because you'd run away if you knew.

The Best Friend tries to soften the blow, of course. She hugs you and feeds you some warm pudding right out of the pot. She holds you by both shuddering shoulders and tells you how wonderful you are, how beautiful and funny and affectionate and loving and talented, and how the cosmos won't let all that go to waste, it just can't. And you whine and moan and cry and go, Really? And she says, Of course! He's the one who'll lose out. You're gonna be *just* fine. Oh hell. Why bother showing all that. You get the gist.

FOURTEEN

Dylan called when he got back from L.A. If that's where he was. L.A. is awfully close to San Diego.

"Really sorry," he said. "Busy busy. Got called to a conference and couldn't manage to ring you."

"That's all right," I said. "Steve told me where you were."

Silence on the other end. I guess Steve hadn't told him I'd "popped by." Steve, after all, didn't want to have to admit that he coughed up Dylan's entire story and must have thought things will find their own level sooner or later. I liked Steve, all in all.

"You met Steve."

"Oh yes. He's an interesting guy."

"He is that. I hope he —" Dylan cleared his throat of a few spare coins, it sounded like. "Toned himself down for you. He's a bit extreme at times."

"He was a real gentleman," I said. "I fed him the Chinese food I brought over for us to have. He thanked me profusely."

"So he told you how I had to go with no notice, did he."

"Yep. For a colleague."

I could almost see him nodding as the hideous possibilities dawned on him. "Well, luckily," he said, "it all worked out for the best. I made some terrific connections and did a bang-up job on the presentation too, I have to say."

"Bravo."

"It was bloody hot down there too. Must have hit ninety every —"

"Dylan, you could have called. Or texted me. Or emailed."

"I know. I'm very sorry."

"It was kind of upsetting."

"Had to be. I wish I would have been more thoughtful."

"You're closer to Steve than you led me to think, aren't you."

"Sarah, can I please come over now?"

It took him less than twenty minutes to appear at my door. There he was, a picture of romantic misery, which incidentally is something every woman appreciates seeing in her man. The physical side of realizing he could lose you. The bloodshot eyes, the wan cheeks, the hair mussed as if he's been running his hand through it neurotically all the way over. Warms your little cockles right up.

He dropped a small nosegay of daisies on my floor and kissed me. It was one of those kisses that sucks the self-awareness right out of you, and you come to wondering what year it is.

"So. Drink?" I said, not wanting him to win *that* easily.

"No, no thanks."

"You want to talk?"

"I think so. I think we'd better."

On the spur of that very moment, I decided I wouldn't confront him with what I knew. Now was his chance to put it all out there, like a line full of dirty underthings for all the neighbors to see. He started small.

"Listen." He led me to the couch and sat with me, holding my hand in both of his in that super-earnest way that is supposed to mean, "No, *really*." He looked deep into my eyes. So deep that I was nearly the one who broke the gaze. Somehow I hung in there. "I think it's time I let you in on a tiny little fib I've been telling."

"Dylan, you've been fibbing to me?"

"I'm afraid so. I wanted to impress you, and I thought I might be able to impress you better with my dreams than with actual — how do they put it? Facts on the ground."

He smiled defensively. Sheepish and charming. I put my other hand on top of his to encourage more truth telling.

"Go on."

"So I'm afraid what I did was, I led you to believe certain things. Certain professional details." He closed his eyes and shook his head, like he was fighting off an inner voice. Then he lifted his head toward the ceiling, laughed at his own hesitation, and blurted it out. "I don't run my own shop. I work for a firm. I lied."

"Hmmm. Well."

"I thought you'd be more interested in me if I had my own company. It made me feel — *bigger*, somehow."

"Dylan, I told you size doesn't matter."

He snorted through his nose at that one, muttering, "Funny, very funny."

"You'll have your own shop one day. I know it." I leaned toward him and kissed his chin. I'd wanted his mouth but he tipped his head back and ruined my timing.

"Not sure about that," he said. "Deck seems to be stacked against it. I'm spinning my wheels at Perry, White & Dawson."

"Oh, the green ones?"

"Right. They won't give me my own set of clients. Not yet. They say I'm too —"

"Green?"

"Ironic, isn't it?"

"Poor baby," I said, and now I took him in a hug and let him rest his head on my boobs. Men calm right down that way. Ben always did. "You'll be fine. You'll get your clients, and then your own place, and one day you'll have a young associate who seems a little too raw and you'll think back to these days and *laugh*."

"He nods knowingly."

"Exactly. Old P W & D knew what they were doing, you'll say."

"I am thirty-seven, you know. Not exactly raw."

"Don't talk to *me*. I'm thirty-eight."

"A ravishing thirty-eight," he said, and I cringed a little bit at the word. Lady MacBeth. Gloria. Ravishing.

We both sat there quietly in some sort of tension break. I wanted so much to lead him by the hand to my bedroom, but there was more territory to cover before that would feel right.

"So," I said. "About you and Steve."

"Yes?"

"You're not exactly estranged."

"Well, I guess that depends on what you mean by *estranged*."

"I mean like me and Ella. When you're together, your stomach grows a little sea urchin inside and you feel like you want to tear your own fingernails out with pliers."

153

He pursed his lips. "Then I suppose no. No, we're not estranged. But you saw how different he is from me. We always wondered whether one of us was adopted, and I said it had to be him because he acted like he was raised by a tribe of baboons."

"He was very sweet to me."

"Yes, he can pull that off. When he wants to."

"When was the last time you saw him?"

Dylan knitted his handsome brow and made a production out of "thinking about it." Then he said, "I guess it was last year. I went over there on holiday."

"Ah."

"Mainly to see the old neighborhoods. A few concerts, museums. And the architecture, of course."

"Of course. Where did you stay?"

"With — *aherm*. With Steve."

Vaguely I remembered that he'd told me he hasn't seen his brother in ages. I got up and poured myself a glass of white wine. I brought the bottle over to the couch.

"Dylan?"

"Darling. Please. *Sarah*. I feel so awful about all this. I didn't want to complicate things with too much *mess*. You can see that, can't you?"

"I felt the same way, you know. But I got around to telling you *my* stuff."

"And yours was so innocuous," he said, then changed his adjective. "Innocent, I mean. And righteous."

It was getting late. I couldn't imagine us putting the *mess* behind us so quickly that making love — *screwing* — might be on the menu. I was sad, I admit. The feelings I used to get when it was becoming clear to me that Ben could actually leave fluttered around in my chest like blind, powdery moths.

"I hate to ask this," I said. I was grinning like an idiot and took a sip of wine so fast that the glass rang against my front teeth. "But is there anything else you think I should know?"

The Transition Point had already turned into the Moment of Truth.

After a few breaths, a pause that anybody would have read as "here it all comes," he looked up at me and, to my deepest heartbreak — almost as bad as when Dad died — began to shake his head slowly as he said, "No, dear. That's all of it."

*

The next day I was a wreck inside and just barely capable outside, moving from exam room to exam room like a pacing old hyena at the zoo. The patients tolerated me. One asked me if I needed to lay my head down for a little while, the sweetie. A child — had to be a little girl, of course — told me to take two lollipops and call her in the morning.

Then Mrs. Bannerjee came in for a follow-up.

There was her black and gold sari hanging on the coat rack, a kind of medical scarecrow. She was in the floral examination gown already, her dark legs pendulating over the edge of the table. She smiled when I entered, but then her smile immediately flatlined.

"My goodness, you look terrible!"

"Oh, thank you. It's my conditioner."

"No, no, no. You're not sleeping. I can tell. Whenever my husband can't sleep, he starts looking like a raccoon, and that's how *you* look."

"How are *you* feeling, Lili?"

"Don't change the subject. Tell me what's the matter."

I said it wouldn't be professional of me to talk personal issues during an exam. It would have to wait.

"Then here's what I want you to do. Examine me, and I'll do the talking."

"Uh huh."

"I'll say things, and if I'm getting warm you give me a little tickle. That's what I used to do with Mita when she was a girl and didn't want to say what was bothering her."

"That's adorable. I don't know."

"Please start the exam, doctor."

She lay back on the table, and I began the usual palpations. Her appendectomy incision had healed nicely. Her liver was in good shape.

"I'm going to take a wild guess," she said, "that something is going on between you and that lovely gentleman you brought to the wedding."

I poked her in the ribs. She squealed.

"Aha!"

"That was too easy," I said. "Be quiet for a second."

I listened to her heart. Perfect. Healthy.

"I'd have to imagine that something unexpected has come up. Something about him you didn't know before, when you were in Santa Barbara. You were so *gooey* over him then. Everyone noticed."

I gave a small tickle on her belly. She flinched and squeaked.

"He let a character flaw slip out? He's prejudiced? He doesn't like children?"

I shook my head.

"He's cooled off a bit and you're worried he's no longer interested in you?"

"Let me take your blood pressure."

I helped her sit up. Then I wrapped the cuff around her arm and started pumping. I had my stethoscope in my ears, trying to hear her Korotkoff sounds, but she was saying something and I missed them.

"Please, Lili. Shhhh."

On the other arm I was able to get a reading. She was titillated. Her BP was a little high.

"I said, Sarah, I wonder if you discovered he's been lying to you about something too important to overlook."

With that I went at her bare feet with both hands. She reeled with laughter.

"I knew it!"

Unprofessional as it may have been, I told her everything.

Sitting up now — and this was the strangest confession I ever went through — she took on the wise air of a priest who's heard it all before but still realizes you're a wreck. "I think you are going to learn a lesson about forgiveness pretty soon, don't you?"

I was slumped on my stool. If I looked like a raccoon before I'm sure I looked like a dumpy old sloth now. "I can forgive him for the job thing. And the Steve thing. I already *have* forgiven him for those. But I can't forgive him for something he hasn't asked forgiveness for, can I? He hasn't even admitted it yet. Gloria and the kids."

"He's afraid to admit it."

"I guess he should be."

"Exactly. So that you do understand."

"Oh sure. But how long do I wait? I mean, suppose he asks me to marry him?"

"See, you *are* an optimist!"

"That's not quite the word for what I am. But really. Do I let it all slide until the big moment comes along? Or do I push now and take what comes? I'm afraid *too*, you know."

It was the first time I'd put it that way to myself. I was afraid Jules was right. This was too serious to brush under the relationship carpet.

"He knows he has to tell you one day. He has a time for it in his head. I have no doubt of that."

"How come *I* doubt it?"

"Because you have so much to lose, dear. Simple."

*

A couple of days went by, and Dylan and I mutually begged off getting together in the evenings. He still had Steve to entertain, and I was catching up on some CME material so I could keep being a good doctor.

Then, when we finally did get together, things were a little off. We met at a neutral location on Saturday afternoon, an outdoor café off Union Square, where Dylan ordered tea and bruschetta and I had a mondo plate of fettucini. The contrasts were striking. To overcompensate for my fears, I was talking like a chipmunk on meth, while Dylan sat with his jaws welded together. When he did speak he made mundane comments about the weather and how sad it was that everyone went around sporting tattoos on every exposed inch of their bodies nowadays.

I emptied my wine glass, looking down inside it in disbelief. Then I took a deep breath and tried to get back to some kind of equilibrium. "When does Steve head home?" I asked. "I bet you're going to miss him."

"Oh, right. Like I can't do without a human cyclone in my life."

"I'm sure you two get along fine."

"I haven't been home that much anyway. We're all right. He leaves on Monday, though, thank God."

"Do you guys talk family? Or is it all cricket and football with you."

"You're kidding. I don't follow that rubbish. *He* does, of course. All in for the Hotspurs. He nearly killed a German, he said, during the last World Cup. The Jerry taunted him in a pub over how *ze Inglische hef lost ze vill to vin.* It was a bit hilarious, I suppose."

A small flash of humor, I thought. There's hope!

"So you laugh together. That's good."

"Can't be helped. He's ridiculous."

"Is your childhood off limits? I mean, even before Ella and I broke up we had a standing rule not to go there because we saw everything in complete opposites."

"We don't talk nostalgia, no."

"I don't mean nostalgia, necessarily. Just, you know. Old stuff. How it was. Comparing notes."

"No. We don't."

And that was that.

After lunch, we strolled around a little, sat on a bench near the Ferry Building, watched a scruffy little band play Michael Jackson songs on tarnished brass, and promised to see each other when Steve had gone. Things were still a bit crazy, Dylan said.

I heard my internal bitchy voice say, "They always are in custody fights."

It was later that night, around nine, when the phone rang. Steve Cakebread asking me to meet him the next day. "Someplace where my brother won't run into us by accident," he said.

*

I was there on the pier for the Tiburon ferry well before Steve arrived. When he did come ambling up he was looking over his shoulder to make sure he hadn't been followed.

"Cutting it close!" I said. "Hello."

"He wouldn't bloody leave. I thought he'd make his usual run for bagels and coffee but he was like warmed-over coma this morning. I finally had to lie and say I couldn't go home without seeing Chinatown."

I envisioned Dylan in one of his idiopathic sick episodes. My maternal side flared up like sunspots.

"He's okay?"

"He's in bed watching Ingmar Bergman films."

"Oh no."

Under his Woody Allen fatigue jacket he wore a faded blue T-shirt that said *Forget the Whales — Save Yourselves!* His hair had been teased into a dark corona by the waterfront wind, and if I wasn't mistaken his socks didn't match. Still, he was smiling with brother-in-law affection (premature, obviously), leaning close to kiss me on the cheek.

"I hope I didn't ruin your Sunday," he said. "I thought since I'm leaving tomorrow, though, it might be a good idea for us to spend some time chatting."

"I'm glad you called."

"This the tub?" He nodded toward the red and white ferry.

"I bought the tickets already."

"Then lunch is my treat." When I made fussy noises, he took me by the arm and said, "Least I can do. You're keeping my Dill on the right side of sanity and doing a fine job of it too."

I was about to say I didn't quite imagine Dylan's sanity was on the line, but Steve grabbed my hand and pulled. We boarded the ferry and took a seat on deck instead of running indoors where it would have been warm.

On the way across the bay to Tiburon, Steve told me about himself. I didn't have to ask. It all just poured out like a favorite joke he loved telling. He was indeed a construction worker who manned a variety of heavy machines — cranes, bulldozers, cherry-pickers, that sort of thing — and indeed did love his hours at pub after work most evenings. As much for the camaraderie as the beer, he claimed.

"And I do love women," he said, "but I never shall marry."

There was a song I recalled with those words. I didn't want to live them myself.

"Why not? You seem like a good guy."

"I like my freedom too much! I couldn't abide a woman waiting for me at 'ome, standin' there with her rolling pin as I come in besotted and jolly. 'Where you bin, oy? I said to be 'ome by ten, and 'ere you are crawlin' in at one-*firt*-ee!'"

The way he put on the sloppy Cockney accent would have made Dylan shrivel.

"You must have girlfriends, don't you?"

"Oh, I get by." He winked. "You see, what I've figured out over the decades — I am forty-three, you realize — is that I'm far too eccentric to impose myself on some innocent lady. Damaged goods, you might say."

I didn't like the sound of *that*. Jules would have elbowed me in the ribs if she'd been there.

"Why — why damaged goods?"

"You know about the old man, I take it."

"The accident? Dylan told me."

Steve's head bobbed and he pursed his lips in an odd way. "It hit us all pretty hard, yeah? Dill was a little one, but I was eleven or twelve. Mum was the worst."

I should have understood sooner. I'd had a tough time when Pat died, and I was an adult. What it was like for a little kid — Dylan had to have been six or seven — had to be terrible. And seeing his mum in that kind of grief.

"I'm sorry. It must have been awful."

We were passing Angel Island, with its ghostly Civil War era outpost in a south-facing cove. They were convinced the Confederates were going to come steaming in from the Pacific in those days.

He looked over at me, shoulders slumping. I felt like he wanted to tell me something else, but he finally laughed through his nose and forced his back straight.

"We had nothing to complain about," he said. "Lots of people have worse hardships than the ol' Cakebreads of Clapham."

I delved into my heart for something reassuring to say. "Sometimes you don't know how bad it was for years and years. Because you suppress your feelings."

It didn't come out right.

"You're a doctor. Of course you think that."

"Well, I mean, I'm not a psychiatrist."

"Working class like us? We don't have the luxury of feeling bad over old news."

It struck me how easily Steve accepted, even embraced, his station, for want of a better word. Or ran to it to compensate for his own disappointments. Dylan, on the other hand, grabbed for the elevated things he could only vaguely recall from childhood — the music, his father's fondness for poetry. Both just wanted to survive.

"You know what Faulkner says."

"Some bloke?"

"A southern writer. He says, The past isn't dead. It isn't even past."

He seemed to be thinking that over for a moment or two. Then he said, "Cheeky."

It wasn't long before we got off at the Tiburon pier and walked for a while among the little shops there, and then on out into the main loop of town. Steve saw Irish fisherman sweaters in a window and said, "Too dear. I can get one for you cheap."

We had lunch at a popular waterfront place where you can sit outside and look across the bay toward the city, but somehow neither of us was especially interested in the view. I was working on a bouillabaisse with no enthusiasm, while Steve devoured a hamburger. We both had a local microbrew, which Steve deemed "tolerable."

The overwhelming theme that kept coming to mind as we sat there in the sunshine (and chatting about benign things like the 49ers — he was mad for American football) was how we never fail to put off confronting the biggest issues. They sit there in your brain like a burr, causing a chronic infection — sorry, I *am* a doctor — that spreads until your whole being is poisoned by it. Your body, your soul, even your face, which everyone else can read. Ella and I, for instance. I knew, just sitting there with Steve, that we weren't finished with our big deal. Not by a long shot. And I knew that my anxiety over it, my anger, showed in my eyes. I could try to be my funny, outside self but there was no hiding the toll that our estrangement had taken on me. And Steve, likewise, couldn't hide the thing in him that wouldn't let go, his grief, I was sure, how he must have had to become a man far too soon because of Mr. Cakebread's early death. I looked at him. It was in there. His speech was animated and full of humor, but his eyes, made shimmering by alcohol (and not just the beer he'd had there), showed me that he was not over it and would never be. The same, it occurred to me, could be said for Dylan.

"All right then," Steve said, throwing awkward punctuation into our chat. "I might as well stop beating about the hedges."

"What's wrong? Did I say something?"

"No, dear. It's me. I've been trying *not* to say something."

It wasn't going to be good, I could tell. His cheeks were flaring red over that dark Elizabethan beard of his. His eyes darted to the water and back, squinting at the bright daylight.

"What it is is — I'm sure Dylan hasn't told you. In fact, he *told* me he hasn't told you, and I happen to think that you need a clear eye before the two of you go much farther along —"

I held up my hand to stop him. "You told me about Gloria. I can handle that, and he'll tell me about it in his good time. I trust him."

"It's not that. I know he'll take care of business with Gloria. She's a bit of a pisser anyway. And the kids — he'll cope, in the end. I wanted to tell you, though — where Dad is concerned." For a moment I thought he meant Dylan. As dad to those two kids, Andy and Vanessa. "The thing of it is, Sarah, our father killed himself. He ran his car across the lane divider and straight into a lorry. A big one, hauling steel. It was clearly intentional, even if the coroner didn't say so on the death certificate. The lorry driver said so. Witnesses. But you see —"

"My God."

"It was Mum who fell apart. She drank. She stopped taking care of us. And truthfully? I don't believe she ever recovered, and Dylan's never forgiven her."

I'd noticed he spoke of her very rarely. I didn't ask much because it felt like probing, and Dylan a reticent one anyway.

"He never accepted that Dad did it on purpose, so — I suppose he thought Mum ought to have come round eventually. Year of mourning and all that. But she didn't. And he blames her for the *pall* over us."

I felt myself starting to cry. I reached out and took his hand. He squeezed back, but gently, in control of his own emotions over this old old story.

"And now this," he went on, like a newscaster's segue. "Gloria's the one who kicked him out. He was drinking too much. He'd changed. She was only trying to spare the kids, yeah? And when he *resisted*, is the polite way to say it, she filed for divorce and he came up here. I'm sorry, Sarah."

He didn't let go of my hand. He kept it in his for as long as I needed, the same way I did when I had to tell a patient something awful, something that would change her life.

A small hungry bird skidded onto our table, cocking its head and looking up at me with a strange sympathy in its black little eye.

FIFTEEN

I was glad that Dylan would be occupied the next day with getting Steve to the airport, then making up the lost time at work. I would put in a long day too. I'd make sure I got home after nine that night. Even if the rigors of doctoring didn't demand it.

I wasn't ready just yet to look into his eyes and see the truth that Steve had given me.

Mom made a dinner of her famous Irish stew. She serves it with horseradish, the way Daddy used to love it.

"You're upset," she said.

"Just tired."

"No. You're upset."

She knows me too well.

"I don't feel like talking about it, so we might as well pretend that I'm tired, okay?"

"Okay. I don't mind. I'll just assume it has to do with your boyfriend..."

"Now stop it."

She watched me reaching for the wine bottle and did that little tsk tsk sound she has for such moments of motherly disapproval.

"I'll stay here if I get too looped, how's that."

"Fair enough. But how come you want to get looped?"

"Stress, all right?"

"When did that kick in?"

"God, you're like a district attorney on *Law & Order*!"

"I'm worried about you, that's all."

I filled my glass. I finished my stew. I looked at her there across the table, and when I tried to make one more remark about how much of a snoop she was being, I couldn't do it. I told her everything.

At the end of which she said, "Dear sweet Sarah."

I've always hated that. She does it whenever I'm faced with insurmountable problems, like, in the old days, acne. Then, later, divorce.

Between the lines I hear, Look what you've gotten yourself into.

"Mom. No."

"I want to tell you something. About Pat and me."

I didn't think I could handle a long-hidden story about infidelity or something even worse between the two of them. "Please no?"

"It's not sad. It was a misunderstanding. He was — well, you know he was in the service."

"Yes. What does that have to do with anything?"

She was smiling, resting her chin in her hand with the look some photographers used to make young ladies pose with. Her eyes had a warm nostalgia in them, dipped in caramel. She looked surprisingly young to me at that moment.

"He was in the *service*, honey. And so, well, by the time I met him he was experienced to a certain extent, if you know what I'm trying to say. But he didn't think I could accept that. I might think he was, *you* know."

"You mean he wasn't a virgin."

"Bingo."

"But he wanted you to think he was?"

"Exactly. So, on our wedding night —"

"Oh, Mom. I don't think I need to hear this."

It sounded like a genuine TMI moment to me.

"No, it's charming. He was so sweet. He fumbled all over himself and acted like he had no idea what went where or how he ought to act. And so finally I said, 'Pat, you understand this is how babies are made, right?' And he couldn't take anymore. We both fell apart laughing."

I wondered if that was why I've always associated sex with laughter. Of course I didn't go there with Mom.

"So he lied to you about his sexploits. Big deal. It's not the same."

"All I'm telling you, sweetie, is don't keep this behind the curtain. *Talk* to him. He'll open up to you."

"How do you know?"

"Because he loves you and he doesn't want to lose you." She leaned over and kissed me on my formerly acne-sprouting forehead. "You're utterly lovable, remember?"

Sometimes it was hard to remember that. But it was even harder to think that Dylan and I really were at that point, where it was time to make or break.

No relationship novel can be without its make or break moment, right? It's always right on the heels of the Moment of Truth, and ours was coming on fast.

*

At work the next day, I was up to my elbows in phlegm, mucus, hemorrhoids, pinkeye, palpitations, loose stool, and anything else grimly but fundamentally human you might care to mention, when I spotted Mom out in the waiting room. Since I'd just seen her the night before, I thought something was wrong — something medical — and my heart tried to wring itself out like a washcloth. She was the one person right now I really couldn't do without.

"It's nothing," she said as I ran over. I already had my stethoscope in my ears. "I just wanted to come by in person for this."

"Oh God. What now?"

"Is there anyplace we can sit?"

She was in one of her old Marin lady outfits, the white pants and baggy Nelson Mandela top, with huge sunglasses parked on top of her head. I led her back to my office, which isn't much more than a cubby hole with a desk and file cabinet. Mom sat in my chair and I rested my butt on the edge of the desk.

"What's happened? If it's bad news, just blurt it out because I can't handle —"

"Ella and the girls are moving up here."

She'd blurted it. That meant even *she* saw it as bad news.

The upshot? Ella had decided that she did not want to live in that house anymore, the house Tucker had "built for her" in tony La Jolla as a gesture of eternal love, or whatever bullshit he'd dished out at the time. She figured that the place deserved to be empty now, that Tucker could deal with selling it and parking the proceeds directly into her bank account as part of the settlement, and that the girls needed to be as far away from that son of a bitch and his skanky hedge fund analyst as possible. After all, she'd grown up in the Bay Area and knew her way around. And she had a support system up here, as it were. A support system of one — Mom.

"They'll be staying with me till she finds an apartment in the city. She wants the girls to have an urban experience, she says. And, Sarah?"

"What." My tone was like a bag of roofing nails.

"She wants to be close to *you*."

With all that was going on in my life at the moment, the last thing I needed was Ella popping up around every corner, reminding me of one of the worst periods I'd ever been through. Not just Daddy dying, but the little girl with sepsis too. Right around the same time.

Didn't I mention that?

"I can't right now, Mom."

"Please, honey. She wants to make an effort."

"Well, see, I don't particularly want to make an effort right now, and besides, it's not fair."

I felt so childish saying that. But it was true.

"What's not fair?"

"She's having a bad time. I'll have to be nice to her no matter what. I'll have to cut her such slack she'll think I'm over it all. And I'm not."

Mom looked out the window at my dismal view of the parking lot. Her face had a perfect expression of compassionate contemplation on it, very Mother Teresa, and the light was like a goddamn Vermeer painting, so I was overmatched by circumstances. "See, dear," she began, not looking back right away, "the thing is — you're doing better than Ella. You've always been able to find happiness —"

"Off and on."

"— but she has a problem being happy. You're in love. She's losing everything."

"Everything but a few million dollars."

"And she knows that all she'll have from now on is the girls. You'll have so much more. You know that." Now her eyes were probing into mine, daring me to complain about Dylan. I wasn't going to. I was going to cling to the last of my optimism and imagine a life with him, a *long* one, after this rough patch. A beautiful happy life. Unlike Ella's. "What it boils down to," Mom said, "is that she's always envied you. And now she'd like to be close to you, so something might rub off."

Too much. I was shaking. Anger, sadness, fear, general pissiness. It was lousy timing, and once again I had to be the bigger person, which, given the whole thing with Dylan, I was sick and tired of. Everyone else gets to be a basket case, why not me?

She put her hand on my wrist, a dry gesture, all things considered. A frank one.

"You've always been the lucky one," she said. "Know why?"

I wasn't feeling all that lucky. "Why."

"You're your father's daughter. You got all his good stuff."

That did it. I sobbed a lot of garbage out of me, in the quiet way I'd worked out over the years so I'd never get caught at it. Mom held me through the worst of it, then left me alone to recover before I saw my next patient.

*

I'm going to fast forward here a couple of weeks, into October, and past a few encounters between Dylan and me in which nothing monumental happened. Reason being, I decided to postpone the make-or-break confrontation. I wasn't ready to wake up, it turns out.

We screwed a few times in there, though maybe it was more like making love now. It was more delicate and less hilarious (from my end of things, I mean), and more than that it was laden (again from my end of things) with the air of possible finality. Possible that when I did confront Dylan over wife, kids, alcohol, suicide — we wouldn't be doing this anymore.

I'd be sad when we stopped doing this. It warmed me, inside and out. Seemed to help him too.

But I have to admit that things felt different between us. How could they not? I was in possession of facts that Dylan had no reason to think I'd ever stumble upon. Steve had obviously lied to him if and when Dylan asked, "What did you tell Sarah?" I treated Dylan, I'm sure, with a bizarrely happy-peppy fizz, trying to hide the truth, while he kept his cards close to the vest and regarded me with, I think, a bit of suspicion. Like he thought I was taking drugs, possibly. Nonetheless, we went out, talked, held hands, made plans for next spring and summer, trips here and there, maybe even one to England so I could see his old stamping grounds. Tahoe for sure, since I skipped it this year. We were together, so all this was natural. To accomplish it, though, I had to ignore reality.

In the meantime, Ella and the girls had arrived. They were bivouacked with Mom in Mill Valley, a place I'd avoid until absolutely necessary.

Busy busy busy!

Naturally, I felt like the sword of Damocles was hanging over my head, or more like it, the guillotine of Damocles.

Jules, for the time being, was steering clear of me. In a verbose email, she'd told me that I was not playing a good defensive game so it was only a matter of time before I'd find myself splat against a brick wall. She was talking about Dylan, not Ella. She said that because she had offered me her best advice, which was to force the issue, get the truth out, bathe in the sweet sunshine of honesty, and make Dylan understand he couldn't withhold key information from me without paying the piper, she would have to bow out until after.

After what? I wrote back.

"After your life-altering heartbreak. In theaters this Christmas. J xoxo"

*

The next time I saw Dylan was at his place. He cooked for me.

169

Nothing elaborate — just some broiled salmon fillets with sautéed green beans and a heap of mash on the side. The English and their mash. He had chilled two bottles of a nice prosecco.

"We're actually celebrating something tonight," he said, pouring generous glassfuls. I didn't comment on the booze. Premature. The fact that there was something to celebrate pushed that back.

"Really? What happened?"

Standing in front of me with a kitchen towel folded over one arm, continental style, he was red-cheeked and elated. "Old man Perry actually deigned to offer me a client. My own, from start to finish."

"Dylan, that's fantastic!"

I leapt up and threw my arms around his neck, kissing him all over his face until he had to push me away or suffocate. It was just what he needed. It would help him think about the future and not his botched-up past. His marriage — I mean his divorce — would fade into the woodwork and he'd troop through the custody fight with a new sense of strength and direction. Soon, within the year I was sure, he and his children would be reunited and their relationship better than ever, and the two of us? We could begin looking ahead. A long way ahead. The truths he was afraid to let out would have come and gone.

There'd be nothing but smooth sailing. Blue skies. Baubles bangles and beads. You name it.

"Tell me," I said. Then, casually, as he popped the salmon in the oven and flipped the beans like Mario Battali, he gave me the rundown.

The project was a modern building in a block of old industrial structures South of Market, something that would offer him lots of elbow room in terms of design and innovative touches but a challenge too, because of the context.

I loved it when he talked architecture. *Context*, for God's sake!

"Of course, there are height restrictions, materials, that sort of thing, and I'll have to jump through hoops at City Hall over some of these green concepts. They can be so retrograde sometimes — even in San Francisco."

I hadn't seen him so ebullient. Ever. I mean *out* of bed, obviously, since he'd always been a zesty lover with me.

Between bursts of enthusiasm, he drank down his prosecco. The second bottle needed opening by the time he served up our salmon.

There'll be time later, I thought. To wean him off the sauce. Happiness'll go a long way with that.

After dinner, I made him put on the Ben Webster and Oscar Peterson, and we danced in his tiny living room. I felt like Daddy was looking over my shoulder. Somehow, he'd helped me dodge a big fat relationship-murdering bullet.

I whispered to myself, *I love you too, Dad*.

When we lost our clothes and ended up flungeing on the sofa like rushed horny teens after school, I had the most amazing feeling that life might very well have a script, that its highs and lows are written in ahead of time and are going to come along no matter what so that you don't have to worry: when your butt is scraping the asphalt, just wait a spell.

Your balloon will take flight again, guaranteed.

SIXTEEN

So I was feeling more or less fine. I even called Jules and told her how everything had changed in the wink of an evening, and I described how all things would be revealed in their time.

"But what if they aren't?"

"Huh?"

"What if he doesn't confess? Will you keep seeing him?"

"You mean, like, how long into it?"

"I don't care how long," she said, her voice brewing with impatience. Married women are bad about lecturing their single friends. "Say a year from now. Say on the night he asks you to marry him. What then?"

"I'm not looking that far ahead." Of *course* I was. "Things change in a year. Look at me a year ago compared to now."

"Right. You were miserable. But you're going to be even more miserable if he doesn't tell you the truth. Just the way it is. I mean, Sarah, the man has two kids he hasn't told you about. His ex is rolling him out like pie crust. He's possibly an alky. Plus, I hate to remind you, he was really really sick for no reason."

I was getting angry. She wasn't going to see it my way. "I'm giving him some time. That's all. I don't know how much time, and I don't know what'll happen if he doesn't want to tell me."

After an unusually long pause (Jules has never liked dead air), she said, "Come on, Pookie. You know I'm hard on you just 'cuz I love you."

We'd called each other Pookie since childhood, though not, I admit, in a long time. It came out only in times of stress or panic.

"I love you too, Pookie. Just stop pissing on my pretty cake."

I know she meant well. She didn't want to see me hurt. But she didn't get that Dylan had turned a corner. Steve must have given him a pep talk. Now he was confident, reinvigorated, dynamic, gung ho — all of that stuff — and there would come a day, I was absolutely sure, when he'd sit me down and say, "Darling, I have something I need to tell you."

My general sense of delirious well-being took a big hit, though, when Mom called on a dark night of Dylan's and mine and said there was going to be a family dinner: two words that have struck me as grotesquely incompatible for many years now.

"Before you say no," Mom said. "Just listen to me. I have something to tell you."

"*Mom.*"

"I *need* this from you. I need it. I haven't begged you for anything, or to do anything, or *anything* since you were fifteen, but I *need* this, Sarah."

She could probably hear the sparks shooting out of my nostrils. When I didn't respond right away, just trying to gather my black black thoughts, she jumped in again. "Dylan's invited, of course." The two of them met earlier, for Mom's birthday in late August. He charmed the old Marin lady pants right off of her. "He can be your safety net. You know Ella will behave if he's there."

True, true. My mind began to calculate the social metrics. I could show Dylan off. I could be the ant of the ant and the grasshopper, or the tortoise of the tortoise and the hare. (Would I rather be an ant or a tortoise? I'd figure that out later.) Slow and steady wins the race, see, Ella? Sarah, here, didn't grab for a shiny pot of gold that turned out to be an asshole like you did, and now she's been rewarded with this classy English architect who happens to look like Jude Law (and don't say he doesn't because you *know* he does!), so who's better off, eh?

I mean, some of that might be apparent in my face. I'd never lord it over her like that. Not intentionally.

I knew what this was, of course. It was Mom trying to make sure that Ella and I could at least occupy the same room after she was gone. All mothers get morbid about such things in their old age, I guess. But I knew it wouldn't work. Even if I still felt sorry for Ella — and I did — the two of us were so different in the way

173

we saw the world, in the way we *lived*, that she'd never be more to me than one of those acquaintances who never seems to drift away. Always popping up and annoying you. In fact, one thing I always asked myself about her, even back before she nailed it with Dad, was simple: would I know this woman if she wasn't my sister?

The answer was no. No, I'd steer clear of someone like her. I'd ban her from my Facebook page (if I had one). I'd cross the street if I saw her coming. I'd say bad things about her to my friends, and I'd probably even get some vicarious pleasure when I heard something bad happened to her. A little bit.

And yet, here I was, feeling bad enough for her over Tucker's infidelity and the divorce that I had to agree to Mom's dinner. It was a week away.

Dylan said he'd be delighted to go. Naturally. He was polite and amenable, what else would he say?

"Just so you know," I told him over tacos at a Mission District taqueria, "I'm going to be manic. You won't recognize me. I'm going to have this hideous smile all evening — I might have to have my face completely botoxed the day before — and I'll be talking way too fast and laughing inappropriately at everything the girls say. You too. So just be ready."

He was working on his third Corona. No big deal. Beer to an Englishman is like tap water.

"Sounds like it'll be quite memorable."

"Oh, I'm sure *I'll* never forget it. I just don't want it to change your idea of me."

"Not possible."

"Really?"

"You'll always be the girl with the 'Land of the Giants' lunchbox to me."

"No matter what?"

"Please. I'm meeting your sister. How could that possibly change my idea of you?"

"She brings out the worst in me, that's all. And you haven't seen the worst in me yet."

"Well, it can hardly stack up against the best in you, so."

I felt myself blushing on that one. His expression made me

think he was talking about sex. I was a "terribly generous" lover, he liked to say.

"I'm just saying. I apologize in advance for all the stupid things I'm going to do next Sunday. Please don't take notes."

That week at the office was a blur of maladies. I saw them as metaphors, in a Dantesque kind of way.

Nilesh came to me and declared he'd never seen a case of flesh-eating bacteria like the one that came through that week. I diagnosed it without thinking twice. Nilesh was impressed.

"*Staphylococcus aureus*, wasn't it?" he asked. "The poor man's lucky to have two legs to stand on, thanks to you."

"My sister made me think of it."

"How's that?"

"Never mind."

As the days went by and the "family dinner" got closer and closer, I began to feel like I was coming down with every strange bug my patients brought in. Psychosomatic, sure, but I had no energy, I was turning yellow, my eyes retreated into my head like shy lichee fruit, and all I wanted to do was lie down in a dark room. Friday came. I took my own temperature and found I was running a 100 degree fever.

"It's nothing," I told Becky. She was worried about me. "I'm having dinner with Ella tomorrow."

"Ah. That explains it."

Everyone knew of my backstory with Ella. Over the years I'd purged to anybody who would listen.

Dylan and I would not see each other that night. We both needed to rest up.

*

I had to do a half-day stint at the ER because a staff doc was involved in a car wreck overnight. Now and then we're summoned by the HMO management to step in when such cases come up, so this was nothing unusual and in fact I welcomed it. Distracted all morning and into the early afternoon by emergency medical situations. It helped put things into perspective.

When the shift ended, though, I was already beginning to tremble.

"You're in the catbird seat, remember," Dylan said as we crossed the bridge. He wore a nice two-piece suit, dark gray with a soft blue shirt, no tie. Looked scrumptious. I had on my navy skirt and jacket with a white silk blouse that had a plunging neckline that made me look supremely cocky, even if on the inside I was a wilting dandelion.

"Really."

"She's the one whose life is falling apart. She needs *you*. You don't need her."

"I guess I've proved that over the years."

"Absolutely. And if she doesn't treat you the way you want to be treated?"

"Off with her head!"

"In a manner of speaking."

I was driving, so I couldn't let myself drift into a full vision of how it would be if Ella didn't show a little humility. Wouldn't be fun. I said, "I hope we don't have a scene in front of the kids. That would be the worst."

"I have a feeling she wants the same."

"She does love them. They're like her little dress-up dolls. All that velvet. She's spent a fortune on velvet these last few years, judging by her Christmas pictures."

In the middle of the Waldo tunnel, he said — and this is one of the reasons I loved him — "Her loss if she can't figure out a way to keep you."

All I could think at the moment, with my palms starting to ooze perspiration like a nice vinaigrette, was that I hoped he used the same logic on himself.

*

Another ten minutes and we were pulling up in front of Mom's house. The cute yellow bungalow with its ivied trellis showed no signs of the tasmanian devil inside, other than Ella's Land Rover parked on the street out front. Mom's sensible blue Honda was in the driveway. I saw a welcoming light in the living room window, but I decided not to trust its soothing message till I could see the whites of Ella's eyes.

Dylan took hold of my hand and gave it a loving squeeze, the way any respectable significant other would do for his hysterical mate. I even noted, in spite of the stress, that I actually *had* a significant other, and I'd had him for some time now. He was still here. Somehow I had managed not to scare him off with my lunchbox and Il Divo poster, with my zillion eccentricities, or even with my quotidian workahol habit, which every doctor has. He was still here with me, and he was going to get me through this evening and hold me afterward in my own bed as I shuddered in frustration over all the nasty things Ella will have said.

Confidence level going in: negative ten.

Dylan did the doorbell honors and held in his other hand the bouquet of red and yellow chrysanthemums he'd brought for the hostess. In a very short time the door flew open and there was the younger niece, Gretchen, in (what else?) an adorable velvet lederhosen sort of outfit and with an edelweiss or something pinned into her blond hair. She was right out of *The Sound of Music*.

"Auntie Sarah!" she cried, and threw her arms around my legs with her head pushing into my stomach. Dylan was already smiling the permanent crampy smile of a new beau meeting the family for the first time. His jaws would be so sore by the end of the evening.

Gretchen could hardly have remembered me, by the way, since she was only three or so when I last saw her. This reaction had been prepped, by Mom most likely.

I could hear her from the kitchen, shouting, "They're here!" Utterly delighted. Completely oblivious to the fear pulsing in my left ventricle.

The older girl, Olivia, appeared, dressed not in lederhosen but more of a horsey, country-clubby get-up, with the red jacket and the dun-colored riding breeches, high shiny boots. All she lacked was helmet and whip.

"Auntie Sarah?" she said, looking up at me with big blue tiddly wink eyes, "Mama says you're a doctor, is that true?"

"Yes, sweetie. I'm a doctor."

I realized that Ben was still in the picture when she was born. He'd written a sweet poem for her christening card, which no doubt Ella had kept to use as ammo against me one day.

"So we can come to you if we get sick here?"

"Of *course* you can. I'll take really good care of you too."

Mom showed up just then and told us to come inside. Olivia took my hand and led me in, while Dylan came in behind us and stood there grinning with his flowers. Mom saw them and squealed, "Chrysanthemums! My all-time favorite! Dylan, how'd you guess?"

"Sarah told me," he said. "I had my eyes on carnations, I'm afraid."

No sign of Ella yet, who I'm sure was hiding out in the bathroom till the fuss died down. She always did like her elegant entrances, timed so that all eyes are on her.

"I smell your famous ham," Dylan said. I'd prepped him well. "Pineapple slices on top, right?"

"And brown sugar too. You're hungry, I hope."

"Girls," I said. "This is my friend, Dylan."

"He's from England, I can tell," said Gretchen.

"A proud south Londoner," Dylan said, reaching out his hand to shake hers. Instead she ran to him and gave him a colossal hug. Poor thing, I told myself. Tucker leaving has her looking for daddy substitutes already.

"Well, isn't this something?" Dylan gave me a helpless look.

Mom rescued the flowers from Gretchen's tough-love hugging, beckoning us toward the kitchen as she went and saying, "Drink orders? We have red and white wine, beer, gin, vodka — a little bourbon, Dylan, if you're a bourbon man."

Oh hell, I thought. Here we go. He'll be tempted to get looped to self-medicate the stress that had to be building right about now.

Instead: "Actually, I'm the designated driver tonight, Mrs. Phelan. I thought I'd let Sarah celebrate this reunion."

"You angel," I said.

"Not a problem."

"I'll have a vodka tonic, Mom. Half and half."

She shot me a look but didn't want to make a scene in front of Dylan already. "Just tonic then for you, Dylan?"

"Perfect."

We all headed for the kitchen through the modest dining room that was still furnished with the things Mom and Dad always had. Hand-me-downs from the fifties, table, hutch, the charming mismatched dining chairs. Each place at the table had been set already — Mom going whole hog with her nicest dishes, what I always called the "blue plate specials" but were just your basic Dutch Delftware. She loved them and hadn't had them out much since Daddy died.

Ella was in the kitchen stirring a pot. She looked up and gave me one of her famous raised eyebrows that always seemed to say, "Oh, it's just you."

"Hello," I said. Prompted by Dylan's nudge, I even went to her and gave her a peck on the cheek. Her cheek was blazing hot too, pink with flushing, and she stiffened noticeably at my hand on her arm.

"Thanks for coming," Ella said. "This must be Dylan."

"It is. I mean, *he* is."

"A pleasure to meet you," Dylan said, and he too, guessing somehow that a handshake wasn't quite right, leaned toward her and offered a reasonable first cheek-kiss. How he always finessed these things I didn't know. I was just glad he did.

"Mom's been telling us all about you."

"Oh I have not, Ella. I only met him the once, after all."

"Dylan's from England!" said Olivia.

"Yes, I hear his accent, sweetheart."

"Actually I've been in the states since I was twenty-ish. I've lost a lot of my proper English habits, I guess."

"And you're an architect?" Ella asked. She was stirring that sauce pot so hard I was afraid of hot splashes.

"I'll get your drink, Sarah." Mom brushed past me and whispered, "It's starting off nice, isn't it?"

To be honest, it was. But mainly because Ella was pretty much ignoring me. The girls were clearly attracted to Dylan and began to cling to him like he was an enormous plush toy. He trotted out one of his funny voices, a trick that I knew must go back to his own fathering but that he explained to me as "just something I've always done." It was the voice you could imagine coming from

179

a cute little mole or possum, with an English accent of course. And it was sweet. The girls went gaga.

Mom handed me my drink. I took a series of wee sips, as Dylan might say, so as not to look like I planned to drain it in one slug. I noticed a tumbler of what was probably a gin and tonic on the counter near the stove and knew it was Ella's fortification to deal with *me*. Well well well.

It didn't take long for Olivia and Gretchen to take my safety net away from me, dragging him toward their room by both hands.

"Apparently I'm being abducted, Sarah. You all right?"

"Fine. Don't let them do a Gulliver's Travels on you."

"Oh dear."

Suddenly it was just the Phelan girls. Alone in the kitchen.

"Sweetheart," Mom said to Ella. "I think the white sauce has been stirred plenty by now."

Since June, when I last had seen Ella, she seemed to have put on a bit more weight. Quite a bit, actually. She wore a pair of black tights with a gray tunic that went to her knees and hung on her like a dry-cleaning bag. It was meant to hide her hips and belly, no doubt, but that couldn't be on my behalf. It had to be Dylan's. She didn't want him thinking she was *fat*. Her hair, gone substantially gray lately, it seemed to me, was pulled into a tight ponytail and held in place with the one dab of color she'd bothered with, a lavender scrunchee.

"How are you holding up?" I asked. "Is the divorce going along?"

"If that's how you want to put it."

"I just mean —"

"He filed. I answered. It's in the bowels of the San Diego County family court. That's all I know."

"Has the house sold yet?"

She went to her glass and took a big dose. I took a bigger one from mine. We looked at each other across the table against the wall as Mom poked her head in the oven to look at the ham.

"Just about ready!" she said with too much exuberance.

"Not on the market yet. Tucker wants to wait for prices to go up again."

"That could take a while."

"I'm going to take it away from him and sell the shit out of it, regardless."

I nodded. "Good for you."

"I'm sending those girls to fucking Harvard if I can. Anything to remove truckloads of cash from his bank account."

"Ella!" Mom said. "Let's watch the F-bombs with the girls nearby."

"Sorry."

What was coming through to me as we stood there — neither of us relaxed enough to sit quite yet — was that Ella might always have been a dry and bitter person, like some kind of repellant Chinese herb, but Tucker had managed to intensify it. Her brow was knitted with hostility lines, her eyes dark and fiery at the same time. She hated being in her own head and her own skin, but to admit it to anyone would be an even bigger defeat in her life than Tucker bailing out on her. In her company, it was hard to keep my own hostilities toward her at a rolling boil. Sympathy is a very effective tranquilizer.

"The first year is the worst," I said. "When Ben left —"

"Can we do without the saccharine advice? I'm forty-two, for godsakes. The first year is how it's going to be for the rest of my life. I don't need to hear how lucky you are now, a few years down the road after Ben."

I was caught a little off guard. The simmer came back up. Mom looked at me as if to beg me not to take the bait.

"You know what?" I said. "You're absolutely right. It's probably not going to get better. I've always been a Pollyanna about this sort of thing, and I'm usually wrong."

I was smiling, for some reason. Daring Ella to come up with a pithy response to that. I felt air on my teeth. Inside I was thinking how I still had my own bridges to cross with Dylan and that nothing was exactly assured before we crossed them. Together.

"I'll carve," Mom said, trying not to get between her daughters. "Or should I have Dylan do it?"

*

I have to confess, things got a little better after that. The mutual brushback pitches we threw were enough warning that an all-out Armageddon here and now was in nobody's interest. The girls might be scarred for life. Dylan's feelings toward me might cool if he saw me fierce-eyed and ruby-throated, screaming at my sister that she's always been a sociopathic cunt and I'm sick and tired of it. So we backed off.

Over dinner, Dylan was the centerpiece. How could he not be? He was the exotic. He was the noble foreigner who might help us see ourselves clearly. And the girls adored him.

What do they eat for supper in England, Dylan? they asked. What kind of clothes do girls wear? Do people have dogs for pets there? Have you been up in the giant ferris wheel yet?

He patiently answered each earnest query, offering us Phelan adults a mugging sheepish grin throughout. I poured vodka patiently down my throat.

When we were finished eating, and before dessert, Mom happened to mention that she'd just had Dad's old piano tuned.

"In case the girls want to take lessons," she said. "While they're here."

"I don't want to spend the money on something like that," Ella said. "Not right now."

"They can fiddle around on it then. For fun."

"Maybe I can pop for some lessons," I said. "Every family has to have at least one piano player."

I was thinking of Daddy, who was not a terrific player, but because he loved music so much he always impressed me with his simple playing. Little chords, melodies plinked out from memory. I always recognized some of his records there under his hands.

Sitting beside him on the bench, I'd ask if I could play some. We had a little joke between us.

"Only if you play with Phelan," he'd say. "Get it? With P-H-E-L-A-N."

"I play a little," Dylan said. "Of course, I haven't been near a piano in quite a while, so I'm no Horowitz any longer."

"Oh, you *were* Horowitz!" I said. "You never told me you could play."

"I guess it never came up."

We all went to the spare room, where Dad's old upright was

parked against the wall like a panel truck. Its former peanutty color had gone a kind of tobacco tinge over the years. Some of the keys had a yellow cast, and on a couple of them the ivory had been chipped off somehow. Who knows how. I didn't think *I'd* done it.

Dylan sat on the bench while Mom and Ella and I stood back, near the door. The girls hopped onto the bench with Dylan and started pounding away at random keys.

"Lovely," he said. "It's a scherzo, right?"

Ha ha ha! they cried.

"Settle down," Ella told them, and they both looked over their shoulders, mouths sewn shut.

"Let's see." Dylan played a long scale from the low end to the high. "How about this?"

His scale turned into a flourishing segue right into "Make Someone Happy." I was floored. He played it just like Bill Evans on a record my father loved. My hand went to my mouth as the tears started squeezing out and turning my vision to mirror mist. He had it down and made no mistakes that I could hear. Purely from memory too, which meant he had the chords in his head and the sweet little trills and runs, even if they were slower than the record.

As he got near the end of the first chorus, Mom began clapping and so did the girls. Ella said, too close to my ear, "One of Dad's favorites."

Coming from her, it didn't sit well.

"How would *you* know?" I said, glaring at her with hot eyes. I felt my whole body starting to tighten up and my stomach turning. I was going to cry and had to leave the room.

In a few minutes they all came back out and sat with me in the living room. Ella pretended nothing had happened in there. The girls were mopey and quiet, clinging to Dylan's sleeves.

As I sulked and walked back my mood to near-normal — my rattled family there all around me, my buttoned-up boyfriend at my side with his warm, sturdy weight against me — I got the strangest feeling that *I* could very well be the one with a problem.

*

On the way home, though, I wasn't in a brown study. Strangely enough, it was Dylan who couldn't bring himself to speak.

He was very good with the girls. They'd loved him. If they were going to live in the city, they would enjoy seeing him now and then, and I had to admit (my issues with Ella notwithstanding) that the little Sterno in my own uterus was flickering at the way he'd engaged them. He was father material.

Maybe because he was already a father.

He was driving, of course, since I *had* indulged in more booze than was probably a good idea. My head was swimming a lazy sidestroke as we went through the tunnel and down onto the bridge, where the lights of the city made me think of sugar sprinkles on dark cake.

This might be a good time for him to tell me, I thought.

"Is anything wrong?"

"No, why."

"You're not saying anything."

"Tired," he said. "Exhausted."

"They can be exhausting, all right. Kids."

"Yes."

"Run you ragged. All that energy."

"They were better than most."

"Ah, but you're a bachelor. You can always go home to your bachelor pad and regroup."

After a fairly long silence: "I suppose."

Then I said, "Dylan, you seem like you have something big on your mind."

This time, instead of getting terse with me as he had in his apartment, he turned his eyes in my direction after we'd gone through the toll lanes — the saddest eyes I'd ever seen in that lovely head of his. I knew his secret but he couldn't let himself think I knew. The only confession he could offer at that moment was showing me without words that he wasn't ready to talk about his pain.

It was all I could do not to blurt out, Dylan, I know everything. Steve told me.

Somehow I resisted. In spite of the vodka on board.

"Anyway," I said, opening the escape hatch, "you were lovely with the girls."

"Thank you. I tried."

A quiet laugh. And then he added, "You were pretty good with Ella too. She's exactly what you said she'd be like."

"Queen of the She-Bitches?"

"Not that. Just, very very unhappy."

"Always," I said. "Since my first inklings of her."

"It's not that uncommon. There's always the possibility that she's suffering inside but can't bring herself to tell anyone."

I knew he was talking about more than Ella. He meant himself too.

Like the insensitive oaf I am whenever I'm tipsy (drunk — I'll be honest), I said, "For forty-two years? You keep it inside that long and I think you must *like* the way it feels. And it keeps people at a safe distance too."

"You're right about that," he said.

I didn't expect it but I wasn't surprised when he asked if I'd mind terribly if he went on home instead of sleeping at my place. He was utterly knackered.

I kissed him with a sweetness that might have raised alarms under any other circumstances. Too momentous. It was a kiss that had a simple tag on it, though: You're wonderful. I'm waiting as long as you need me to wait. If you'll have me.

SEVENTEEN

B ut let's face it. That was pure weapons grade BS. No woman, especially not in the middle of her own relationship novel, can wait indefinitely for her lover to come around and honor her with the truth. And I say honor because the longer it took, the more he made me wonder if he'd *ever* tell me the truth (some men can keep major secrets their whole lives — Honey, I'm gay! — and not bat an eye), and the less respect he must have for me. It takes a big toll on the feminine ego. We want to be a goddess in our lover's eyes, right? You worship a goddess. You don't keep her waiting. And you don't let her think you're Mr. Perfect when you might be, end of the day, just another dud English architect who looks like Jude Law.

I was thinking a lot about Ben after the family dinner. He just came to mind as I was driving home from work one evening that week, and I got this strange desire to pop in at a bookstore on Chestnut Street, where, you guessed it, his new novel was on display right there on the front table. New Arrivals. It was called *The Frostbitten Man*, and I gathered from the jacket flaps that it was about a man who finds himself in middle age to have become so isolated that he suffers an emotional sort of frostbite and begins losing crucial parts of himself. His feelings. His dreams. His sense of identity. All very post-modern and dark, it seemed to me, and then, there on the back cover, was his obligatory black-and-white photo, my old Ben ten years on, bald as a newel post, sporting a Just For Men goatee and a pair of nerd glasses, like all the male writers seem to favor these days. I thought, Oh fine: He had to leave me to get what he really wanted.

His bio was abrupt and sad. Ben Cargas lives alone in Brooklyn, New York.

The sick and sickening thing, as I stared into his always-lovely eyes — the kind that make you want to melt all over him like warm caramel — was that I hated not being with him for this. He'd wanted it so bad when we were together, and even though I never believed in it as much as he did, being the practical doctory type, I always imagined the day I'd sit in a small crowd and watch him reading nervously at the podium from the work he'd slaved and worried over for so many years. I'd have been overflowing with pride, dripping with love, oozing smugness over being that man's wife and muse, but now here I was, thousands of miles away from him and feeling a definite, smarmy satisfaction that he was alone. He sacrificed *me* to get his book out, and God damn it, there ought to be a price for that.

Hated myself for it, but what can you do?

Naturally, I bought the book.

What would he make of a congratulatory note from me? Would he smile to himself and think something sweet? Or would he wonder if I was trying to insinuate myself back into his life, now that he was a success? (Not that getting a book out made him a success. Novels die in obscurity every day, he used to tell me.) Maybe he'd write back something self-deprecating like, "Managed in spite of myself. Hope you are well."

That wouldn't help me any.

*

Dylan and I had made tentative plans to drive up to Mendocino later in the month. Long weekend, B&B kind of thing. Winery tour, walks on the beach, screwing in front of a crackling fireplace — the whole nine yards. We hadn't made reservations yet but we knew when we could both go. Then he went and vanished for three days. Again.

Just like the earlier time, when he had to "go to L.A." for a meeting, he never told me about a possible trip. I half wondered if he was actually in his apartment, wiped out in bed with his mystery disease and unable to answer his phone. We hadn't exchanged keys yet. I couldn't go in and check. Seemed premature to call the cops after only a day or two, but by the third day I was frantic with anxiety over him — when I wasn't imagining him in a San Diego family court arguing his case for shared custody — so I phoned his office. The receptionist, a young woman with a drippingly honeyed voice, said he was out of town. When I asked where she said, "That's private information, rilly."

"I'm his —" I wasn't sure if he'd told anybody there about us. "I'm his friend, Sarah. Dr. Phelan?"

How stupid. Like being a doctor would get me through her perimeter.

"I'll tell him you called."

"When does he get back?"

"That's kind of private too. He tells the people who need to know."

Ooh, that was a bitchy blow. And so low it made me think of something. Could Dylan possibly be seeing someone else? Could he be playing the field after Gloria so he doesn't make a big marital mistake again? I could just picture him with this receptionist girl — how convenient for him — with her cascading hair to match her honeyed voice, her stiletto heels, her camel-toed white pants, and fake tits to complete the cliché. My absolute opposite.

After work that night, I went to his place. No answer. No lights on. No telltale music from inside. My old Middle Eastern pal at the corner store remembered me from last spring, when I was trying to run into Dylan after examining his prostate.

"You come back! I knew you come back!"

"Can I just get a coffee to go?"

"You still not marry? I expect you go away because you marry the boy."

"No, I didn't marry the boy."

"I take you to movie? You like the Brad Pitt?"

"Oh, no thanks. I don't really have time for movies."

"I treat woman very nice." He smiled and showed a gold framed tooth right up front. "I buy her the flower, I take her to good restaurant. No monkey business till marry."

"You're an old-fashioned guy. That's sweet."

I paid for the coffee and left him to fantasize about me for ten minutes. Till the next lady came in.

The building next door to Dylan's had a stoop with high stucco walls on the stairs. I sat there out of the wind listening to traffic sounds and theme music to the eight o'clock TV shows. Conversations going on in the near apartments, little snippets of which reminded me that life goes on. *He did so! No he didn't. He did. He took her checkbook out of her dresser and cashed a check for three hundred dollars so he could buy some cocaine. I thought he was over that. You kidding? He's a fuckin' coke machine!*

That people had bigger problems than mine was not what I wanted to admit right at the moment. But what did I even think I was doing? Sitting there on Fell Street, I never felt less a part of things going on around me. I was going to be thirty-nine soon. And then forty. If I was lucky, *if I was lucky*, I'd have rounded the bend with Dylan by then and settled into some kind of mundane happiness, which *is* the best kind, you know, and I'd have stopped thinking about my age and my stats and my dumb sister. I'd just *live*. I'd have arrived, like Ben's book. All the things that bothered me — here, now — would have fallen away like Dad's old autumn leaves, but here I was, still caught in the old here and now and Dylan doing everything he could to keep me trapped in it. My coffee was getting tepid way too fast. A couple of teen boys walked by in their black leather and giant black boots, mumbling something lewd as they glanced down at me. I thought I heard something like "one pathetic prostitute," but I could be wrong.

It just kept hitting me — standing still is no way to live. I might as well be Ben's frostbitten man. Could he have had me in mind when he wrote it? I always used to say to him, we're in love. That's all we need. (Don't quote me Beatles lyrics, he'd say.) No, no, you know what I mean. When you're in love you don't need all the connections everyone else is scrambling for. You can be boring if you're in love. Love plugs you in to everything good that life has to offer, so thank you, Mister Writer Man (a nod to Jules). Thank you for loving me.

That's what I used to tell him. And I believed it.

I loved Dylan too. He came along at a time when I was *this* close to admitting that I didn't quite believe in love anymore. I had almost gotten a dog — that's how bad it was. (I was going to name it Cliff.) But then he showed up with his lethargy and jaundice and his physical need of me. Maybe that was it. He seemed to *need* me, and the idea that love actually exists and I could get me some of it was ignited again. Against my better judgment.

I stared out at the buildings across the street with their warm evening lights on and the different lives inside going along like the orderly business in ant farms. Envy, that's what I was feeling. Envy for normal. Just plain old living, till death do us part, dull as watching water boil but at least there's someone to laugh with.

A cab pulled up while I was in the middle of these maudlin thoughts, and at first I didn't notice that the man who got out and whipped his wheeling suitcase to the ground was in fact Dylan. I heard him say, "Keep it, mate," in his distinctive accent. I perked up, but for some reason I didn't stand and go over to him. Instead I sat there and watched. The distant observer.

He slammed the cab door and turned, going toward his apartment with his head down and the suitcase rumbling along behind him on its little wheels. He looked worn out, hair hanging over his brow and a puffy weight to his cheeks that wasn't usual for him. Two days' growth of whiskers too, when he was so meticulous about his shaving.

For a moment I think he glanced in my direction, but the staircase walls would have blocked his view of my body and shown him only a sad-looking woman who was trying not to wanly smile but couldn't help herself.

Anyway, he looked back down and went to his door. I heard the luggage thud over the threshold.

What to do, what to do? Should I go on home, now that I knew he was safe? Or should I go to his door and reveal that I'd been stalking him all evening? Maybe I could make it look like a coincidence, like I'd been really really busy myself and hadn't had a chance to pop by in three days.

Impossible. My eyes'd betray me.

I let him have a minute to himself. Then I went to his door and knocked. *Rapped*, actually. Rapping is harsher than knocking.

He opened fairly quickly, as if he'd phoned ahead to have a pizza delivered and was expecting some kid in a baggy uniform and not the woman he was currently fucking.

Sorry. I can get a little coarse when I'm upset.

"God. Sarah."

"Hello, Dylan."

It was so like movie dialogue.

"I just got home," he said. "Didn't expect —"

"Can I come in?"

"Oh. Absolutely. Please."

There beside his kitchen table was the suitcase, its handle still telescoped up, and his sport coat thrown over the back of a chair. He'd had time to pour himself a too-tall scotch, neat. He saw that I saw and asked if I wanted one.

"Oh, absolutely," I said. "*Please*."

He took a tumbler out of the cabinet and poured a couple of fingers for me. Much less than he obviously intended to swig down. He couldn't look me in the eyes as he handed over the glass, and when I said, "Well. Cheers," he just nodded and drank from his glass with a certain parched urgency.

Then, abruptly, he turned toward me, put down his glass, and took a deep breath. "All right," he said. "Look. I owe you an apology, I know. I'm sorry."

"What are you sorry for, Dylan?"

"Oh, that's how it's going to be?" A nervous grin came out. "Okay. I suppose I deserve it. Fair enough. I'm sorry for going away again and not telling you. I'm sorry that it might look like I don't care. I do care. It was all very sudden, that's all."

"Sudden. Ah."

"Mr. Perry sent me to Arizona to look at a building. He wants me to incorporate bits of it into the SOMA project I told you about. Very *modden*," he said, emphasizing that goddamn accent of his, and I couldn't help snorting. Almost passed ninety proof scotch through my nose.

"Bullshit," I said.

"Pardon?"

"You heard me. I call bullshit on that little story."

"You can't call bullshit."

191

"Of course I can."

"Well I won't accept it. It's not bullshit." He took a deep drink. "Besides, I don't need to run my plans by you down to the nanosecond, do I? We haven't reached that pitiful stage, have we?"

"No, but three days? I was picturing you in some ER with your mystery disease, or worse — in a morgue, John Doe-ing your way right out of my life."

"Oh, how dramatic, Sarah. Just because you're a doctor doesn't mean people might die without your *mystical* ministrations!" The sarcasm was thick as Spam.

"Mystical ministrations? I write twenty prescriptions a day for Lipitor and Prilosec. There's nothing mystical about it."

"Shite."

I took a drink and tried to lower the intensity. "Look, maybe you went to Arizona, maybe not." The SAN tag on his luggage was a big clue he hadn't. "But I call bullshit on the way you didn't *tell* me. It's lousy. It makes me feel like you don't think I'm worth the fucking courtesy."

The cussing seemed to jar him out of his belligerence. He softened. He came to me and tried to hug me and dot my face with little apologetic kisses, mumbling under his breath, sorry, so so sorry, sweet Sarah.

"Your breath smells like booze now, no thanks."

"Yours too! Christ!" He pulled away, clenching his fists in exasperation.

I decided it was time to flash my poker hand at him, a tiny glimpse of an ace or two.

"Dylan, I think you're keeping secrets from me."

"Oh bugger off."

"You disappear — twice now — for *no* goddamn reason and leave me wondering if you're dead or alive. Then you're defensive when I complain about it.

"I've *apologized*, haven't I."

"Are you seeing someone else? Some other woman?"

This seemed to stun him. He faced me again and looked like he wanted to come close. Afraid to now. I was too angry. His eyes did a mesmerizing mood ring spectrum of colors, from a warm, contrite, sympathetic blue to a dark, affronted, stormy black. Then back to the sympathetic color of a robin's egg, alone and fragile in its nest.

"No, Sarah." His voice went low and tender. Soft as love-nothings in bed. "No. I love you. I don't want any other woman."

I started to cry. I couldn't help it. And I hate to cry. Doctors don't cry. Plus, when I cry I don't actually make any sobby noises. The tears just leak down, like they were starting to do. They leaked off my chin and spilled on my nice beige satin top.

"I love *you*," I said. "I do. But you have to tell me what's going on."

"I can't."

"Why not?"

"Because right now — I'm sorry. Right now it's none of your business."

It was the last thing I expected to hear. I expected, finally, to hear the truth, because whenever things get to the point where you're crying and the yelling has stopped and the future seems to be on the line and it's either get to the truth or lose everything, the truth comes.

He was leaking tears too. Mine had stopped. The starkness of what he just told me had cut them off, and my cheeks were now flashing with a different emotion.

I had to get out of there. I walked out and left the door open behind me.

*

Jules came over within ten minutes of my call. I could always count on her to want in on a disaster.

We were lying on my bed, under the impossibly manly chins of Il Divo, looking up at the ceiling as if some gypsy had spurted tea leaves up there.

"What you don't seem to understand," Jules was saying, "is that he's scared out of his fucking mind that you'll leave *him* the minute you hear the truth."

"So I should tell him I know?"

"God, you'll lose him in a flash if you do that."

"Why?"

"Because he'll know you've been holding out on him. He'll be too mortified."

"Do you want some ice cream balls?"

"Yes."

"They're low fat."

"I said yes."

I got up and fetched the tub of ice cream balls from the kitchen, chocolate covered antidepressants. Back in bed, I put the tub between us and left the top off so we could just munch away.

"You're saying I can't win. How can that be? I thought I was doing the right thing not telling him."

"And he thought he was doing the right thing not telling *you*."

"At least he could tell me, Sweetie, I have to go out of town for three days!"

"You'd want to know where."

"Sure I would. He could tell me."

"No, you'd get suspicious. San Diego again? *Dylan, you don't even have work down there anymore*. So he'd have to lie."

"So he's not telling me because he doesn't want to lie?"

"Right."

"He lied tonight. He said he was in Arizona."

"Shit. Why'd he have to go and do that?"

I took another ice cream ball. So did Jules. I don't know how we understood each other, talking with our mouths full of ice cream balls.

"Anyway, that's not the problem. The problem is the 'none of your business' thing."

"That's truly screwed."

"Everything about me is his business. Even my dysfunctional family crap with Ella."

"And you told him all about Ben, I'm sure."

"Of course."

"How's the book, by the way."

I'd been reading it for a few days now. "It's — it's really good. He's a different kind of writer than he was ten years ago."

"I don't think I can read it. As your best friend, I don't want to like it."

"That's fair. I don't want you to have to choose."

"Guess what."

"What."

"I found out I'm pregnant."

"Holy!"

She wasn't smiling. She just kept staring at the ceiling, her cheek bulbous with a cold chocolate ball. One arm went over her forehead, and I thought she might start to cry.

"Total accident," she said. "This was not something we were pining for. Either of us."

Yes, frankly, I was shocked. Jules had always been a stickler for birth control. The pill *plus* the rhythm method — poor Wayne. But worse than that, I realized I was weirdly jealous of her. No logical reason, since I didn't want kids, never wanted kids, thought (and still think) that kids turn perfectly wonderful adults into babbling blobs who have to care about things like Hannah Montana and perverted teen text messaging. Maybe I've been overcompensating for my own fears, but it's just as possible that I was born without maternal hormones or something. Or I'm just not generally responsible enough to be a parent. Still. I envied Jules right then, thinking of Dylan as daddy to my own babes.

Here was another Life Stage that someone else was going through and I wasn't. I must be literally retarded, I thought — held back. Frozen in time at around fourteen years old and never wanting to grow up. Never able to, anyway.

It was clear soon enough that Jules wasn't happy. "Wayne's scared," she said. "I guess I am too."

"Are you guys sure you want to keep it?"

"Abortion? No. Been there, done that. Not again."

She'd never told me. I tried to hide my reaction. "Uh huh."

"Truth is," she said, "Wayne and I haven't been doing too great lately. He's getting mid-life crisis wandering eyes and I'm — I've been jealous."

"Of Wayne?"

"No. *You.*"

I put the top on the ice cream tub and set it on the table by the bed. Let those balls melt, I didn't care. Then I went back to Jules and curled up beside her, she on her back, me on my side with my head tucked between her shoulder and neck. She smelled like the garlic and onions she must have chopped at dinner. And the citrusy shampoo she used.

"Don't be jealous of me, Pookie."

"Can't help it."

"Trust me, it's not all it's cracked up to be."

"Sometimes I wonder what it'd be like to start over," she said. "And then I tell myself — this is scary — You *can* start over if you really want to. Have to."

It would break my heart if Jules and Wayne ever split up. I was trying to find a way to get where they were. More than anything, I was beginning to think, I wanted to be a girl who had *this* said about her: At least she found someone who loved her enough to marry her.

You reach a point where it doesn't even have to be reciprocal.

"You need to stop thinking that way. You love Wayne. He loves you. Now you have a baby coming."

"Blah blah blah." She made a puppet of her hand. "No. Don't worry. We're solid. Boring but solid. Wayne's like one of those moles on your shoulder that grows into a human head right next to yours. Can't cut it off without killing both of you."

We both had to laugh at that. In a strange and wistful kind of way.

"I admit, it's nice at the beginning, but Dylan and I are past that now. I called you tonight because I'm so fucking — *miserable*."

And I began to cry into her neck. Hard. With uncharacteristic sobbing this time. It was a cathartic deluge of self-pity and saline.

"I wish I could make it all better for you," she said. A warm, syrupy bromide that didn't help.

"I'm going to lose him," I said, certain of it. The acceptance of this didn't even surprise me. "You said so yourself, right?"

EIGHTEEN

The next week wasn't so bad. Dylan was back in the swing of things, telling me about the minor and major dramas surrounding his building project, the various impossible hoops he'd have to jump through to please the firm, the building department, inspectors, and his own perfectionist instincts. It was clear he was stimulated by the whole thing, running on all eight, as the boys like to say.

I wanted to let things go along smoothly for a while. Our skirmish when he got back from San Diego had me a little bit gun-shy, to be honest, so the last thing I needed was a repeat of that evening. The way I called Dylan the next day and pretended like it was all just part of being in a relationship — all is forgiven, hon! — still gave me a bad taste in my mouth, but I needed at least a week of normal if I was going to be able to control myself.

Meanwhile, Mom told me that Ella found a house to rent up there in Mill Valley — she had changed her mind on a city place — so I could go back to my old pop-ins if I wanted to. She missed me. But she also let slip that Ella was mad over the way I treated her at the "family dinner." She felt like she was on best behavior and I jumped down her throat for no reason — in front of the girls.

My dander went up. I won't recount the predictable conversation Mom and I had. Enough to say that I ended it with, "The next time I have to see her is going to be too soon, I just know it."

To which Mom said one word. "Thanksgiving."

Well, with any luck Dylan and I would be in a better place by then, Ella would be a little less tense and bitchy, and the sky might be a little bluer. I couldn't think about it now.

The other thing that upset me during that week, while Dylan and I were trying to ignore our elephant in the relationship, was that we continued to make love. And I mean *make love*. He was tender and gentle and deliberate, as if I might flinch if he made a wrong move and eject him from my body. His kisses were soft-petaled appeals for mercy. One night, his hands touched me like I was a butterfly made of sheer tissue paper, and at the moment of his orgasm? — he whimpered. He whimpered as if his soul were about to jettison his body and fly off into space without saying good-bye.

You remember how I need a good laugh at times like that. Didn't get it.

We had entered a period of self-consciousness that would tear off, bit by bit, pieces of our hearts until what was left couldn't feel anything at all, much less love.

That was the night I knew the Last Stand was coming.

*

It's important to distinguish between the Make or Break Moment and the Last Stand, according to the complex nomenclature Jules and I had worked up over our many years together.

The Make or Break Moment by definition is a threshold to second chances, right? In fact, there could be a whole series of Make or Break Moments, assuming they always fall your way, but in the system Jules and I made up, there's only one Last Stand. Once you've had the Last Stand, the very next infraction is that ultimate Capitalized Event nobody — neither you nor him — ever wanted to happen. The End.

The Last Stand is more or less the climax of the book, and after it you'll get either a denouement and happy forever after, or you'll get The End. The women in relationship novels postpone the Last Stand as long as possible, but they always come to see they're only killing themselves that way. After all, they think they're completely lovable, but they're killing this lovable person who ought to be reaping this man's devotion in spades. The only thing to do is force the issue. Or more accurately, *let* the thing happen that she's been desperately trying to keep at bay for weeks, months, or sometimes even years.

How to do it is always the thing.

*

Behind Dylan's back, I emailed Steve.

I told him, as pithily as I could, that I hadn't imagined using his email address so soon after he gave it to me. It was meant as an emergency thing, like your floating seat cushion in an airplane crash. In fact, he'd said to me as he jotted it down, "Just so you know, right? I'm not one for basic correspondence. I don't want to be anybody's mate, yeah? But if you think I ought to know what's going on with him, you can write me."

Instead of emailing back, he phoned. It was ten p.m. my time. Had to be five or six in the morning there.

"So it's hitting the old fan, is it?"

I was tired. Luckily Dylan wasn't at my place. Lately we'd been going to our separate homes after seeing each other.

"I'm afraid it is. I don't want it to, but I don't think I can do this his way."

"I want to tell you something, Sarah. I wish I'd never have told you the whole story. I wish you were still going along with your head up your arse —"

"Gee thanks."

"Figure of speech. Sorry. I mean in the dark. I wish I'd let Dylan tell you in his own time."

I thought about that alternate universe. But in that one I would have learned about his family — when? Months, years from now? And I'd have had to wonder if I knew this man at all and whether I could even stay with him. My innocent happiness would have been shot out of the sky like a lazing dove. In some ways, this was actually better, that I knew the truth up front and required a proactive step on Dylan's part to bring our understandings into unison like focusing a camera lens. I was sure that if he'd just cough up the facts, I'd be satisfied. Thrilled. Commence the bliss. In that *other* universe I'd be devastated by the news when it finally came. We probably wouldn't survive its, I'm guessing, accidental release.

"What should I do? I feel like he'll bolt if I tell him I already know. And *I'll* bolt if he can't bring himself to tell me."

"Look," he said, his voice clear and resolved, "you will have to bolt, and it's God's truth that nobody will blame you when you do. The only worse thing he could keep from you is killin' a bloke."

"I don't know about that. I think I'd have dumped him by now if you told me he killed a — a bloke."

"You know what I mean. But here. Listen to me."

"Oh God."

"I'll be dead honest with you. The bottom line, I hate to say, is this isn't the best time to try and get good with Dylan. He's found out lately — me too — that Mum's not doing so well down in Florida. Brain tumor, I'm afraid. Not good. I'm flying out to see her next week, but he's still fighting the old battles. Can't bring himself to go. At least not yet. I'm afraid he won't be very happy with a challenge from his other flank, meaning you." He paused for that to sink in. "But that's what you need to do. I get that. Confront the little prick."

Anybody's toothiest secrets are bound to rise up and go for the jugular eventually. Dylan had kept this piece of news from me too. "I don't know if I can do that to him now."

"Well then. Maybe not. Or maybe you could couch it in wanting to be there for him. You know. Dumbshit Steve told you about his mum, and you'd like to be his rock. Or some such rubbish."

The cynical bite there seemed appropriate somehow. There was no good angle to this. Either way, Steve saw, I'd be bullshitting Dylan or myself. Or it would seem that way to one of us in the end.

"I do want to be there for him. I love him."

"Sweetheart, here's the thing, though. I know my brother better than you might think, considering the distance. He's stubborn. He's got a resentful streak. And he will not hear things he doesn't want to hear."

We hung up promising to talk some more before I did anything, let's say, final. And afterwards, as I lay in bed thinking not just about Dylan and his mom but about Jules, her baby, Ella's kids — uncertain futures all around — I told myself I had to find a way to help Dylan lean in the right direction. He wasn't alone, and, if I could believe the rumors, he loved me too.

*

I saw him the next night. We met, like we'd been doing lately, at a restaurant more or less midway between our places — neutral territory. We were both trying to stick to best behavior rules, steering clear of conversation that might lead back to that "mistake" of his — San Diego II. Only *I* knew where else we could be led.

I spotted him waiting outside the tapas bar in the Inner Sunset as I walked from where I parked the car, a few blocks away. An N-Judah train made the big curve from Ninth Avenue onto Irving and blocked my view for a few seconds, and when it was gone so was Dylan. Mirage time. I wondered if I had imagined him out there, sexy and subdued, looking like a morose philosopher with something weighty on his mind. When I went inside the restaurant, though, there he was by the host station, chatting amiably with a young dark-haired woman in skirt and prep-school blazer as she grabbed two menus. He made her laugh. I couldn't hear what he said. Something charming, I'm sure. My jealousy antennae went up, what, with everything that had been going on. She was twenty-three, beautiful, easily seduced, no doubt, and way too much competition for me. If he'd lied about seeing other women, or even the desire to, I was going to be toast. Without crust, the way the English like it.

"Sorry I'm late," I said, hoping to abort their little flirtation, if that's what it was. He hadn't tried to make *me* laugh in quite a while.

"*Hola*," said the girl, all beaming-white fresh teeth and glistening fire-engine lipstick, and Dylan turned toward me. I watched the smile he'd been wearing for her fade into a serious flatline, though he did lean close and kiss my cheek. Good form. Bad feeling in the pit of my stomach.

"Hello, darling," he said. "You must have had to park in Ulan Bator."

"Just about. I hate this neighborhood for that."

"Would you two like a table or booth?" the hostess asked in a luscious Catalan accent. *Elena*, said her name tag. She was from the mother country.

"A booth," Dylan said, without consulting me. Oh well.

"That's fine."

"In back then," she said. "Away from the street noise, so you two can talk."

Was it that obvious?

Once we were safely ensconced in our deep red Naugahyde booth, serenaded by overzealous Spanish guitar piped in overhead, I felt a little calmer and a little less competitive. A pitcher of sangria would help. We ordered an array of small plates, then sat there with our big goblets full of wine and fruit with, apparently, nothing to say.

"So," I said.

"Yes."

"Busy busy."

"Always. Never a break nowadays."

"Same here. I saw a rectal prolapse today. Don't see those all the time."

"I can imagine."

"And how's SOMA going this week?"

He gave a faint shrug and an insouciant wrinkle of his brow as if to say, Oh, you know. As if I wouldn't be interested in the minutiae, but I'm all about minutiae, I wanted to say. I love minutiae. I live and breathe minutiae, for Christ's sake, *talk* to me.

His eyes floated out toward the front window. I leaned to one side to get back in his sightline.

"Sorry. A Rolls just went by. Silver Ghost, if I'm not mistaken. Midnight blue."

"That's a song. My dad loved that song."

"Silver Ghost?"

"Midnight Blue."

"Ah."

Luckily the food came.

It's not pleasant when things start becoming clear in a youngish, troubled relationship. Not exactly sad. Just not pleasant. You think you might get through this rough spot (even when the Last Stand is looming), but in the meantime it's just not very pleasant sitting through the discomfort and angst of it. And of course I had all the information and Dylan had none, so I couldn't say anything like, What's bothering you, sweetie? Or, Penny for your thoughts? Because I didn't want to go where those questions went. Anyway, I knew perfectly well what was bothering him, as he sat there with his lips sewn shut like a shrunken head's. (Oh, they opened fine enough to let in the sangria.) Added to the matter of Gloria, Andy, and Vanessa was the really sad matter of Mum and her brain tumor (inoperable, Steve had told me), and Mr. Cakebread could probably think of nothing else. Not even SOMA. Not even me.

When we finished eating and Elena came by again, I watched his eyes drifting up to her youthful chin and cheeks, the flawless olive skin, the magnificently earnest brown eyes, the silky long black hair. I was about to say, Dylan, at least *try* to be discreet, but it dawned on me that there was no lust in his eyes, no desire, no raw attraction. He was looking at her, as she tried very hard to sell us some dessert while the waiter was getting our coffee, the way a proud father would look at his daughter in her graduation gown. He was seeing Vanessa a few years from now. A lovely young woman he had helped bring into existence.

His glance swept back to me and then to the table, guiltily. He was afraid I'd caught him scoping.

"I'll have to pass," I said. "I'm stuffed."

"And me." Dylan looked up at Elena, glassy-eyed, knackered again from the wine and the mix of thoughts cycling through his head. I felt for him. "Sorry."

"I'll have Fernando bring your check."

"Thanks!" we both said, too eager, too awkward. We couldn't look at each other right away.

I realized at that moment, that I could be his rock and trusty shoulder to cry on only if I hurt him by revealing what I knew. And I started to, as soon as Elena left us alone.

"Dylan, there's something I need to talk about tonight."

He looked up. Anguish on his face like a tattoo of reds and deepening blues. He couldn't even gulp a response.

"It's just that — it seems like there's something going on that you don't want to tell me. I think you must be afraid I won't take it well, but I promise. I'll be fine. I want you to feel like you can tell me anything."

He bit his top lip as if to keep from crying. His eyes implored me to stop right there and to let him be graceful about this "something" I'd detected. The only times I'd seen him look so miserable were his awful episodes with the mystery disease. Wiped out. Flattened by what his own body was doing inside.

"Please," he said. That's all he could manage.

"I want to be able to help you. I never want to hurt you or make you feel —"

"I don't especially want to feel anything. Not tonight." Then a horrible, forced, desperate smile weaved itself across his mouth — involuntary, like a cramp — and he said, "Would that be all right with you, Sarah? Can I just, can I take a rain check on this tonight?"

That was despair on his face. Utter, and deep as his organs.

I'm a doctor. I should be able to understand.

"That's fine," I said. "I'm sorry. I just thought we could talk about it."

"I know." He was standing and taking out his wallet. Cash, so we wouldn't have to wait. Fernando would be getting a big tip. "I understand, but could we just."

Outside, I took his hand before he could slip away. He looked like I'd hunted him down to stab his heart right there on Ninth Avenue.

"You can trust me, okay?" I said. "I *love* you."

He didn't really give me a nod on that front. Instead, he apologized in that disproportionate English way and said that he had to get home to finish up a few things for work tomorrow.

He blew me a kiss into thin air. Too anxious, I had to think, to feel my cheek against his lips and understand how this must look to me.

And it looked godawful. It looked, suddenly, almost hopeless.

*

The next day was Friday, and we both agreed to a dark night before the weekend so we could get caught up on all the things piling up around us, two workaholic professionals. That trip to Mendocino seemed to be on the back burner now.

Why wasn't I surprised when, on Saturday afternoon, Dylan phoned to say he was under the weather and couldn't see me? A cold, he said. Not the illness. He sounded a little stuffed up, but maybe he was faking it. At midnight I called Steve.

"Mum's in hospice," he said. "I rang up Dill myself this morning to tell him."

That was it.

"Is he going to see her?"

"No. Or, I want to say, doesn't look like it. Everything with that little bastard is wishy-washy, have you noticed?"

I had. For a long time I thought he was just polite. Now it looked like he was paralyzed over making choices that could change his life.

"I can't believe he's going to let her die without trying to — shit, what's the word?"

"Kiss arse?"

"No. No. Without trying to reconcile with her."

"He's not inclined toward reconciliation, dear. He's an island unto himself, *he* thinks. I tell him he'll regret it for the rest of his life, losing Mum like this, but he won't hear it. Says she's the one who lost *him*. Do you know what the last thing he ever said to her was?"

"No. I don't know much, it turns out."

"He said, vis-à-vis Dad's suicide — he said, If he did kill himself, you must have drove him to it."

I knew Dylan would have said *driven*. I landed on that tiny grammatical point so I wouldn't have to think of the larger disgrace.

And I began to cry.

Again. I'd cried more in the past two weeks than I had since Daddy died. And shit, I told myself as Steve went through some other grim stories of Dylan and his mother, how am I supposed to get through to a guy who's heart is in this kind of trouble? Love isn't cutting it. He needs a fucking catharsis.

"I'm going to tell him," I said, interrupting the brother who had turned out ironically normal. Hard-hat sensibilities. Common sense. There's nothing complicated about forgiving your mother when she is about to die. "I have to."

"I know, sweetheart. It's the only thing to do."

Steve said he'd be in Tampa the following weekend. If I were to talk to Dylan before then, maybe he'd change his mind and go — that was Steve's thinking.

"There's something you need to know about me, Steve."

"What's that, dear?"

"I'm a big fat chickenshit."

In other words, no promises. I couldn't be sure that, confronted again with Dylan's melancholy eyes, I wouldn't up and choke.

NINETEEN

A summary of the next few days. A lot of interior monologue. Pros/cons. What-ifs. Don't you dares. Work was my saving grace, twelve hour days, another stint in the ER one night, where I saw gunshot wounds, broken glass embedded in scalps, broken bones from obvious domestic violence, myocardial contusion in accident victims who were thinking about something else when the light changed, self-administered poison, pit bull bites on little kids' limbs, children, in fact, with every kind of infection and boo boo you can imagine, and the eyes that looked at me with the thing, I suppose, that must have subconsciously led me to become a doctor in the first place — complete and abiding trust.

Jules told me that Wayne had turned the corner on the baby front and was now all into it. He'd seen his therapist — an on-again off-again relationship there — who planted the idea, apparently, that Wayne's genetic packet would now go forth into the exciting future, like some kind of space probe. Wayne was into sci-fi, so this intrigued him. There could come a time, he told Jules, when one of my heirs has access to time travel or something like that, and he might send me timely stock tips or ideas for the Next Big Thing. "What a gas!" he said. To my mind, and Jules's too, this was not a terrifically good reason to become a parent, but Wayne seemed to need it as a procreation crutch or he'd fall apart over the gigantic responsibility of fatherhood. This was fine with Jules. As for herself, she still hadn't come to grips with the idea that in six months she'd have this seven pound appendage depending on her every moment for its very survival. She wasn't thinking in emotional, maternal terms. Instead it was more of a philosophical thing. Existential. This creature wouldn't have existed at all if it hadn't been for an accidental lapse in her birth control regimen, and yet, now, a life of seventy to ninety years was pulling into the station. A body, a consciousness, another human being. "To think it's all that random," she said. "It blows my fucking mind."

"Food for thought," I said. My concerns were so prosaic by comparison. He loves me, he loves me not.

In a year she wouldn't be thinking like this, and Wayne would have dropped his hopes for a time-traveling great-great-great-grandson. They'd be deep in the swing of caring for an infant, changing pea-soup diapers, wiping up milky vomit, taking shifts on the nighttime feeding schedule, videotaping every little syllable the kid utters. Jules has always prided herself on her practical cynicism, she calls it, but I bet that it will have vanished forever by then. There's something about the introduction of a child to a cynical pair that makes them see the light.

She wished me luck at the Last Stand.

"Just remember," she said before hanging up the phone. "It hardly ever goes the way you think it will."

"I don't expect it to go very well. Maybe I'll be surprised."

"Before you do it?"

"Yeah?"

"Make absolutely one hundred percent sure you know what you *want* to happen."

This too was food for thought.

On the Wednesday, I called Dylan and asked how he was doing. Not so great. He'd missed a day of work with this damn cold of his. I didn't believe him. I chalked it up to the wrenching moral dilemma he had on his hands, visit Mum in Tampa or keep this stern Ice Man exterior on board till it was too late. Steve would arrive in Tampa on Friday. I asked Dylan if I could see him on Thursday evening. At our bench, Marina Green. It would be another warm day in October.

Earthquake weather, we call it in Frisco.

San Fran, I mean.

*

I was jelly with nerves all morning Thursday, so I went to Mom's for lunch. I didn't tell her what was going to happen that night on the Marina Green, but she could tell I was a mess.

She thought something was going on at work.

"I'll be fine. I'm taking a CME exam soon. You know how I used to get for exams."

"You'd throw up in the azaleas."

True. I did that so nobody would know how upset I was.

All I wanted from Mom was the familiar face of my own lifelong caretaker. She wouldn't know what to do about Dylan if I told her. Whatever you think is best, is probably what she'd say. And that was the way it was, more or less. I just needed the sound of her voice and the soothing impact of those Shirley MacLaine eyes of hers, the kind of lady who can make you feel better just in the way she lays out the sandwich bread in an orderly grid. (Which is what she was doing as we talked.) Then, a layer of mayonnaise on each, then precisely three slices of ham on each, then skim-milk cheese slices, then the iceberg lettuce she never lost her loyalty to. She cut the sandwiches diagonally, which we always said was "like a train" because Daddy told us sandwiches came that way on trains when he was a boy.

I was about to tell her that Jules was pregnant when Ella showed up.

The moment I heard her voice as she came through the front door, I bailed to the bathroom. Mom stage whispered, "*Sarah's* here, sweetheart. I wish you would have called first."

"That's ridiculous. You're my mother. I can pop by and see my mother without calling first, can't I?"

I was fuming as I sat there on the toilet lid amid the rosy soap smells (Mom collected decorative soaps in a glass bowl on the toilet tank but never actually used them). Half an hour with my security blanket. That's all I wanted. Now I had to put my bigger problem off to one side while I dealt with the smaller but definitely more irritating one — the permanent love/hate thing with Ella. Which, I'm sure you've noticed by now, had been woefully short on the love part for a long long time. For God's sake, I thought. Can't I catch a break on the day I tell Dylan to shit or get off the pot?

The irony that I was sitting on the pot didn't strike me at the moment.

"Sarah?" Mom called. "Your sandwich is ready. Your diet Dr. Pepper."

"You can come out, Sarah." Ella's voice had its typical sarcasm. "I'm not going to chew your nose off."

I washed my face. In the mirror I looked — thanks to one of the light bulbs burning out — like a patient with one foot already in the autopsy suite.

When I presented myself in the kitchen, there was Ella looking at me with her eyebrow raised, as always, and an angry blush flaring in her cheeks. She leaned against the sink with her arms crossed, forcing *me* to go to *her*, as usual, and make the ceremonial peace gesture — a quick mwah-style kiss. I did, but from at least eight inches away. She snorted through her nose as she turned her face to one side and all but stiff-armed me to keep a safe distance.

"So you'll have to come out to the house one of these days," she said. "It's nothing like La Jolla, but there's a view of the water."

"Super."

"Do you want a sandwich, Ella?" Mom asked. She was clicking her fingernails in fear. "Diet Dr. Pepper?"

"No thanks. Can't stay too long. I have to pick the girls up at school, but I wanted to drop by those old pictures we were talking about."

I sat at the table and started eating. Luckily I had the excuse of work to get me out of there in a hurry.

Ella fished inside her enormous knitted purse and pulled out a plastic grocery store bag of photographs.

"Sarah," Mom said, "these are a bunch of the old snapshots I'm always talking about. I don't know how Ella got her hands on them, but I mentioned them last week and she said she's had them for years."

Mom sat across from me. Ella sat to my right and emptied the bag of pictures onto the table.

Right away I saw that this wasn't what I needed. Nostalgia is actually a disease. The first picture that caught my eye showed Ella and me in horrid pink Easter dresses posed against the back redwood fence and grimacing into the stark sunlight — Daddy's natural-light method. It got so bad that somewhere in there I began wearing sunglasses for all photo ops. In this picture, Ella had managed, like she always did, to maintain some degree of poise even though her face was melting, while I was in the process of raising one hand to cover my eyes. It made me look like I had a wispy bit of angel's breath for a hand, since Daddy snapped the picture while I was in motion. I was such a geek, too. That dress that fit me like a body bag.

"Burn this one," I said.

Mom got wistful over some of her own wedding pictures, reception photos after the ceremony in which Daddy — a skinny young devil in a white suit with an ink-black bow-tie — seemed to have had too much to drink. (And he was only nineteen at the time!) In the background of some of them you could see the jazz trio he got for the occasion, the drummer a friend of his, the story went.

Ella shuffled through the photos like they were pinochle cards, remarking as she did that what struck her about looking at them was how nobody ever turned out the way you'd have thought they would. "The older I get and the more crap I go through, the more I realize that it's all the luck of the draw."

"I think Daddy turned out exactly the way he looks in those pictures," I said. "He looks like a nice, funny kid, and he turned out to be a nice, funny man."

"He was," Mom said in complete innocence.

"That's not what I see. I see a boy who could have done anything he wanted. Look at him." Ella lifted a shot of Daddy leaning against a door frame that made him look a lot like pictures I've seen of a young Arthur Miller. Smart, confident, cocky, unstoppable.

Ella's implication, of course, was that he was a failure. And then he died.

My blood was bubbling up. I didn't want this. Not again, and not today.

I had just taken a bite of my sandwich, a big bite to keep myself

211

from saying something dumb. I said something anyway, mouth full, hardly understandable.

I said, "Dylan has a wife and kids, and he still hasn't told me."

God, the look on Ella's face.

*

My last patient of the day was a child. Six years old, she was lethargic and feverish, pale, and mainly unresponsive when I asked her questions. Obviously her mother was worried, but not much more than I was. The poor little thing reminded me too much of the girl from before.

What a horrible omen.

Even after that tragedy, I was disciplined enough to handle similar cases with a rational approach, the usual diagnostic tests, when I thought they were necessary at all. Most kids' fevers are harmless and treatable with a little ibuprofen, and even when they're higher and a little scarier for the family, routine exam and blood tests are all I need to do. More often than not it's just a touch of flu or a mild bacterial infection.

But I was upset that night. I was emotional. I'd had a terrible time of it after I left Mom's. Ella thought I was worse off than her. I was pitiable, in her eyes. She felt sorry for *me*! I cringed at the self-satisfaction in her eyes, and the soft murmurs of so-called compassion coming through her lips, and the goddamn patronizing Mother Teresa words of wisdom, that everything would turn out fine and at least I had family close by to take care of me if it didn't. I had to clap my hand over my mouth to keep from saying something ugly. Mom was whimpering my name as I went out the door.

It was all too much. The little girl was sick. Dylan would be waiting for me at our bench. Ibuprofen wasn't going to cut it.

"I'm going to send you down to ER," I told the mom. Her eyes became two tarnished nickels. "They'll want to do some blood work and a full physical, just to rule out some things, all right? I'm asking for a lumbar puncture too. I don't want to ignore the possibility of meningitis."

"Oh God," she said. Her cheekbones seemed to be creeping

their way out through her skin. Ashen. She might have known that a lumbar puncture is more commonly known as a spinal tap, and I'm afraid *The Exorcist* ruined that for all us innocent clinicians.

"It's not terrible," I said. "She won't feel a thing. They do a topical, and the actual procedure only takes a few seconds."

An overabundance of caution. I had to do it. There was no way I'd have this little girl on my conscience in the middle of a Last Stand.

*

There was no time to go home. I tried calling Dylan from the hospital parking lot but he didn't pick up. He was probably in the middle of his own last-minute crisis, wondering how long I'd have to sit on that fucking bench with Alcatraz hazy in the gloaming while he raced down Van Ness in nightmare traffic. But if he was, why hadn't he called *me*?

I got there fifteen minutes late and he was nowhere to be seen.

The earthquake weather had held up into the evening, warm and close and more like Wisconsin in July than San Francisco in October. I was sweating from the trot over from where I parked, blocks away on Fillmore (I might as well have gone home), and frankly my hands were shaking. I was angry. And not at Dylan so much as *about* Dylan, in both senses. I was mad about him. He was perfect for me. I didn't want to lose him. I deserved him. The way we were together, the way he loved me *for* my eccentricities, or in spite of them, the way we laughed, the way — crap, *everything*. So I was mad about what he was doing to me by not sharing his life with me. The whole of it. Secrets and warts. I wanted to be worthy of his secrets, but he wasn't having it.

My cell rang after five minutes or so. It was him.

"Where are you? I've been here —" Five minutes didn't seem all that long, but since I was fifteen minutes late myself I could fib if I wanted. "I've been waiting."

"To be honest," he said, "it occurred to me not to come."

This was a stunner. As I looked out at the bay and the bridge, feeling like a person should never be unhappy in a place like this, so full of boilerplate beauty it was practically kitsch, I thought, Oh how perfect, to be stood up at my own Last Stand. Classic.

"Why wouldn't you come? Did something happen at work?"

When in doubt, play dumb.

"No. No," he said. "In fact I got off early today. I went to the building site and took some photos. Then I had a — a gin and tonic. At some place on Third Street near the ballpark. To talk myself into coming."

"Are you home now, Dylan?"

"No. I'm on my cell."

"So you are coming? I mean, I feel like an idiot sitting here with this fuzzy pink sunset all to myself."

"Sarah."

"What."

"I was getting a bad feeling about tonight. About meeting you at our bench."

"Why?"

"I thought you might be inclined to confront me about something."

"What do you think I might want to confront you about?"

Let's see how far he's willing to go, I thought. Maybe it's easier this way. At a distance.

"A million things, for all I know. I realize I've been a prick lately, as Steve would say. In fact, he did say."

"You've talked to Steve?"

"Constantly, it seems."

"I just wanted to see you here. Old time's sake, I guess. We haven't been talking much, and I just thought —"

Somebody came around the end of the bench and sat down beside me. It was Dylan, his phone at his ear. He must have been within ten yards of me the whole time.

I put my phone away. I took his from his hand and tucked it into his jacket.

"That was interesting."

"I wanted to see how you looked. If you were loaded for bear or something."

"How would I look if I were loaded for bear?"

"I don't know. Pacing? Gesticulating?"

Had I ever gesticulated in front of him? I don't know. God, you question everything at times like this.

I pressed my lips to his temple, cupping his head from the other side. He was warm and moist from the heat, just like me. Nerves too. Somehow he had sensed, correctly, that I had to ask him something big tonight.

Instead of jumping into it, I told him about the little girl. How upset she had me. "I'm probably making her go through a lot of unnecessary crap tonight because I'm afraid. I was thinking as I sat here, it's just a stupid fever, it's not meningitis. I mean, there's what, like a one in a million shot? What are the odds it hits *my* office? She has the flu, that's all, but I couldn't take the chance."

He was nodding in that contemplative way of his, looking out more or less in the direction of Sausalito, though his eyes seemed unfocused. The water shined like aluminum foil. I told him I felt guilty about Vanessa, which happened to be the girl's name (just like his daughter), and he turned toward me very deliberately, as if I were trying to trick him.

"She's innocent," I said. "I shouldn't have let my own anxiety rub off on her."

"All right. Look. Just do it," Dylan said. "Just go ahead and fire away, why don't you?"

"What?"

"Hit me with whatever it is you've got to hit me with tonight. The suspense is killing me."

That line can only be delivered with enormous sarcasm, and it was. He was smiling a wide mock smile now. Sad and a little bit sickening.

"Fine. I do have something to say. I wanted to say it the other night, but you didn't seem up to it."

"No. Indeed. I've got some shit on my plate, all right."

"Just tell me what I need to know, Dylan." I sounded too whiny. Spineless. "I've earned it, haven't I? Tell me what you think is none of my business, because it *is* my business. I want to spend my life with you, God damn it, and if I'm going to do that I need to know what hurts you."

That didn't come out exactly the way I meant it. Maybe he took it as a threat. All he said was, "There's nothing to tell."

One of the saddest moments of my life had arrived. The Last Stand, and he failed me.

After a minute or two of total silence — during which I was saying things to myself like, "I've had my finger up your ass, for shit's sake, why can't you tell me!" — I took his hand and held it in mine on his knee. There should be physical contact. There should be subconscious communication, or subliminal, or *something*. He'll feel the heat in my palm. He'll feel the tremor.

"I know."

"What do you know?" he said. "What do you *think* you know?"

"I know about Gloria. I know about Andy and Vanessa — and yes, my little girl tonight is really named Vanessa. I know about your drinking. I know about your father."

"What about my bloody father?"

"That he killed himself. Steve told me everything. And he told me your mother is dying and you won't give her a chance to say something that might make a difference. I know everything except why you couldn't bring yourself to tell me."

If he was angry, he battened it down so hard it smothered. Under his breath he said, "Fucking Steve." But he didn't try to explain himself. No story to make it all make sense. No apology.

"You might be tempted to think I don't love you," he said. "Not true. I do. I have loved you —" Now tears poured out of his eyes and he sobbed the last word out. " — desperately."

I stood and looked down at him. He was small and crumpled there on our bench. He couldn't force himself to look at me. He leaned with his elbows on his knees and gazed at the grass as a sleek young woman jogged by. She was like some kind of magical ocean creature in her black form-fitting Lycra, but he didn't seem to have seen her.

"I won't be able to —" That's all I could say before I left him there.

You can fill in the blank.

*

I called the ER. My Vanessa was fine. The spinal tap was negative. The blood work showed no generalized infection or abnormalities, except maybe a touch of dehydration. They'd sent her home with children's Tylenol.

My room was very dark that night. The darkest it's been in a long long time.

TWENTY

November arrived, carried in on sheets of rain like clipper ship sails. Every day was a new shade of pewter. It felt like my armpits were growing a crop of heavy moss.

He didn't call.

The first few days went by in a stormy blur, no contact, no news. I hadn't even heard from Jules, other than the text she sent within hours of the Last Stand: ur 2 gd 4 m.

Then Steve called. He was in Florida.

"Believe it or not, he's here."

"What? Dylan?"

"Flew in last night. Doesn't want a thing to do with me, mind you — I'm persona non grata for now — but he's been in to see Mum."

"I didn't mean to tell him how I knew. I'm sorry."

"Where else would you have got it? He'd figure it out. But anyway, dear, I wanted you to know that whatever you said to him had quite the effect."

"I miss him already."

"I know, love. I know. But listen." I heard him take a deep breath. Maybe he was tense in the middle of all the drama down there. "Like I said. This isn't a great time for him. He's a mess. It's a shame when people meet when one of them is totally hatstand."

That was a new one on me. I got the gist though.

"Has your mom told you what he said to her?"

"She won't do me the honors. Says it's between her and him and I'm to keep me nose out of their business."

"I think he might take after her."

"Oh, he does. He does, but he'd have to be shitfaced to admit it. Me? I take more after Dad, but then again I knew him longer than Dill did."

I have to admit, I was beginning to feel the buds of optimism sprouting inside me. It sounded like Dylan was in the process of "turning himself round," which would lead him, I had to think, back to my door, where he'd present me with another fistful of sunflowers and a "Get Smart" lunchbox to make up for his poor judgment. And I'd take him back in a flash, of course, I'd have his clothes off in no time and we'd screw like the old days right there on my living room carpet, laughing our ridiculous heads off. But I had to be patient. It *was* a process. It wouldn't be instant, like pudding.

"Steve?"

"Yes, dear."

"If you see him. If the time is right and he seems like he might listen to you?"

"Fat chance."

"Just tell him —" Fucking tears. Shit. "Tell him I was anorak for him at first sight."

*

Jules finally came over the next evening, dripping wet and shaking the beads of rain out of her hair like a collie. Pregnancy had no apparent effect on her overall demeanor. She was still the jaunty wild child I'd always known.

She'd brought a batch of sushi over from Ace Wasabi's, along with a large Kirin for me and a two liter cream soda for her. Already the cravings kicking in. We both sat on the floor at my coffee table, negotiating the maki with chopsticks.

"You couldn't have picked a better spot for the breakup," she said. "Marina Green's beautiful at sunset."

"I wish I would have picked someplace that's more in line with the way I was feeling. Mission and Sixteenth? Someplace that smells like urine."

"No. It'd follow you for the rest of your life. This way you have a nice view to remember at least."

"I'm not going to be single for the rest of my life, Pookie. I hope not, anyway."

"You know what I mean."

"Obviously it's pretty much out of my hands."

"Careful what you wish for, babe. *I'm* not single."

She grinned around a piece of California roll.

"Please. You and Wayne are going to be fine."

"If mediocre is fine, then — fine. It's just that I never thought of myself as being happy with mediocre."

"Wayne's not mediocre."

"No. Not really. But it turns out I am."

"How can you say that? You're goofier than *me*!"

We were laughing. For the foreseeable future, my laughter wouldn't have much to do with sex.

"I mean, seriously. I'm pretty square when it comes to family stuff. I *want* the kid now. I want the house and the white picket fence — though I'm sure there's no such thing in San Francisco. But you put a kid in the picture and suddenly all the goofing around becomes what it always was, I guess. Just entertaining yourself while you wait for something big to happen."

"I'm shocked," I said. "My Jules is a soccer mom deep down?"

"Crazy, huh? Wayne's already shopping for a used family van."

"Used, no less."

"We have to save for college. By the time little Harry Claire is eighteen, Berkeley's gonna cost two hundred grand a year."

"Harry Claire?"

"That's what we're calling him/her for now. If it's a him it's Harry, if it's a her it's Claire. Harry Claire."

"You could always have an ultrasound done and end the suspense."

"Too easy."

I could tell she was happy.

I was happy *for* her, I suppose.

"I hate to say this." I watched the rain pelt my front window for a beat or two. In the streetlight it looked like the window was shattering into tiny bits. "I really really wanted to be Mrs. Cakebread."

"Oh, Pookie. You could never have pulled it off. Sarah Cakebread? I mean, come on."

"No good?"

"Sounds like a plump middle-aged lady who sells home-made pastries at county fairs. Sarah Cakebread's Guilty Pleasures."

"Yeah. It's a stretch."

I didn't tell her how I was nursing the fantasy that Dylan would reinvent himself after his big catharsis with Mum, how he'd ride in with that fistful of sunflowers and haul me up on his horse's haunch, how we'd live happily ever after in a house of his own design. Blah blah blah, she'd have told me.

"One thing you have to get through your thick head." Now Jules gave me one of her rare serious looks. "You're special. Not everyone can handle a special mate. That means you special people are especially hard to match up because you need someone as special as you."

"All right already. I'm special."

"Hell, if I were a dude, *I'd* marry you."

"That means you're special too. See, you're not mediocre."

"Maybe you're right."

We had our fun. I let myself imagine we'd have our fun even after Harry Claire came along.

*

More time passed, and if it's starting to feel like this relationship novel is winding down, that's because not much happens after the Last Stand. If there's no Happily Ever After, what's the point?

But I wasn't convinced on the whole Happily Ever After thing. I told Nilesh at work one day that I was giving Dylan plenty of time to put all his love ducks in a row, though it was all I could do not to call him up to encourage him.

"Going to see his mom was a big deal," I said. We both had on our white coats and our stethoscopes. A couple of love doctors. "I think the whole thing with his mom was keeping him from committing."

"Men are mysterious," he said.

221

"I thought men think *women* are the mysterious ones."

"Women are mysterious too. Humans are mysterious."

"Seems so."

It was nice to float along thinking that in a few months' time, I'd get a call from Dylan saying he was ship-shape, ready to carry on, sorry for all that chup-chup we had to get through, what, but darling, can we meet at Davies for a concert this Saturday night?

Then Nilesh threw me a wicked curve.

"Oh, I meant to tell you. Your friend's been reassigned to me. As a patient."

"Dylan?"

"Isn't his last name something a little odd? Cakepan? Breadbasket? I can't recall."

"Cakebread."

"That's it. I just got the notice. He asked for a new primary, and I assumed you had suggested it."

"No. I didn't know."

"Ah."

"I mean, it's not a bad idea." I was trying like hell to hide my real reaction. I felt like my stomach was full of bees. "Probably for the best. If we're going to —"

Couldn't finish.

"Well then," Nilesh said. "Don't worry. I'll take good care of him."

As soon as I got home I called Dylan's number. I was going to basically tear him a new one for not at least discussing this with me before going ahead with it. I deserved a chance to at least act like a professional, didn't I? To say, No need to switch doctors, Dylan, I can be completely objective about your care, and I'll be absolutely discreet with your private information too.

The *least* you could have done was get a new doc in the city, but no.

His answering machine picked up. I couldn't bring myself to leave a message.

In fifteen minutes I was at the corner of Fell and Steiner. I could see his stoop from there, but unfortunately the Corner Store Casanova could see *me*.

"Hey, you come back again! You never stop thinking of me,

and now you want the dinner and the movie, eh?"

He had been sweeping the floor but now came out and approached me as if I really had entered his fantasy. I wanted to say, No, I have a fantasy of my own I'm working on, but it didn't seem fair.

"You look sad. You look like the dark clouds hang over the head."

"Big time," I said. "How much for a bottle of gin?"

"Little nine-nine-nine. Big one nineteen-nine-nine." He looked at me with real concern. His one dark eyebrow wriggled like a worried caterpillar. (Not to disparage him. He was being sweet to a damsel in distress.) "But you don't want to swim in the alcohol. Trust me. No good. You need a nice man. I am Rashid."

He smiled so big and kindly that I was disarmed for a moment, finding him to be just the kind of good Samaritan that you need at a bad time like this. But then I saw a car pull up in front of Dylan's building, and in two seconds Dylan emerged from inside the apartment, with his children, one at the end of each arm.

They'd spent the weekend with him or something. Visitation. He was their father. Their mother was in the car to pick them up.

I slid into the garbage alley beside Rashid's store, watching like a trench-coated voyeur as Dylan led the two kids toward Gloria's blue Lexus sedan. She must have spent the weekend in town to be close, rather than flying to and from San Diego. I saw a shadow behind the wheel, and it leaned toward the passenger door and popped it open.

As Dylan approached her, I could see and hear from where I stood that the children had begun to cry. Vanessa, was getting tall and innocently elegant, with her hair combed out down the back of her coat. Her profile was lovely — pale skin, a nose just like Dylan's, small budlike mouth. She wasn't letting go of Daddy's hand. Andy, meanwhile, wasn't letting go of his leg. He clung, a little bantam of a boy in a puffy down jacket and stocking cap, and as he twisted and contorted himself around Dylan's leg all I could really make out of his face was his gaping mouth, roaring how he didn't want to go.

I had no business seeing this. Dylan was right.

The mother got tired of the fussing and got out of the car. She came around and took Andy by the hand, peeled him away from his father, and packed him into the back seat even while he continued thrashing and screaming. For some reason, she reminded me of the gamekeeper's nasty ex-wife in *Lady Chatterley's Lover*, that destructive cow. Cold, calculating, and brutally efficient when it comes to lacerating her former mate. But she was pretty too. In a freckle-faced English kind of way, though I knew she was American. Strawberry blond hair, where little Vanessa got hers. Narrow-nosed, but with high cheekbones and dark eyes that must dazzle a man when they look at him in love, or in anger. She was in a crisp gray raincoat and black boots up to her knees, stylish but not showy. I could see why Dylan was attracted to her in the old days. She broadcasted: I can be the mother of your children, young man.

Vanessa turned and gave Dylan a forlorn hug, burying her face in his chest. He was crying as he bent down to kiss her on the forehead, his own mouth twisted involuntarily. I couldn't hear what he said, but he must have said something reassuring because Vanessa nodded and wiped her eyes. Gloria watched the two of them. Andy had begun to shout from the backseat, "Bye bye Daddy!"

Gloria helped Vanessa into the front seat and closed the door. She said something to Dylan, not in anger, not even emotionally. Just a remark or an order. Be on time from now on. I can see they had a nice visit. We'll try again soon. Who knows?

Finally, the capper. The thing that made me turn away.

As the car pulled out, both kids waving through the fogging windows, Dylan was so overcome he covered his face with one hand and sobbed as if there were no one else on the street, on the sidewalk, near enough to witness his pain.

As if, in fact, no one existed at all but him and those children.

TWENTY-ONE

There's something about the rainy season that really gets under my skin. It's not that dubious "seasonal affective disorder" you may have heard about (SAD — give me a break). I never gave it much creed as a doctor. Everyone is a little blue in the winter, after all, and life just gets more annoying. My problem with the rainy season has always been practical. I hate getting wet.

That, and my old Volvo doesn't handle especially well in the rain. I have white knuckles as I drive up and down the Waldo grade, cars flying by me at twice the speed. I call the left lane on the bridge the "death lane," and I creep along to the right at no more than thirty-five. Other drivers hate me. It's always a long walk from the car to my office too, across a wide parking lot that's also a wind tunnel, so that by the time I hit the door I'm soaking wet in spite of my wide-ass Mary Poppins umbrella. (I never did get a chance to see how Dylan was with his umbrella etiquette.) On top of that, at home, something about my apartment holds the moisture in and gives the place a smell like turtles live inside the walls that doesn't really fade away till July. Everywhere is one reminder or another that I have six months of getting wet ahead of me, when the November storms start rolling in one by one like God's bowling balls.

Then there's the thing with Dylan.

That — not your measly old seasonal affective disorder — was SAD.

Sometimes it hits me that life, in general, might just be sad. *Bearably* sad, and our pursuit of happiness is really on the order of building a dam out of toothpicks. I hope not, but there is evidence.

Professional that I am, I threw myself into my work in a way that left hardly any time for self-pity. This was what Ben always complained about, all those years ago now. How I kept myself so busy so I wouldn't notice certain things. Things like, ultimately, how unhappy he was.

Oh, and his book? *The Frostbitten Man*? I'd finished it recently, since I wasn't going out in the evenings anymore. It was lovely. It was a genuine work of art. The main character comes to achieve a literal and metaphorical transformation when he realizes that if life has no meaning, as he has come to believe in his emotional isolation, then there is no reason to be alive. He'd been reading his Sartre and Camus, I guess. And he takes this to its logical conclusion, a suicide attempt, but in the act of it (pills) he has a revelation. Not a religious one. A plain old practical one: that as meaningless as life might be, *being* alive meant experiencing pain, and alleviating pain was the one thing that might offer him something to do with his existence that didn't make matters worse. Is that enough? he asks. Is it worth being alive if all I can do is help a handful of people who suffer more than I do?

We've heard the story before. Jesus et al. chide us to follow that line of thought. Countless movies take us there. But something about the way Ben wrote made it seem new to me. I was crying through the last ten pages, after our frostbitten man phones 911 to save himself, then sells all his earthly belongings and goes to Darfur (hot climate — perfect cure for frostbite), where he becomes an aid worker delivering food and medicine to remote villages and refugee camps, and he is fulfilled.

I could just see Ralph Fiennes in the role, dressed in his khakis and sweating, shirtless of course, as he hauls sacks and sacks of life-saving grain from the bed of a truck.

But here's another SAD thing. Nobody bought Ben's novel, I'd come to learn. He didn't make the bestseller list, didn't get the author tour. *Publisher's Weekly* called the book "derivative and lacking a dramatic soul," and the only major print review poor Ben got was in the *Denver Post*, claiming, "Mr. Cargas is obviously a talented writer, but he has let himself, in this debut effort, fall in love with his own prose rather than offering up the kind of dynamic structure and scene-making that could have made *The Frostbitten Man* a must-read. Instead, the reader slogs through page after page of internal monologues that wind up sounding like a schizophrenic's diary."

I wanted so badly to call him up. I wanted to tell him how much I loved the book, how much it had moved me, how unfair its reception was, and how much, in ways I had almost forgotten, I really missed him, because we met when we were young, and we were such sweet blank slates back then. (I've relived that night of his reading many many times.) But I didn't call. I imagined how it would look to him, how self-serving of me. And if he took the bait and wanted to see me? How crummy of me to use my ex that way. The bloom would fade from that rose in no time.

Also, how arrogant of me to think my reappearance was all he needed. I'd just spent a few months trying to make a man happy, without much success. I wasn't just what the doctor ordered for Dylan — why would it be any better with Ben?

*

The next patient on my roster was Lili Bannerjee. The chart in the door pocket of her exam room said she'd come in for a referral.

There she was, in full Bengali regalia, a minty green sari with purple bordering and minute embroidery, sitting not on the exam table but in the side chair with her legs crossed as if for a coffeeklatsch.

"So what's this all about? You don't look under the weather to me."

"Psychiatrist," she said. "Believe it or not."

"Oh no. What's bothering you, Lili?"

I sat on the stool and wheeled over to her. She looked fine enough. Tired, maybe. Sometimes a run of insomnia can make you *feel* like you need a psychiatrist.

"Actually it's not for me. It's for Mita. She's four months pregnant and isn't having a very easy time."

"Well, her OB should be able to —"

"I was hoping you could recommend someone. It's not

227

physical. She's afraid of motherhood."

Her accent made it sound kind of intimidating: *mother-hude*.

"Poor thing. And she's so young."

"That's why I told her not to get married so soon! I said let it sit for another year and see where things are."

I asked if Mita was enrolled in the HMO.

"She's on Palu's insurance. I haven't told her I'm getting her some help yet."

"To be honest, I only know our own therapists," I said. "Maybe I can ask around, though."

"Ah. I should have thought."

"It's not rare, what Mita's feeling. Motherhood is a big responsibility."

"Ha. Tell me about it." She laughed.

"I have a friend who's pregnant right now. Same thing. A little less severe, but she's definitely anxious over it."

"And what about *you*?"

"Pardon?" I sounded like Dylan. I'd picked up a lot from him, apparently.

"You and the Englishman. When's *your* wedding day? You don't have much time to start on the babies."

"Oh. Well, long story there, I'm afraid."

"Don't tell me!"

I filled her in on the latest. Twenty-five words or less, so I wouldn't get too upset.

"I told him to get you straight to the altar, didn't I? I was afraid something like this would happen."

"He just needs some time," I said, believing it. "He'll come around. And meanwhile I'm busy enough to give it to him. Some time, I mean."

Her face tried to tell me not to be so naïve. Maybe she was right. But at the same time, after seeing him with his kids, there was no way I could put another ounce of pressure on Dylan.

"Now you see that we Bengalis are right, don't you? Marriage should have less to do with love and more to do with practicality," she said. "I'm telling you, love is a mental illness!"

"Hmmm. Not sure about that."

I gave her a scrip for something to help her sleep better. And I promised to get the name of a good therapist for Mita.

"Tell her it'll be all right," I said. "Look what a good mother she has. Perfect model."

"Please. She's a young American girl. Since the wedding I can't even get her into a sari, much less teach her how to be a mother."

When she was gone, having thrown my mood into an elegant tailspin, I jotted on her chart, *Insomnia re Mita's peripartum depression.*

There is a lot to worry about in a young American girl's life. For a fleeting moment I was silly enough to put myself in that category.

*

One Saturday night I went to the movies by myself, something I hadn't done in years. Usually I went with Jules or Jules and Wayne — perennial third wheel — but on this occasion I had to get out of the turtle-stinking apartment or commence the serious drinking. There was a spectacular new 3D film at the Presidio on Chestnut. I could walk. The movie would be vapid enough that I could vegetate behind my 3D glasses and unhook my brain for two hours.

For once, it wasn't raining.

Jules and Wayne, by the way, were already starting their birthing classes. Adorable. She'd told me it was actually refreshing, giving in to all the baby-making clichés that have been cooked up over the years, starting with the family van and Lamaze and proceeding directly to that premature obsession over which nursery school to apply to before the child is even born. She'd painted their spare room a sickly lavender color, like grape juice mixed with milk, so it would be gender-neutral for little Harry Claire. They bought a crib at Costco. She was thinking about breast feeding and whether she really wanted to be one of those women who whip it out in public — "But discreetly," she said, "I'm nothing if not discreet." — or more like our own moms, who used to boil the bottles and rubber nipples on the stove and feed us "formula."

I didn't really like thinking about her life. Here I was, stuck in park while she was moving right along in the grand promenade of life. It's much more unsettling for women than men, I think, to be stuck in Park. Men are more content with "the way things are" than women, at least if things are more or less comfortable. Women always look ahead. Or around. At their friends, and at other women. And we compare ourselves — in spite of ourselves.

Things were flying out at me from the screen. It was slightly nauseating.

About halfway through the movie, I felt my phone vibrating. I figured it was Jules, back from her class, so I was tempted to ignore it. Something told me it could be someone else, though. Someone important. Dylan? I can't say I went that far. But I looked at the backlit screen on the phone and saw that a text was coming in, from the hospital. They could use another pair of hands in the ER.

What else is new? The movie was dull. I didn't care for the overblown sound effects and the sardonic military laugh lines, so.

Real life. I chose *it*.

*

The place was rocking, as the regular ER docs liked to say. "It's M-A-S-H in here tonight, Dr. Phelan," a too-young-for-me PA called out when he saw me come in. "You ready to get your hands dirty?"

There is a camaraderie in the ER that Nilesh and I don't really share at the clinic. He and I are friendly but not friends. We sometimes eat lunch together in the cafeteria and talk the politics of health care, how the Giants are doing, or the bizarre decisions being made by the suits in Phoenix, where the HMO's corporate headquarters are based. In the ER it's more like a team of death-defying rogue soldiers, Kelly's Heroes. They make bad jokes and tease each other about their love lives, so I always fit right in. Since I'm a GP, though, with some training in emergency med, I mainly follow orders when I work there. That night the head honcho was Dr. Beaudry, a gray-faced, sixty-ish man who reminded me of George Clooney (he played a doctor for a while).

Dr. Beaudry saw me as I signed in. He was in a green scrub top that revealed his tanned upper arms in all their late-middle-age glory, and he happened to be carrying a trach tube.

"Nice to see you, Sarah. You look hypoglycemic."

"Gee thanks. I was at the movies earlier. Sitting in the dark."

"Have a donut, why don't you. Spike that glucose."

And off he went to see about the suspected food poisoning in number 8.

My first patient of the evening was a man in his seventies, complaining of shortness of breath. Since it could be a myocardial infarction just beginning to roll, I had a nurse take blood for an enzyme panel and asked one of the nursing assistants to prep him for an EKG.

"Don't worry, Mr. Yellin," I said. "This is all precautionary. You might be having an allergic reaction or maybe an asthma attack. Are you asthmatic?"

"Hell no," he said, imploring me with wide rheumy eyes to get him back to his La-Z-Boy as soon as possible. "I was an athlete when I was young."

His BP was high. Pulse near a hundred, but nowhere near v-tach. He was anxious, that's all.

"The blood test will tell me whether you've had any damage to your heart muscle. The EKG's going to show how things are ticking along in there, okay?"

Mandy, the EKG tech, came in and started wheeling Mr. Yellin away.

"You're pretty," he told her. "I get to say things like that at my age."

"Your wife is right outside. I'll tell on you."

"You want a witness, Mandy?"

"I'll be fine. He talks the talk but he's in no position to walk the walk."

"Hey now," Mr. Yellin said, in relatively good spirits for a man whose life might be changing forever tonight. I'd see him again in an hour or so — or much sooner if his creatine kinase was up, in which case he'd be off to the cath lab for a clot buster and a shiny new stent in his left anterior descending.

In spite of the fact that every curtained treatment space was occupied, the joint was bizarrely quiet. Soft voices of docs asking their questions, patients answering with meek trepidation, nurses reassuring family members or speaking with EMTs and cops. I could hear the TV in the waiting room playing the theme song to *Law & Order SVU*, so that meant it was nine o'clock. No idea who got kicked off the island on *Survivor*. The triage nurse gave me the chart for a woman who had severe abdominal pain.

She was lying in a fetal position on the gurney, small and scared in the gown she'd changed into already. She was petite and wan, very young to my eye — early twenties, maybe. There was a garish tattoo on her neck leading down along her spine, kind of a serpenty thing, and for some reason I began to think drug overdose. The way her hair was done — choppy, black, with spots of different colors dyed in — made me think she was a victim of the Haight homeless-kid lifestyle, which hadn't changed much since the sixties. Girls like her loitered around over there like gypsies, panhandling, buying and selling and using dope, hanging with boyfriends who look like ex-con zombies with pit bulls at the end of a heavy tow chain.

"Hello," I said. "I hear you have a bellyache."

She rolled over to look at me. Her arm went over her forehead to shield her eyes from the overhead light. I scanned them as furtively as I could for needle marks but didn't see any.

"It's not that. I know what it is."

I began to palpate her lower abdomen under the gown. "Sometimes people think they know what it is, and it turns out to be appendicitis or something. Or worse."

"It's a fuckin' miscarriage," she said, just as I lifted the gown and discovered that her panties were glistening with blood.

"Okay, take it easy, sweetheart. We'll take care of things for you."

I called a nurse over to help clean her up so I could see what was what. The soiled panties made a sickening soppy noise as they went into the bio-waste bag. The girl tightened into a ball with cramps and forced out a helpless whimper. I'd have thought she would shriek to the cosmos, Fuck you all! But no. She was one of those who became a child again when she was in pain.

I heard some commotion out in the reception area that usually meant the arrival of an ambulance and the initial evaluation of trauma. Dr. Beaudry ran by behind me, oblivious to the girl — Karen was her name. A couple of nurses and beefcake orderlies followed him out front, where voices were raised over the sound of the television for the first time since I'd arrived.

Mandy stuck her head in and told me Mr. Yellin's EKG was normal.

"Thanks," I said. "See about the blood too. And do you mind calling up to obstetrics to see if they can do an exam and possible D&C?"

"I'll let you know."

I began to examine Miss Karen, trying to determine what, if anything, she had passed. There was no tissue visible, no products of birth or anything other than the bleeding, so it would be up to the gynecologist to make the assessment. She might not have miscarried after all. Could be hemorrhage, which is not always something to worry about. The amount of blood wasn't reassuring, though.

When I lifted the gown over her pubic area to do a digital exam, I saw something that made my heart shrivel. Between her belly button and her mons was a blossoming contusion, going dark blue with sickening violet around the perimeter. It was fist-sized, or doorknob-sized. Either she'd been hit, or she tried to hurt herself. A home abortion. SAD.

"So how come you didn't tell reception you thought you were having a miscarriage?"

"I don't know. I wasn't sure what it was."

"You told me."

"I just figured it out."

"Do you think you know what caused it?"

She turned away from me, then all but sank her teeth into one wrist — from a new cramp, or from a thought. I couldn't tell which. Tears seeped from her clenched eyes.

"What happened, Karen?"

"I can't tell you."

"Why not?"

"He's out there."

"Who's out there?"

"My boyfriend."

Shit. I hoped there was still a cop around. A little while before, they'd brought in a drunk driver who split his lip on the steering wheel. I looked out past the curtain to see if I could spot a uniform without upsetting Karen — I knew she wouldn't want me to say anything — and saw Dr. Beaudry following a gurney into the room next door. The sheets were bloody. An assault. A crime. There'd be cops.

"We're going to send you up to see the gynecologist now, all right, honey? Don't worry. Everything's going to be fine."

I left her, heading for the front. A Hansel and Gretel path of blood spatters from the new patient led the way. That bright red arterial blood. It always gives me an automatic cringe in the stomach, one of those things the human body does on its own. Red is danger. Be afraid. It's always good to respect what the human body is telling you.

At the front counter, thank God, was a sturdy looking policeman filling out the paperwork on the bleeder. And there, sitting like a goddamn slob-monkey, was the fucking creep who had socked Karen in the gut to get rid of *his* baby.

It's a goddamn sick world at times, you know that? It's easy to forget, I suppose, tucked away in our safe little turtle-smelling hidey holes, but bad things are going on every minute of every day and there are times I am sick of it. I know. I know. I'm a doctor. I could have been a barista or a tour guide. But once in a while — sorry, Ben. Helping people is hard on the old psyche. With all the self-control I had, I kept myself from going up to the asshole and sticking my thumbs in his eyes, the skinheaded, tattooed, white-supremecist motherfucker.

"Officer, can I talk to you for a second?"

Strangely enough, the cop and the creep had the same haircut. What to make of that?

"Whatcha got?" he said, all business. He let the clipboard with his paperwork slap against his thigh.

He was one of those pink-cheeked men who look pretty much like they looked in high school. Blondish, a neck like a fire hydrant. He had varsity squad written all over him.

"In here," I said, and took him into the vending machine alcove off the waiting room. "I've got a domestic violence victim back in back, and there's the guy who did it." He glanced over, one eyebrow slightly rising.

I told him about Karen's injury and probable miscarriage. He listened without showing in his face any kind of opinion. A nod, that was it.

"She make a statement?"

"Sort of. Not really."

"She'll have to make a written statement."

"She's scared of him. Did you see the guy?"

"Want me to talk to him? Maybe he'll say something dumb."

"Good. Perfect. I'll fill out the domestic violence report. But she can't go home with him, okay? I'm making sure she stays overnight for observation."

We were both startled by the code blue alarm. Cardiac arrest, and a voice over the intercom gave the room number where I'd left Mr. Yellin. *Shit.*

"I have to go," I told the cop. As soon as I got back to the treatment area, Dr. Beaudry was there to meet me.

"I'll do the cardiac. They've got the crash cart and defibrillator there already. I need you to maintain hemostasis on the guy in number 4 till we can move him to an OR."

"Yes, chief," I said, my head blasting thoughts at me like a Gatling gun. I was worried about Mr. Yellin and sick that his blood work was late, but Beaudry was a master with cardiac arrest. The problem could be an intermittent arrhythmia the EKG hadn't detected, but Beaudry would take care of him. "Was it a stabbing or something? There's a lot of blood."

"Worse," he said. "Suicide attempt. Did a helluva number on his left radial. We just need to stabilize him for surgery."

"Got it."

"His wife called it in. He'd be on ice now if she hadn't."

"Dr. Phelan?" A nurse came out of the room, blood dashed all across the bib of her scrubs. "His heart rate is going up. He's unconscious."

I went in, spotting the pressure bandage as thick as a deck of cards on his left wrist and a bright orange tourniquet the EMTs had placed above the elbow. That's a last ditch kind of thing. They use it only when they think the patient might not survive the ambulance ride to the hospital. I followed the streaks of fluorescent blood up the man's chest and to his chin, where the clotted blood was already turning a deep orange and darkening the creases in his neck so that he looked like he'd been dipped in lurid ink. And I saw then that his eyes were rolled back into his head, showing just the whites like a Greek bust, and I saw that he looked like Jude Law would look unconscious on a table, drifting away on a bad dream.

It was Dylan.

*

The morning was still dark when I went to see him after surgery. They'd put him in a semi-private, with a completely comatose motorcycle accident victim across the room, breathing rhythmically on a gurgling respirator. When Dylan woke up he'd wonder if he'd managed to send himself to some dully antiseptic limbo instead of the peaceful void he'd been hoping for.

There'd been no sleep for me, of course. All night long, waiting while he was in surgery, I kept saying, Jesus Christ, this is the climax of my relationship novel! And if that sounds a bit distant and self-absorbed — all from nerves and fear — maybe that's about right, because it finally hit me as I wandered the halls (checking in on Mr. Yellin, who survived, thank God, and Miss Karen, who *had* lost a baby, it turned out) that Dylan's mystery illness had been depression all along and I was too wrapped up in myself to see it. All I'd wanted from the moment I laid eyes on him back in May was to fall in love with the man.

Maybe Lili was right. Lovesickness ought to be in the DSM-IV, for godssakes.

There are moments when you have to shed your outer costume like a pea pod and look at the nuggets of you left inside. I did that that night. I decided I was too ridiculous to be a doctor. I wasn't even a reasonable person. First, the oath goes, do no harm. But I was thinking, First become a fucking human being. *Then* you can try and save the world.

I thought about Pat a lot overnight too. Everything he taught me about being a *mensch*. (And an Irishman speaking of *menschen* will never cease to warm me.) *You put yourself aside whenever you think of it, Sarah,* he'd tell me. *Let the other guy talk a while. Let him have his moment. Anytime you can give somebody something rather than taking it for yourself, don't even think about it. Just give.* So there I was, charged with taking care of the sweet and suffering Englishman last spring — *his* moment — and all I did was dwell on how to sink my teeth into him. He was trying to tell me he was in trouble. I couldn't see past my own pathetic wants, my fat-assed ego.

Pat would have forgiven me, I'm sure. My divorce troubled him a lot. He wanted his little girl to be happy, but he'd probably have said, "The way your mom and I did things, love comes easy. You don't even have to work to find it, much less keep it."

Meaning, Sweetheart, stop trying so hard.

Forgiveness was much on my mind that night.

Around six, I went out to check again on my other two charges, happy to find that they were both resting well. I'd want to talk with Karen later, after she was finished sleeping it off. She probably hadn't slept so soundly in months.

Dylan was just waking when I returned. He saw me come in the room and turned his face to the wall.

"Nice mittens," I said. His arms were wrapped to the elbows in heavy surgical gauze, a superficial wound on his right arm, the almost-fatal one on his left. He'd be feeling some awful pain shortly.

"Thanks. They're all the rage this year."

I sat on the edge of the bed. Instinctively, my hand went to his brow and caressed it, then his cheeks, but still he wasn't willing to look at me.

"Dylan," I said.

"No need." He was groggy on sedatives. I knew they'd be sending him to psych for evaluation as soon as he was up to it.

"I'm sorry. I'm so sorry. I didn't know you were — I didn't see what kind of pain you were in."

"I was hiding it from you."

"I should have shipped you off to a therapist that first day."

"I was still hiding it from myself back then. Please. Don't beat yourself up on my behalf."

I was crying, of course. It came on suddenly. I let myself fall onto his chest, his injured hands rising to avoid being bashed. He tried patting my back with them, not very successfully. He muttered, "There now."

"Why?" I groaned. "How come you couldn't talk to me? Wasn't I good for you?"

"You were wonderful. You were all I could have asked for."

"But."

There was nothing I could say that wouldn't have been all about me. My stupidity, my failure, my selfishness, my baggage. So I didn't say it. I let my head rest on him and I just sobbed it out in wordless words.

"I didn't deserve you," he said. "And then — you know. The rest of it."

The children. The wife.

As if on cue, a nurse came in and announced that Mrs. Cakebread had arrived, was it all right to let her in?

I got up, trying to make myself look borderline professional as fast as I could. I leaned down and kissed him on the forehead. He had tears in his eyes now, but what emotion they were coming from I couldn't really say. All I know for sure was what I was feeling, and I hid it for for his sake. For Gloria's sake too. There she was.

"Doctor?" she said, like they all do.

"He's going to be fine. They patched him up better than new."

"Oh my God." She looked past me toward her husband in the bed — the i.v. line and the heart monitor there, his big white mittens.

She was prettier this close than she'd seemed to me before. Less arrogant looking, less pinched and flinty. Her heart was visible in her face. She'd been in despair all night, trying to get up here from San Diego.

"Dr. Phelan's been taking good care of me," Dylan said, and that's when I left them alone. The last thing I saw as I looked back from the doorway was Mrs. Cakebread taking Dylan's face tenderly between her hands, like she was lifting a new ostrich egg from its nest, and then kissing him on the lips.

TWENTY-TWO

Thanksgiving came and went. I put in my time at Mom's house in Mill Valley, with Ella and the girls, but thanks to the mood of the season and the weather like a dream of wet army blankets, it went fine enough. Ella and I kept arm's-length from one another. For the girls' sake.

On the Sunday after Thanksgiving, two weeks after that traumatic night, I learned from Steve that Dylan was recovering well from his injuries.

"Lucky bloke," he said over the long phone connection. "If Gloria hadn't called 911 he'd have bled out in his bath."

"How did she know?"

"He was on the phone with her just before. Out of his bloody wits. Weeping like a newborn at the fucking affront of being alive. He told her what his plan was, said he had a straight razor on hand to do the deed, and all he meant ringing her up was to say good-bye and plead with her not to tell the kids the truth. She tried to get him to call the suicide hotline but he wouldn't have it. He was wild. Mad. I don't know whether he even remembers it, in actual fact."

Gloria, he went on to say, kept him on the landline while she called SF 911 on her cell. At some point, when the pint of whisky he'd thrown back told him it was time, he hung up and went to the bath tub, where he made the two cuts and waited for the big dark to come over him. "In bloody excruciating pain, by the way." The EMTs who found him (the poor drunk man had even failed to lock his front door — or maybe he *wanted* a close call, who knows?) said that he was actually laughing to himself as they pulled him from the still-hot water. He had about five minutes to spare, they figured. His heart would have gone into v-fib and that would have been "all she wrote," as Steve put it.

"I don't quite know how to tell you this next bit, dear." Steve's voice got low and pebbly. He might have been drinking a bit himself at that hour, late Greenwich Mean Time. I could hear the rumble of the Underground beneath his flat, ominous as thunder. "He's moving back to San Diego to be with Gloria and the kids."

The blood flushed out of my brain. I had to sit on the edge of my bed or I'd have fallen. Totally unprepared for this, even though I hadn't dared to think yet when I might see Dylan again, or how I might be able to ease my way back in with him. I'd let myself assume that Gloria's tenderness with him in the hospital was out of sympathy more than love. Apparently the tragedy had kindled something in them both.

"He asked me to tell you," Steve said. "Gently. Looks like I've mucked that part of it up."

"I'm okay." A lie.

"He didn't think he was up to the task. Still on the fragile side, really. But Sarah."

"Mmmph."

"He does care about you. He wanted me to make sure you know. If you don't know it, I need to drive it home. It's just that, he understands now what he has to do."

I felt myself beginning what Jules and I like to call a Temporary Total Collapse. Thank God it was a Sunday. I'd have lost my license to practice if it happened at work.

"Sweetheart? You all right?"

"No." Monosyllabic, sobby, snotty. I grabbed a pillow and shoved my face into it. "I feel like I've been loving in circles my whole life, and it's not fair."

"Well," he said. "Be sure you get off at Piccadilly, dear. Eros lives there and he'll do right by you. That's a promise."

Of course it was raining at the moment. It was raining hard. Inside and out.

*

Just so happens that Jules was on vacation in Costa Rica that week. She and Wayne had decided they might not be able to afford a trip for a long time, and Jules realized she wouldn't look good in a swimsuit ever again. She had started to show a little bit, so now was the time.

When I was off the phone with Steve, I was good for nothing. Prostrate on my bed. The subtle change from daylight to dusk went unnoticed, thanks to the crummy weather out there, so it was kind of a shock when I managed to lift myself up and look at the time. Eight fifteen. I'd wallowed in self-pity for almost four hours, a new Phelan record.

The thing about the TTC — Temporary Total Collapse, sorry — is that even though it's temporary, you never know how long that is. At least your classic dark night of the soul ends at sunup. *These* things can go on for days, weeks, like certain chronic infections of the bowel, and you walk around like the living dead until either the TTC passes or some loved one or colleague slaps you around and says, Buck up, you twerp! And that's what I needed that night, because I knew I couldn't show up at work the next day with a gray caul over my head and the scarlet letter tattooed on my chest: B, for bamboozled.

But had Dylan bamboozled me, really? Or had he pulled the wool over his own eyes more than anyone else's? Maybe I bamboozled myself.

Turns out I was never the hero of my own relationship novel at all. It was Dylan's relationship novel, and I was the transitional character, the rebound girl. A walk-on.

I thought about all our moments together — a grand total of maybe (this is what you do at times like this) six hundred hours, which sounds like a lot but really isn't. Not when you'd been imagining a lifetime. Not when the hours flew by like itinerant geese. And not when nearly every minute of every hour was so sweet and easy and calm (except for the wonderful screwing, which could never be described as calm), and fun and fulfilling and, you'd like to think, *deserved*. And God damn it, I wished I had some alcohol left in the house as I relived those hundreds of conversations and those languid hours we spent after the screwing, nested in each others arms with our bodies touching all along their lengths from temple to cheek to shoulder, my boobs to his pale English pecs, to belly to hip to thigh to knee, and even our feet tangling in offhand pleasure. There was nothing but warmth between us. My memories were so touched with it, the warmth that makes you tell yourself, You can do without everything but this, that I forgave him right there for all his trespasses where I was concerned, all his secrets, his errors in judgment, his failures, his flaws and flukes, and all his future wrongs. I'd absorb them all. I was bargaining with the cosmos, like the stages of grief, begging whatever force it is out there that controls the meandering paths of people who belong together to make it happen again.

Followed by an irrevocable silence that strangled my heart.

Jules was away. I couldn't inflict this on Mom, but I had to call someone. I couldn't be alone that night.

I picked up the phone and called my sister.

*

The tap at my door an hour later was surprisingly timid and polite. I didn't peek out the peephole. I opened right away, and there I found Ella in pressed jeans and one of her bright knitted Rastafarian shawls (there really *is* no accounting for taste) over a baggy blue cashmere top. Rain drops clung to her naturally frizzy hair, tiny glass worlds. And in her hand was a frosty bottle of Belvedere vodka.

"Let me guess. I read your mind," she said, raising the bottle.

"You read my fucking soul."

I let her in. Before she could get to the couch, I had two jelly jars filled to their lips with the miracle cure.

"Let's get things straight," she said. "You're going to have a colossal headache tomorrow."

"I know."

"It's pain therapy. Worked wonders for me. The headache chases away all those bad thoughts."

"Let's begin, doctor."

"Skoal."

We clinked glasses, sat together on the couch, and drank like a pair of gunners on the battleship *Potemkin*.

Ella looked tired, but her cheeks were pink from the chill outside and there was a certain shine to her eyes. It wasn't her usual holier-than-thou. It was different for her. Not sympathy, I thought, so much as empathy.

"Why don't you just letter rip," she said. The girls were with Mom. She had all night.

So I did. I railed. I wept. I let my hair down. I whined about how unfair it all was, till I remembered what Tucker had done to her. She didn't remind me. She just listened. We drank and drank while in the background played the Ben Webster and Oscar Peterson CD on a perpetual loop. It made me feel like Pat was there in the room with us, the Phelan girls' daddy listening in on their sad love stories.

"I'm sorry," I told her. "I haven't forgotten what you're going through."

"Oh that. Well."

"How are you holding up?"

"My instinct for revenge gives me enough of a reason to get up in the mornings. I have a good lawyer. We're going to get a very good deal."

"I'm glad."

"He'll wish he'd have joined a monastery." She laughed. Ella actually laughed. I had a hard time remembering when I last heard her really let one go. "At least I have the girls to justify kicking his sorry ass."

"I don't know how you do it."

"Do what?"

"How you manage to be such a good mother with all of this *crap* going on."

She swallowed the last of the vodka in her glass and offered one of those puckering smiles of hers, the kind I always took as sarcastic. Turns out it's more of a sheepish thing. "I hide a lot from them," she said. Then, looking at me with more intensity. "So you think I'm a good mother?"

"Hell yeah."

"How come?"

"I can see how great the girls are. If you weren't a good mother, they'd be wrecks by now."

"That's nice of you to say."

"I envy that about you. I'm jealous."

This was pretty much news to me. It just came out.

"Really?"

"I mean, I wouldn't trade places with you."

"Oh thanks."

"Just, it wasn't till I fell in love with Dylan that it even occurred to me to think about kids. He made me kind of want them. A little bit. But I decided it was too late — for me, anyway — and I realized I'd never be as good a mom as you are, so."

I hadn't really admitted to myself till then that loving Dylan might have spiked my maternal hormones. Not sure it was true or whether it was losing him that made me think, There went my chance. Either way, it was true what I'd said. I couldn't be the mother Ella was to her girls. She was strong. I was a mess.

The bottle had another four fingers in it, but I felt like I'd had about all I dare. Work in the morning. Nilesh looking at me funny. Patients who'd want to have some level of confidence in their doctor.

Ella was quiet for a while. Me too. We listened to the music. Daddy's ghost doing the breast stroke around the room.

"You remember the time he took us on that vacation in the desert?" she said at last. I knew who she meant.

"Yes. Not very successful, was it."

"I loved it. Actually it's one of my best memories. Not because of anything vacationy we did. But I remember one day he left Mom at the motel to soak in the tub or something — she said she had sand in her underpants — and he took us out driving."

I did recall. Vaguely. I was probably about six at the time, and I was with Mom on the whole desert experience. It was icky. Hot, dry, dirty, pointless, as far as I could see, and we had bypassed Disneyland to be there.

"The Volvo had no air conditioner."

"Really? You should know. Anyway." She laid her hand on my thigh and looked up toward the ceiling. Maybe she was seeing that vision of him up there, swimming around. Guilt might give her more access to him than I had. "He drove us up into the mountains and pulled over at one of those overlooks, a vista point, and we all got out of the car."

"Right. I think there's a picture of it."

"No. We didn't have the camera with us."

"If you say so."

"We just stood there looking out at the view for a long time. I think he was working something out in his head. Not sure. He wouldn't have told us. But after a while he looked at us and just said, 'Listen to that.'"

"I don't remember."

"He did. He made sure we were paying attention. He said, 'Listen to that. You know what that's the sound of?' And we both shrugged. One of his quizzes. It was getting hot and we wanted to go back to the motel. He said, 'Listen, girls. What's that the sound of?' And the funny thing was, there *was* no sound. There were no cars. No people around. Just the sound of the wind, I guess, and whatever the inside of your own head sounds like."

"A fricking circus lately."

"I said, 'I give up, Dad. What is it?' And do you remember what he said?"

"No."

"He said, 'Life on earth.'"

*

So this is the end of my relationship novel. Me perpetually unlucky in love, but the relationship I did get out of it all is the one with Ella that we'd both turned away from, each for our own untidy reasons.

She was too looped to drive, of course, so she slept in my bed with me (good thing I had those two pillows), and we both went in and out of fitful naps all night. She was worried about the girls, I'm sure, but they were safe with Mom. I was feeling the early tentacles of that headache. Rain sizzled against the window in occasional gusts, reminding me that life on earth is an insecure thing and the discomforts of being alive are always right behind the nearest pane of glass.

Sometime in the middle of the night — maybe Ella didn't even know I was awake — I became aware of her whispering. It's what people do in the night, even if they mean to be heard, because there's something about the dark that seems to demand it. She was facing me.

"You know I loved him," she said. "All I wanted to do was help him get something *solid* that would make him happy. I handled it badly. I overreacted when he sent the check back. But I loved him. I did, Sarah. And I miss him a lot."

I didn't say anything, but I took her hand. This time she let me. The night was still dark, and under the covers our hands were both as warm as bread.

If you enjoyed this book, please consider posting a review at Amazon.com, Barnes & Noble, iTunes, Goodreads, or any outlet of your choice. Nothing warms the cockles of an author's heart like unsolicited reviews by readers he's never met.

Follow the author online at:

http://kevinbrennanbooks.wordpress.com
http://www.facebook.com/kevinbrennanbooks
Twitter - @kevinbrennan520

Cover by Max Scratchmann
www.maxscratchmann.com

Also by K E V I N B R E N N A N

KEVIN BRENNAN

Yesterday Road

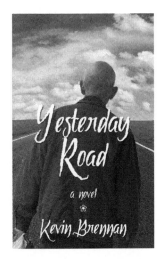

All octogenarian Jack Peckham wants to do is make his way home. But "home," it turns out, is a tough nut to crack.

In this "coming-of-old-age" tale, Jack finds himself on a journey into his distant past, helped along the way by Joe Easterday, a young man with Down syndrome, and Ida Pevely, a middle-aged waitress with her own mountain of regrets. Jack has a hundred grand in cash that he can't explain, since he can't remember yesterday much less forty years ago. He's not entirely sure, either, how it is that he got separated from his daughter, Linda. She'll be worried about him.

Setting out from Northern California for "points east," he gets lost, carjacked, abandoned, and tangled up in dreams, but he's always homing in on the one object of his inner drive — home.

Ida takes charge, but Jack's inner compass that seems to be guiding him to the pastoral land where he grew up makes her task, like her own life as a single mother, complicated. It's a huge moral choice: help Jack get home, or turn him over to authorities for his own safety? Things get even stickier when Jack and Joe vanish with her car, and she feels like a lady Job, tested and taunted for her own bad choices.

With humor and plenty of unexpected turns, this lyrical and poignant tale of memory and identity reveals how it is the whole of experience — pain and regret along with love and pleasure — that gives life its fullness.

We all tow our histories behind us as we make our way down Yesterday Road.

4.8 stars -- Amazon.com

"A wonderful story written with beautiful language, gentle humor, and warm insight."

"Mr. Brennan writes with quite a rare gift."

"[Brennan's] writing is lovely, with passages so true that they almost hit you in the gut."
Cinthia Ritchie, author, *Dolls Behaving Badly*

Available as an e-book at Amazon.com, iTunes, Barnes & Noble, and everywhere e-books are sold.

KEVIN BRENNAN

Parts
Unknown

(William Morrow/HarperCollins, 2003)

As a young man, Bill Argus abandoned his wife, their young son, and his family's dairy farm in the Sonoma County hamlet of Pianto. Now sixty-three, the once-famous photographer is overcome with the need to find forgiveness from those he left behind. Journeying back to the small dreary California town, he is disoriented after finding a ragged skeleton of the boyhood farm he remembers, and a family unmoved and indifferent to his return.

Bill's awkward homecoming is seen through the eyes of his second wife, Nora (twenty years his junior), who has her own troubled family history. Bearing witness to Bill's reception in Pianto sparks in Nora a revisiting of her own complicated past, and soon, she too sets off on a spiritual journey to explore her own parts unknown.

Set against the wild beauty of the California desert, this deftly imagined first novel lovingly maps the diverse terrain of the human heart as it probes the intricate bonds of family and the complex nature of forgiveness and love.

OUR CHILDREN ARE NOT OUR CHILDREN

Five Tiny Tales of Our Times

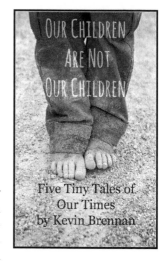

Poet Kahlil Gibran has said, Your children are not your children. In this brief collection of short-shorts, Kevin Brennan (Parts Unknown) turns that simple idea on its head with five case studies in bad parenting. From a father who won't pull over to let his boy pee on the roadside to a couple who unwisely lock their twin toddlers in a closet all day while they're at work, these parents embody the adage that it takes a village — to save innocent kids from idiots like them!

Available as an e-book at Amazon.com, iTunes, Barnes & Noble, and everywhere e-books are sold.

Made in the USA
Columbia, SC
16 June 2017

Critical Praise for Kevin Brennan's
Parts Unknown

"[Brennan's] first novel proves him to be a literary storyteller with enormous versatility, poetic and starkly realistic, able to drift among various voices and various moments seamlessly."
— San Francisco Chronicle

"[Parts Unknown] roasts the old chestnut that male writers cannot convincingly tell stories from female perspectives. Brennan does it with grace, wit and beauty."
— Denver Post

"Intimate...intoxicating."
— Milwaukee Journal Sentinel

"...portrait of an exterior landscape—and how it influences interior mindscapes—invites a comparison to Ivan Doig, whose family novel Mountain Time echoes with some of the same painful whispers among fathers, sons, and lovers."
— St. Louis Post-Dispatch

"A promising first novel...The story is remarkably coherent, considering that it plays leap-frog among roughly a dozen different voices and years. As a story of gentle revenge and the charity of lies, it picks out an original path among the many contemporary novels that focus on dire psychological twists and violent paybacks."
— BookPage

"Brennan intricately interweaves several interrelated stories into a lyrical testament to life, love, and redemption. A powerful debut novel from an exciting new talent."
— Booklist

ISBN 978-1500638399

OCCASIONAL
SOULMATES

Kevin Brennan